When a lion at a breeding park mau[...]
Con steps in as the keeper of Sekhme[t, ...]
maned lioness in the world.

In a Cape Town where fences keep people and wildlife apart, park officials and investors fret about their flagship big-cat project. And while Con grows steadily more bonded to his enigmatic charge, a cult of animal lovers with obscure alchemical aims seeks to claim the lioness as their own.

When she escapes, Sekhmet engulfs the city's imagination, stirring up rumours of terror and magic. In Con's quest to track her down, he must enter the wilderness of a cordoned-off Table Mountain – and his own dark history.

Henrietta Rose-Innes's novel *Green Lion* gleams with stylistic precision as myth and reality fuse in a story that sparks off the page.

GREEN LION

Henrietta Rose-Innes

UMUZI

Published by Umuzi
an imprint of Penguin Random House South Africa (Pty) Ltd
Company Reg No 1953/000441/07
Estuaries No 4, Oxbow Crescent, Century Avenue, Century City, 7441,
South Africa
PO Box 1144, Cape Town, 8000, South Africa
umuzi@penguinrandomhouse.co.za

First edition, first printing 2015
This edition 2016
1 3 5 7 9 8 6 4 2

ISBN 978-1-4152-0959-2 (Print)
ISBN 978-1-4152-0496-2 (ePub)
ISBN 978-1-4152-0497-9 (PDF)

Cover design by publicide
Author photograph by Martin Figura
Text design by Fahiema Hallam
Set in Adobe Garamond

Printed and bound by Novus Print, a Novus Holdings company

For my mother, Ann Rose-Innes
(Ann Schweizer)
1930–2014
Most beloved

I just sit where I'm put, composed
of stone and wishful thinking:
that the deity who kills for pleasure
will also heal,
that in the midst of your nightmare,
the final one, a kind lion
will come with bandages in her mouth
and the soft body of a woman,
and lick you clean of fever,
and pick your soul up gently by the nape of the neck
and caress you into darkness and paradise.

– MARGARET ATWOOD, from "Sekhmet, the Lion-headed Goddess of War, Violent Storms, Pestilence, and Recovery from Illness, Contemplates the Desert in the Metropolitan Museum of Art", 1995

CONTENTS

I. HUMAN THINGS

Last night the lions seemed almost to storm the fort to get at the sheep which are kept inside at night. A large number of them had followed the scent, roaring horribly and loudly as if they wanted to tear everything to pieces — to no avail however as the surrounding walls are too high for them to scale.

– JAN VAN RIEBEECK, *Journal*, 23 January 1653

lion

"Lions," the bus driver called down the length of the vehicle. "This is the lions, people. You got an hour and a half."

Con was seated directly behind the driver. As the tourists filed past him, he lingered, picking at the pilled fabric on the knees of his old suit trousers. Ever since the phone call, he'd been building a wall of reluctance between himself and this thing that he now must do.

"I barely knew Mark," he'd said to Elyse in bed that morning. "It's been twenty years. I can't imagine why his mother asked me."

"Maybe there's no one else. Maybe she can't go herself."

And it was true; on the phone Margaret had sounded frail, distressed. Con frowned at the ceiling. "God. I can't get there, anyway."

Elyse might have offered to lend him her car, a sleek little Audi that still smelt new, but she didn't. She had a solution ready: "The tourist bus. It goes right past the bottom of our road every day. Make a plan."

He'd pulled the pillow over his face. The linen was suffused with Elyse's scent – potent enough to cancel out his own. A bright synthetic note, tempered by the musk of her underarms, her sex, a fusion of what she applied and what she secreted.

"Don't be childish, Con," she'd said, tugging at a corner of the pillow. "When something like this happens – something awful – you can't say no. You have to go. It's the human thing to do." A moment of peevish silence. "Anyway, it's not like you've got anything else going on."

And Con had wrapped his arms around the pillow and pressed the sweet and cushioning dark against his eyes.

"Coming or not?" said the driver.

Con roused himself and stepped down from the bus. The first thing he saw, not two metres away, was the fence, standing between him and the mountain. Its silver finish was tarnished now, but still it sang with power.

He turned away from it and crossed the road. This much was familiar: the wooded mountain behind, the university below. But the parking area was brand new, paved in interlocking brick. A walkway led down to a smart modern complex, all pale stone and glass. The gloomy old Victorian zoo, he realised, used to stand on just about this spot. It was a strange mirage, these bright new buildings floating on grim foundations. He looked around for peacocks, but of course they'd have got rid of those: alien species.

Con tried to walk through his unwillingness, but it travelled a step ahead of him. The air was still and mown-grass fragrant. Not an animal smell, as he'd imagined. Not blood and meat.

At the entrance stood a tall sign in the shape of a rampant lion, cut from golden metal. *The Lion House* was engraved beneath the lion's back paws. After Con had explained his business, the heavy-armed ticket lady let him through without paying. Here were the cafeteria, gift shop, toilets. The buildings were pleasingly designed, arranged comfortably around a courtyard where people could sit in the sunlight with their cafeteria trays of tea and muffins. Everything light and bright and open, sandstone and pine. At the opposite end, bright specks flitted against the sky; he recognised the elegant art nouveau lines of the original aviary.

There were no obvious signs to an office, so Con followed a group of Germans from the bus through a doorway on the right. *The Den*, this building was called, the words etched into a plaque of the same bright metal. Below, in smaller lettering: *Back from Extinction! Come and meet our breeding pair, Dmitri and Sekhmet – the first black-maned lions in the Cape since 1858.*

Inside, it was entirely unlike the ominous pit of a lion den he remembered from the zoo of his childhood. This lion house had high ceilings and educational posters, documenting the usual: climate change and the countrywide drought, species loss, habitat decimation, the importance of keeping the fragile Table Mountain ecosystem closed off to people. In front of him, a party of schoolkids was being shepherded past the displays. Con noticed that many of them had toy animals dangling from their backpacks: tiny zebras, dogs, dinosaurs. The newest craze.

A doorway led into an inner chamber, where a broad, lit window floated in darkness. The glass was streaked and dusty, as if nobody had cleaned it for a while. Children clustered around it. Con peered between the heads of two Dutch tourists. A veld scene. Around him, he could feel the human herd sniffing, staring, ready to dart away or perhaps thrust someone else between themselves and danger. The weak, the lame. But nothing moved in the window, and soon the party was muttering its dissatisfaction and moving on.

"Where are they?" asked a tiny child who remained, hands splayed on the glass. "Where are the lions, Mama?"

"I don't know, Azi. I don't know." His mother tugged him away.

Con wanted to explain: this clearly wasn't the real lion cage. The lions were somewhere else. This was merely a diorama. An unnaturally bright, flat image of Table Mountain was pasted against a blue-painted backdrop; specimens of fynbos flora had been arranged in the foreground. It was well done, if a little artificial. But as he watched, a stalk of grass twitched in the stillness, and a tiny grey bird flew off into the backdrop, which turned into sky. It was real. He was looking out onto a circular enclosure, landscaped with boulders and shrubs. The rear wall, made to look like a rock formation, blocked out the road while allowing a mountain view. To the left, the wall rose higher, its top out of sight. A black metal grid like a miniature portcullis was set into its base.

Con squinted into the vegetation. Come out, he thought. I know you're in there. Each shadow, each blade of grass was suggestive. But nothing moved, no amber eye between the leaves. The bird returned to its perch and opened its beak, mute behind the glass, although its throat was flexed in song.

A square of paper was taped to the window, down near his

knees. *Apologies*, it said in a crooked hand. *No lions today due to unforeseen circumstances. Feel free to visit our dassie enclosure.* Clearly nobody had informed the international tour groups; perhaps they'd booked long in advance. Left of the display, in the corner and barely visible in the gloom, was a door marked *Staff only*. Con pushed, and it opened onto a different, sunlit zone.

Backstage. A grassy corridor was lined on one side with prefab buildings; on the other, the rear façade of the lion den was a wall of old, darkened stone, pierced by barred archways. Part of the original zoo? The smell here was more like what he had expected: old meat and straw, and under it something else, sharp and inorganic. He wrinkled his nose, conscious of breathing it in: particles of blood and bone, urine. He peered through the bars and at first saw nothing at all, just a pulsing blackness. Then his eyes made out shapes in the gloom. The concrete floor of the cage was littered with straw, and he could see a water trough, a knot of ship's rope that seemed to have been used as a giant puppy-chew, and what looked like a gnawed cow femur – the bone of some big functional animal, at any rate, something bred to be slaughtered. Beyond that, deep shadow.

He walked on, fingers trailing across each archway. Bars, stone, bars, stone – and then a CLANG as his arm was smacked back by the force of some huge hot weight throwing itself against the metal. Con lurched away – for a moment glimpsing a snarling mask – and sat down hard, fingers burning, head buzzing with the savage noise. A liquid chainsaw roar. He gaped at the cage.

The creature had retreated but was still there, hidden in the shadows, pacing, growling – a bass note so deep Con could feel the vibration in his chest. He could *smell* it, a feral whiff that jolted his heart all over again.

He got to his feet. His legs were trembling, but he forced himself on, away from the cage. The ground was tilting, trying to tip him backwards. Fuck this, he thought, fuck this whole mission.

The door of the prefab sprang open and someone blocked his

way: a sturdy, dark woman with a clipboard and a long grey plait draped over one shoulder. She wore a cinnamon-coloured uniform, safari style, with a gold badge on one lapel. "Can I help you?"

"I was attacked!" His voice came out comically shrill; he had to catch his breath to laugh.

But the woman's gold-ringed fingers tensed on the clipboard, and immediately he saw his mistake. "No, no – not attacked, just got a fright, sorry. Sorry." He put a hand to his chest, manually restraining his heart. "I'm fine." But he wasn't fine; he was racing.

She didn't smile. "You're not meant to be back here."

"I actually need to see the director. About someone who worked here? Mark. Mark Carolissen?"

"Ah." Her expression faltered. "You've come for his things, of course. We got the message. Wait, please." She disappeared into the building and came back a second later, holding a bag. "It's not much. I'm Amina Kajee, by the way. The director."

Con had imagined this moment with some dread. He'd been afraid to take possession of Mark's grisly belongings: blood-soaked, perhaps. Torn. But instead the woman handed him a clean, sporty daypack. Light in his hands. She kept hold of its strap for a moment. He could feel tension in her grip, as she surely could feel the tremor in his.

"We haven't had any news," Amina said. "About Mark. You've been to see him? He's not—?"

"He's hanging on. But I understand it's pretty bad."

"Conscious?"

"No."

Amina sighed. "Yes. There was a lot of blood." She had a small twitch at the side of her mouth, but her eyes were steady. "I'm sure I don't need to say—" she began, and then stopped short. "You must know how sorry we all are."

Con was shaking his head. "Of course," he said. "A horrible accident." In fact, he wasn't sure of the truth of any of this, had no authority to say it. But the intimacy of this exchange unnerved him; he wanted to be gone, the task done.

Amina released the bag to him. "Mark's one of our best volunteers, you know. So, ah, committed. He adored that lion."

Despite himself, Con was curious. "Was the animal … put down?"

"We had to, of course. When there's an attack on a human, you know."

"So what came at me now, through the bars?"

"Our lioness. Sekhmet is unsettled. She's still not used to us. And she came from a place where humans had not been kind." The woman looked at him. "You know about these lions? They're very rare, the ones that have the ancestral features. The size, the black mane, the ruff going down the belly."

"I thought they were extinct."

"Oh, they are, but you know there were Cape lions all over Europe, even after they were shot out here. In zoos, circuses." She, too, was relieved to shift the conversation away from Mark. "The genes are still circulating out there, but diluted. The idea is to find individual specimens that have the black-maned traits, breed them back. Like they did with the quaggas. We got our boy in a Russian circus. Sekhmet in Namibia in a safari park. Canned hunting, you know." She put her hand to the twitch at the side of her mouth, took it away. "It wasn't easy, finding those two. Right age, everything. And they were just getting used to each other. And now, I don't know …"

"So, what, will you have to close down?"

"Look around you. Certain people have spent a lot of money on this place. Parks Department, government high-ups – it's a big deal. They don't want us to turn away the tourists. No, we won't close. We can't." She sighed. "Although. We're struggling, since the accident. We had lots of volunteers, the American students liked us; but now, with this, most of them have gone. Freaked out. And the other staff … people are superstitious." She held her clipboard across her chest with one hand, as if it were a sheet or a blanket she'd like to pull up under her chin.

"Well, you still have the dassies."

She laughed. "Indeed." She gestured towards the mountain with the clipboard. "There's another exit up that way. Here, I'll show you."

Beyond the prefab was a corrugated-iron shed, emitting chill air and the sound of splashing. Inside, a wiry man in gumboots and a plastic apron was hosing down the cement floor. The shed smelt like a vet's surgery: a chemical tang, and something sweetly rotten. Switching off the water at the wall, the man looked up at Con with a big white smile, at odds with his cold labours. He had a battered-looking bald head, but his teeth were perfect. "Watch out, your feet," he called, and Con stepped back smartly. A puddle of rusty water had crept almost to his shoes, the only good pair he owned.

At the back, on a concrete bench, lay a long, bulky form under green tarpaulin. A hank of dark hair emerged from one end, and for a jolting moment Con saw a human figure there. But of course the body was much too big, with its heavy, obscured head lolling off the end of the block. Blood had collected in the folds of the cover. Looking more closely, he made out the sooty tip of one enormous claw.

"So that's it. The body. The lion?"

The man nodded, pulling a knitted hat snug over his bald head. "Dmitri."

"What will happen to it now?"

A shrug. "I think the people from the Department are coming to take it."

"Why?"

"They use it. Bones and skin."

"He'll be taxidermied." Amina had come up behind him. "In a natural posture."

"I didn't think people did that any more – stuffed animals," said Con. "Seems a bit old-fashioned."

"He's special. There's only a few specimens in the world. None in South Africa." She nodded to herself. "They say he's good, the guy who does it. It'll look real, they say. Maybe … curled up, like he's sleeping." She cupped her hands as if holding a drowsing kitten.

Con, embarrassed, looked away and accidentally met the old man's eyes. He was still smiling, perhaps more a habitual teeth-baring than a grin. The teeth were dentures, too white and even; maybe they were giving him pain.

"Well," Con said. "I can see the way out now – thanks again."

"Do please give Mark's mother our best wishes," said Amina. She wiped her nose with a knuckle. Brisk now. "And Mark, of course, when you … well. We were – are – all very fond of him here. He was terribly … committed."

That word again, with the same slight hesitation. "I didn't really know him," Con said.

"It was good of you to come, then."

With an awkward half-bow, Con turned away. He was conscious of the two people watching as he retreated, still a bit unsteady on his feet.

Elyse would want to hear all about it.

As he came out into the parking lot, he joined the same group of tourists heading back. But he couldn't stand the idea of getting in that stuffy bus now. Impatient, he jogged around the herd, carrying on past the waiting driver – sitting in the shade with a can of Mountain Dew – and on towards Rhodes Memorial. Its grey pseudo-Grecian pillars came into view, and the bronze lions he'd ridden as a child, staring out across the Flats.

There would have been red deer standing between the trees then, descendants of the deer introduced by Rhodes himself in an attempt to make the landscape more English; and Himalayan tahrs, further up on the crags, offspring of those that escaped Rhodes' zoo.

That was all gone now. The tahrs and the deer were dead. The only animals tolerated were indigenous, and all of those were stashed on the other side of the fence, apparently. Out of sight, and safer that way.

They'd extended the restaurant: a beer garden was built on descending terraces all the way down to the gravel half-moon in front of the monument's imposing steps. Now you could sit and drink under the eyes of eight scaled-down copies of the Trafalgar lions, the naked horseman, and Rhodes' own lugubrious bust in his niche above them all. The old brigand looked dejected, cheek propped on a hand. Above, the mountain rose, dark green from the recent rains, the silver fence necklacing its base. He remembered running among the trees up there, pretending to be a soldier in a jungle war. Safe enough, then, to play those games, when the slopes had seemed to teem with benign and hidden life. Mark and him, lobbing pine cones at each other ... his mind pulled away from the memory, refocussing on the details of the present: the stiff clusters of pine needles, the orange gravel, the granite blocks minutely flecked with black and quartz.

Con felt strange. Sharper. The world had a fine grain, an artificial brightness to it. He knew what it was: the kick of big-predator adrenaline, working its way around his system. Maybe he would run all the way home; it wasn't too far, down past the old wildebeest enclosures and along the highway.

Out across the city, rainwater glinted on the roads from the night before, but it was turning into a fine clear day, and he needed to shake the tremble from his legs. He hoisted the rucksack onto his back. Mark's stuff was light, no problem to carry. Mark's human things.

wolf

It was, in fact, extremely far to run. By the time Con got to Sea Point and up the three steep flights of stairs, the bag felt heavy, saturated with sweat from his back. He let himself in and walked through the rooms, relieved to find them empty. It was good to be alone here in the daytime hours. He'd been staying in the flat for six weeks now, ostensibly looking for a job; but Elyse hadn't yet, he felt, given him permission to call it home.

Elyse's hours were irregular. Some weeks she was on the road doing educational skits, some weeks it was a corporate-theatre do every evening. She started early or stayed late to paint sets, to rehearse, to hang out with other actors.

Meanwhile, Con was meant to be job-hunting. But the first couple of weeks had been fruitless. He had few employable skills. In London for the last few years he'd basically been a security guard, but the gigs were easy: museums, galleries. It was a different proposition in South Africa. He imagined wearing a bulletproof vest for some armed-response outfit – absurd. Most days, now, he didn't even make it down to the Nigerian internet café on Main Road to check the classifieds.

Instead, he lingered in the flat like an aimless ghost, toying with the possessions of the corporeal resident. Sometimes he moved small items of hers from place to place, pens or cutlery, or rearranged the bookshelves – keeping busy, and also reassuring himself that his fingers didn't pass through matter like a spirit creature's. It was possible that these little actions, subtle though they were, disturbed Elyse as much as would a genuine poltergeist. He sometimes saw her looking at a shifted stapler or roll of kitchen towel with a frown of gentle puzzlement. He was aware, also, of touching and holding her too much, perhaps to an annoying degree, and for similar reasons: just to feel her skin against his, his body acknowledged.

He liked to clean when he was alone in the flat. Take all the cups that had been getting dusty in the cupboard and rinse them one by one, then do the cutlery, the plates and mugs and egg-stained pans. Then move through the other rooms, wiping down the surfaces. It pleased him to think that he could run his hands in this way over every one of Elyse's possessions.

He sniffed his palm and caught a whiff of something wild. The reek of the lion cage was on his skin, or perhaps emanating from the rucksack. He regretted bringing the smell into the flat, into Elyse's intimate air. Like a dog bringing roadkill to the door, unsure if he'd be smacked or petted. He put the bag down in a corner, stripped off his sweaty clothes and put them straight in the washing machine. He needed to wash.

The apartment had far too many mirrors for his liking. It felt like he was running a shining gauntlet some mornings, assaulted from all sides by flashes of light as he made his way from room to room.

But this morning, naked after his shower, he faced the bathroom mirror squarely. He looked very pale to his own eyes, his colours barely organic: slate eyes, iron hair, chalk skin. He hadn't quite shaken off the northern hemisphere. In London the light had flattered him, but here in the lush Cape spring his flesh seemed bloodless and cold as stone. Con sighed. He should try for a tan. He should try for something. Like a job maybe, he could hear Elyse say. She didn't mind paying for him, but he could tell she was growing impatient; she wanted him to be something better, something more. Stand up straight, she often told him. You're letting it all go to waste. And she didn't just mean his looks.

Still, not yet thirty-five, and only a few strands of silver in the brown. He wondered how Mark had aged. If the grey had got to him, too. All these years, he realised, he'd been keeping an unacknowledged ledger: his own progress, or lack of it, against Mark's imagined gains.

He observed Elyse's cosmetic arsenal with interest. The mascara, the lipstick, the hair tongs … they seemed clinical implements, or alien tools, not obviously related to the brilliant effects she coaxed from them. Con never tired of watching Elyse at work on these transformations. Before moving in, he'd known that she took care with such things, but the time she spent on it daily had been a revelation.

Con picked up a stick of eyeliner and touched it to the ball of his thumb, then to the corner of his eye. He used to do this when he was a teenager. Mark would shoplift eyeliner from Clicks, or borrow a girl's, and they'd put it on before going out to some school disco, and later the clubs. Tight black jeans. Tin badges pinned to denim lapels. Precocious, he thought now: they were only, what, fourteen? Always the youngest at the party. He'd followed Mark's lead in this as in other things, but he'd never been a natural peacock. Later, he'd drifted back to a neutral style: conventional if elegant drabness, like winter plumage after a brief tropical summer.

Con stroked the eyeliner along his lower lid, flinching from it. He'd never got used to sticking something in his eye. This was not the cheap kohl from his youth; Elyse's products were expensive, and the mark was subtle but effective. With the smallest alteration of the line, his right eye was instantly enhanced, larger and brighter, flirting with its drier left-hand brother in the mirror. He couldn't leave it lopsided, and so he did the other side too.

Not bad, he thought, giving himself a wolfish look. Quite sexy – from the neck up, anyway. Now his face looked clothed while his body was bare. It would work with a black suit; something a bit sharper than the one he currently owned.

He wasn't particularly vain. His body, he felt, was lean but standard, his face quite regular; but he liked his clothes to be trim, to be right. Always dark colours. "Dapper" was a word that had been used about him. When he was working overseas, he'd enjoyed the uniforms. This was another casualty of his unemployment. The good dark suit he used to prefer had worn through at the knees and elbows, and he couldn't afford a replacement. In the slightly humiliating pattern that had arisen between them, he would wait for Elyse to find a new one for him.

Elyse. Sometimes he'd watch her approach through a crowd or from a distance, and be surprised all over again. Tall girl, all legs, with a lunging stride that was, despite her dancer's training, more force than grace. She was beautiful up close: that triangular face, all cheekbone and nose, the large eyes made larger with make-up, only softened by the breath of her perfume. No mistakes, no unplanned effects.

He liked her best naked. The first time he'd seen her that way, her long, pale back had made him think of bones, the smooth curves of the animal skeletons at the museum in London where they'd met. That spare. It surprised him to see her shy. But then he realised, no, the turned back was not timidity. When she rotated towards him it was a measured unfolding. She kept her head bent to the last and her arms over her breasts, so he saw first her hips and her hairless groin, and as she lowered her hands her small white breasts and nipples of subtlest rose. Only then did she fold away the hair – a dense red flag, at that stage – and lift her face. All rich colour. Blue eyes, red mouth, bright as paint.

When he placed his hand against her breastbone, he felt quickened: warmth stealing into the cells of his body, through his palm and up his arm and to his heart. Kissing felt like substance flowing from her mouth into his: warmth and taste and colour flooding his dusty insides.

Waking up with her for the first time at his place, he'd felt ashamed. She was a rare piece of art in a shabby room, one without security or lustre or ambience. It was a tiny walk-up studio: white walls, narrow bed, furniture made out of boxes, some books in a pile. Kettle, a pan, a two-ring gas hob.

He'd watched her stalking through the space, naked but clothed in poise, skimming a hand across the three shirts and one suit hanging on plastic hangers from the picture rail. She turned to him with genuine curiosity, a corner of his old black jacket between finger and thumb. She'd just woken up but had somehow already fixed her face: perfect.

"You wear this? Every day?"

He just smiled, anticipating how she would tease him next. She snorted through her comma-shaped nostrils, flapped the sleeve back against the wall.

That very weekend she went shopping and returned with a beautiful suit, two beautiful white shirts, leather shoes. She dressed him – the sizes just right – and stood him next to herself in the mirror. They looked good, he thought. Not too mismatched. He could see why she'd wanted him to change.

"You see, so handsome. When you try. We must cut your hair." With one hand, not breaking her own gaze in the mirror, she tilted his face slightly, so the light picked out his jaw.

The grip on his chin irritated him, and he ducked his head to softly bite the side of her hand. She laughed and pulled away and looked him in the eye. There were spots of pink on her cheekbones, and he felt a kind of wondering pride in that: he'd kindled a flush in her, even through all that make-up.

In the Sea Point bathroom, he rearranged Elyse's cosmetics, putting them all together in a toiletry bag and then storing that on a different, more logical shelf. He wanted her to come home.

Alone in the bed that night, he dreamt he was a lion, and that he was wrestling with another lion: a sister-lion, brother-lion. It breathed, it rumbled, it pressed its meaty weight into his face. He was trying to open his jaws wide enough to clamp them on a neck, to snap a long bone or pierce a belly, to feel the hot insides. It wasn't a new dream: he had dreamt it often, all his life. But this time it was extremely clear and detailed. Each hair was crisp, each claw-thrust ecstatic; the weight of the body on top of him was crushing. But as he pressed back, he felt the furred skin dissolve into something smooth and gasping, and suddenly Elyse was there with her late-night breath and the coolness of the outside air on her skin.

"Shh," she was saying, confusingly. "Con, it's me, it's just a dream." Soothing but at the same time pulling away from him with alarm, and from this he knew he had frightened her, had shouted out or even struck at her. Ashamed, he didn't open his eyes; he pressed his face into the pillow and pretended to sleep, until in fact he did.

In the morning he could still feel the heat of the fur, and the weight of his claws. The taste of his own breath in his mouth, thick and sweetish like a dog's. And other things too: forgotten dreams within the dream. Running. Seeking. He wiped a trace of saliva off his chin. The dream disgusted him, the sensation of blood at the back of his throat.

The flat smelt of fresh coffee. On the pillow next to his head, cracked open on its spine, was one of Elyse's fantasy novels. The cover was golden, with an embossed dragon. She must've been up for a while, making coffee, sitting reading in bed next to him as she liked to do, waiting for him to stir. Now the flat was silent: she'd already left the house again.

He got up and showered briskly with slightly-too-cold water, drank a cup of slightly-too-strong coffee, heated a pan on the stovetop and fried an egg. He forced it down on toast, even though the rich yolk filling his mouth reminded him of the bloodier parts of the dream. The dream had left him jittery. He could smell its acrid aftertaste, under the coffee, and when the front door opened it startled him so much he actually jumped.

Elyse had effected one of her great changes. Her hair, in silvery ringlets the day before, had been cut in a sharp thirties-style bob and dyed pure black, shiny, as if she'd applied lacquer. It was good, a definite transformation. She seemed revived and full of brisk energy. A doll repaired. She was also dressed in midnight blue: leggings and close-fitting, matching top, made of some rich damask material that held her curvy body tight. It was both seductive and alarming, like reptilian scales. Con wondered if she was angry.

"Hiya," he said. "It's cute."

She flicked her neat head side to side, efficiently acknowledging the compliment. "Betty Boop," she said, stroking the curl on her forehead. "Thought it was time I went dark again."

He smiled at her, admiring her resilience, her belief in the renewability of the body. But then, she was a little younger than him, twenty-six to Con's thirty-four, and there were few defects that couldn't be set right with a lick of paint.

She leant forward to peer at him. "Is that … *make-up*?"

"What? Oh, shit, ja, I was messing around last night."

Embarrassed, he went through to the bathroom and scrubbed off the tenacious kohl. When he came back into the room, though, his awkwardness was replaced with a wave of annoyance. Elyse was sitting on the carpet, long legs crossed like knitting needles, working at the buckles of Mark's rucksack.

"What are you doing?"

She glanced up through newly acquired eyelashes. "Have you looked inside? This is his, right?"

"No, of course I haven't – Elyse!"

He was disconcerted by his own anger. It passed quickly enough but it had been there, a hot conviction that this was what she'd been after all along, for all her talk of *human things* – a chance to pry. He reached for the bag, but Elyse, impatient, was already tipping the contents out on the carpet.

It was a very small array of effects. A thin T-shirt. A thumbed paperback with arcane symbols on the cover – *Alchemy for a New Age*. A packet of breath mints. A postcard. A small bottle of pills. A ring of keys. Stuffed in the bottom of the bag was a bundle of brown fabric. He hooked it up cautiously with finger and thumb, but it seemed clean enough: the trousers of the zoo uniform, gold braid running down one crumpled leg. There was a short-sleeved safari jacket too, with braid at the collar. No blood. A glint of gold caught his eye: a brooch on the lapel. It was in the form of a golden eye, the central dot painted black. Unmistakeably feline, with a tear mark sweeping from the inner corner. The gold flickered in the back of his mind and he remembered: glass eyes.

Amber glass eyes. One glass eye, wrong, in the wrong place, stuck – where? An eye glinting in a boy's palm.

With quick fingers, Elyse tweaked the objects, positioning them in a grid on the carpet like a game of memory or a soothsayer's thrown bones. The pang of outrage he'd just felt was already subsiding – what did it matter, really? But still he felt this was not right, and also, more urgently, that they would be found out, that somebody would sense they'd rifled through Mark's things.

"What is this …"

She was reading the postcard. He snatched it away from her, more roughly than was necessary. "Jees, Elyse. Seriously. This is private." It was a reproduction of an old painting, vaguely familiar. A man in a red robe bent over a desk, in what seemed to be a kind of medieval workstation: neat wooden cabinetry, filled with books and pot plants and other interesting objects. The whole thing seemed to be standing in the nave of a cathedral. The back was blank. Familiar, but he couldn't quite catch the memory …

"It's Saint Jerome," said Elyse coldly. "*Saint Jerome in his Study*."

"How do you know that?"

"Art History?"

He tucked the card protectively back into the top pocket of the rucksack.

"So Mark's into art?" asked Elyse.

"Well, he could draw. He was a pretty artistic kid. His mother knew a lot about painting."

Elyse leant back on her elbows, a pose in which every part of her body tautened: shoulders, calves, thighs. Con felt a stupid flash of jealousy. Mark's attraction still operating, even from his deep slumber. Look how she quivered! Her muscles were hard, untouchable. Con laid a hand on her knee, partly in apology for his harshness a moment ago, and partly for his rough denial of her in the night. (A flash of disturbing waking-dreaming memory: *biting* somebody.) She gave him a cold look and her patella vibrated under his palm.

"Tell me more," she persisted. "What's he like?"

He didn't answer her at once. How to summon Mark – his particular grace, even at thirteen, fourteen? His languid control. It was part of why his accident was so shocking. The mess of it, the negligence. The footsure boy had stumbled. What was Mark like? He might be like nothing, now, like nobody. A coma blank. "Oh," he said, looking away. "Back then, he was the cool kid, you know? Precocious, quite indulged. Spoilt, even. He had his own pad, like a whole outside flat for himself. I'd never seen anything like it. We got up to a lot of shit." He shrugged. "But that was a long time ago. Who he is now, I have no idea."

Elyse flicked her fringe, impatient. "But what does he *look* like?"

And perhaps it was that gesture, or the new hair colour, or the particular crafted blankness of her glance at that moment, but it came to him for the first time. *You*, he wanted to say. Mark looked like you. The long limbs, the eyes, the polish. He'd never seen it before.

Elyse rocked herself backwards and forwards, watching him. "So what went wrong? Why did you two stop being buddies?"

Con shook his head, as if to shake the conversation from his ears. He was tired of the whole thing now. He wanted to drop the memories down a drain. He stretched out on the carpet next to Elyse and reached for her. Her ticklish stomach was an odd, tender part in a body otherwise elastic, hardened by years of dance and theatre training. He loved her little belly though, the way it shrank from a cold hand but was always warm in bed. A sweet surprise, the first time he'd got her naked. He'd hate it if, as she was always threatening, she finally found a way to get rid of it. He wanted to touch it now, but his probing hand could find no end to the nylon sheath of the leggings, which continued up and up under her shirt, transforming into a bodysuit: there was no way in.

"You're tickling," said Elyse, wriggling away from him. "Don't you have things to do? You need to take this stuff." She started to pack things back in the bag.

Con groaned, once more face-down on the rug. The wall of reluctance was back. For a moment he considered asking Elyse to go instead. She might get a kick out of meeting Margaret Carolissen. Elyse was interested in people, and good with the elderly, too: unpatronising, gently cheeky. But no. Margaret had asked for Con.

Elyse pinched his ear with small, cool fingers. "Just get it over with. Come on, she'll love you. Just switch on the charm."

He felt another ripple of annoyance. It was an odd point of pride for Elyse, that he was a charming man – one whom women warmed to. It was true that he'd never had difficulty in that regard, not since school. Elyse had explained it to him once: "You give the impression of being up for anything."

"So a bit of a slut, you mean?"

"Yes, sure, but also that you're not necessarily going to take any drastic action. It's very relaxing, for a girl. It leaves things entirely up to her."

There was perhaps something in that. The man in her description certainly sounded familiar: circumspect, but keen to please. Direct, if not entirely truthful.

But the whole discussion was obscene in relation to Margaret. "She's an old woman," he said from his position on the carpet.

"So? She's probably dying to be flirted with. Come on, you can take the car."

A concession, this. So he forced his limbs into necessary movement. Found his jacket, keys, wallet; wrestled himself out the door.

It'd been a long time since he'd been in the driver's seat of a car, and for a moment he was disorientated by all the knobs and levers. He adjusted the seat angle, the rear-view mirror, but still it felt wrong, a bad fit. He turned into the traffic cautiously, indicating with an old lady's excessive care. The reluctance felt now like he was pressed up against it, nose squashed against its bricks.

Such a battle with the body. It made Con feel that he'd not

completely returned from the lion dream into his human skin. All these clever actions, duly performed; these hands on the gearstick, signalling right and left … and all the time, his lip pulled back in a snarl.

cub

Although he knew exactly where to go, he missed the turn-off to the Carolissen house three times before his rebellious hands could be compelled to turn the wheel. But then there it was: the old house, the tree leaning over the garden wall. Unchanged, it seemed, although now Mark's house was not the only one in the street with high, concealing walls.

Con parked a little way down the road and sat with his hands flat on the steering wheel, observing the front gate. He could feel the heavy metal knocker in his palm, the weighted swing of the door. It had been exciting to come here as a boy, to pass through that gate, to encounter Mark's exotic parents: his elegant mum, his imposing dad. Margaret and Gerard – alone of all his classmates' parents, they were called by their first names.

He remembered, too, the last time that gate had closed behind him, and the certainty that it would never, never open up again. He'd been wearing funeral clothes then: a fourteen-year-old in a black suit, standing on the black tar on a white-sky day. On the other side of the door, he could hear murmur and talk from the guests; and, more distinctly, he could sense the egg of silence around his friend, somewhere inside. Mark, gone quiet. Gone dark.

Con had walked all the way home wearing that suit, over white zebra crossings, feeling more monochrome with every step. In some ways he'd never regained full colour. The borrowed T-shirts, the badges and beads, the posters on the walls – they had all seemed silly, even ugly, without Mark's presence to animate them.

Impatient with himself, Con pushed out of the car and strode towards the gate, biting the inside of his cheek, noting how in fact the door was painted a different shade of green now and how the knocker had been replaced by a plastic buzzer. Possibly someone had stolen the brass. The buzzer made no sound, but after half a minute a crackle emerged from the intercom grille.

"Hello?" called a thin voice. "Who's there?"

"Margaret, it's me, Con. Constantine."

The door clucked as if recognising and forgiving him, and submitted to his push. Beyond the shadowed stoep, the front door was also ajar, and he went through into the entrance hall. It surprised him with its airiness: his memories of the house were shadowed, every room dominated by Gerard's legions of hunting trophies. The house was in fact a graceful Victorian, high-ceilinged, elegantly proportioned; he'd never really been able to see it before. A door leading to the body of the house was closed, but next to it, light spilt down a white spiral staircase.

"Come up, dear," came the high voice again. "Up the stairs!"

It was a sunlit room with tall sash windows. Margaret's studio. He'd never been up here; his interests in the house had always lain elsewhere.

Margaret was sitting in a window seat of bleached wood, dressed in a white cotton shirt and slacks; her hair had grown pure white since he last saw her, and was cut in a short bob. Her face was still fine-featured, delicate. She looked fragile but oddly festive in the strong light, like a clear glass Christmas ornament. There was no light in her voice, though, when she turned to him.

"Constantine." She and Gerard were the only people in his life who had ever called him that, his full name. She held out her fingers and for a moment he saw himself bowing to kiss them. Instead, he went towards her and took her hand.

"Hello, Margaret." He kissed her creased cheek.

She looked frailer than she should, for her age. Her eyes were a milky blue and seemed slightly unfocussed, and he wondered if her sight was going. Had she been ill? Or simply hollowed out by grief?

"Oh, don't stare," she smiled. "I know, it's terrible, I've got so old. But sit, anyway." She patted the pale-blue upholstered cushion next to her, and he sat. It was just right: they were intimate, but not touching. Margaret always had the knack for arranging things.

There were several paintings on the walls, oils it looked like. Pale geometric shapes in white frames. Hers? He'd always known she painted, but he'd never paid much attention; even now, his gaze slid off these pallid abstracts without finding purchase, Margaret herself much more compelling.

She looked at him searchingly for a moment. "So," she said. "It's been a long time, dear Constantine."

"Yes," he said softly. "I'm so sorry, Margaret."

"Oh," she said, and waved the words away as if she didn't care for them.

"How's he doing?"

"They say … at the hospital, they say it's not …" Then she put both her small hands around his forearm, gripping it to make herself understood. "He was *beautiful*, wasn't he?"

Con nodded. "Yes, yes he was."

She dabbed the air with her hand. "A lion's paw – so big, so powerful. Just a swipe, just a careless *pat* – it opened up an artery, here in the arm. He lost, oh, so much blood …" A tiny gasp. "Such a strange kind of symmetry, don't you think? We were … my family … was *full*. Complete. Do you know what I mean? And each one … *taken*." Again, the swipe of the imaginary paw. A disembowelling motion, it occurred to Con. "One, two, three …"

He couldn't speak. Mark's not gone yet, he wanted to tell her.

"The people at the zoo, or whatever they call that place. They were decent." She rested her dry blue eyes on him. "You must think I am cold."

"Not at all."

"You understand – when did you last see him? Mark?"

"In London. Years ago."

She nodded, and turned to a collection of photos, framed in dull silver and gold, on a small side table. Only men in the pictures: her husband, her son. Constrained by the sober frames, held still at last.

She selected a photo and handed it to him. It might have been taken five years ago. Mark as the handsome man he was always going to be. He was standing square to the camera, his hands lightly clenched, an awkward pose. But he was muscular, tanned, his dark hair clipped short against the skull, showing his small ears. If there was anything that connected this man to the dreamy-eyed boy Con remembered, it was those small, surprisingly delicate ears. Strange that Con should remember that. He had a flash of Mark hooking his long fringe – too long for school – back behind his ear, the glossy hair spilling back. A move young Con had tried to practise, shamefully, in his own mirror before grimly discarding it. His hair was curlier, not made to slip teasingly across the eyes.

How Mark had toughened up! Very different to the wild-haired ranter Con had walked across English meadows with, ten years before. Although perhaps something of the same fierce focus. Con didn't feel strong, not nearly as strong as the man in the picture. And yes, he had let himself go; it was easy to do. Mark, on the other hand, had clearly put himself through the opposite process. He had taken himself up, had brought himself together. There was no sign, in this picture, that Mark was flinching from the rigours of life. But still: tension in the pose.

"He looks good," Con said.

"Yes. That was years ago. What you must understand is that Mark hasn't been well." Margaret shook her head. "Con, he wasn't really *here*. Not for a long time. He didn't want to be."

"I thought he was living here."

"Oh, he *lives* here." She nodded to the top of the stairs. "Down there, in his old room. I stay up here." She looked around. "After we lost Gerard, I cleared this space for myself. It's how I always wanted to live – clean."

"It's unrecognisable."

"Good," she said dryly. "The wretched menagerie. All those stuffed heads!"

"I was always quite frightened of them," said Con. The hunting trophies had been alarming. The house used to be alive with eyes, its walls sound-absorbent, shaggy with hairs and horns, moving and breathing and reaching out to touch as Mark's family travelled its dim corridors.

"God, those grisly things. Can't stand to look at them. Gerard disliked them too."

Too late now, Con remembered to say: "I was very sorry to hear about Gerard."

"He was so ill, in the end. Poor man. It was a mercy. He never really recovered." She shook her head, decisive. "You know, I always used to feel sorry for the poor dumb animals. But in recent years I started to *loathe* them. I was glad they were dead. Dead and stuffed!"

"Did you sell them? They must've been worth a bit."

"Oh no, oh no." She nodded again at the head of the stairs, as if that marked the lip of the well of all dark memories. "They're still here! I just … *herded* them into a different part of the house." She gave a little laugh. "Mark wanted me to keep them." She stared blindly out of the window for a moment. "He loved that lion, you know? What was it called?"

An image flashed: an empty-eyed young lion in a glass case. Then he realised what she must mean: "Dmitri."

"It had been horribly abused, you know. Jaw broken, he told me. Some terrible circus owners." She sighed.

Con remembered what he was there for, and reached for the rucksack. He didn't hand it to her, just moved it out into her line of sight.

"Oh, Con," she said, "I'm so thankful. You see, I haven't been able to …" She gestured to her leg. For the first time he noticed the walking stick propped behind her. "It's been hard for me to travel to the hospital. It's not easy to even get downstairs. I've had to let the maid go. And there was nobody else. Nobody I could trust."

"I'm glad you asked me."

She breathed in sharply, wiped her nose with a tissue from a box at her side. "Now, dear," she said, "would you do me one more favour, please? Would you put the bag in his room? I don't think I can bear it just yet – looking through his things. In his old bedroom, you remember?"

Leaves tapping at the glass. Cigarettes and stolen whisky. "I remember."

"He kept it locked. I think there should be a key," she said, nodding at the rucksack.

Con didn't pretend not to have looked inside. He rooted in the bag – noticing, with some irritation, that the brown uniform wasn't there. Bloody Elyse, he thought, messing around. But perhaps it was for the best. Margaret would most likely not want to have those clothes here in the house. As he pulled out the keyring, the postcard came with it, landing face down on the floor. Con's impulse was to snatch it up unseen, but Margaret bent and took it between thumb and forefinger, brought it long-sightedly to her eyes.

"Oh!" She breathed, and looked up at him, eyes bright. "Saint *Jerome.*"

"I'm sorry," he said, feeling another burst of annoyance for Elyse. "I didn't mean …"

"No, no, don't be sorry. It's perfect." She propped the postcard against the silver picture frame, obscuring the photo of Gerard beneath. "I gave it to him, you see, when he started his job. Saint Jerome, Hieronymus – a very serious man. A great scholar. But then there is this terribly sweet story attached to him, about how he made friends with a lion. Do you know it?"

"Something about a thorn."

"Pulled the thorn from the paw, and then the lion was devoted to him after that. A strange fable, isn't it? Doesn't seem quite Christian. Like something from an older time. Animals speaking and repaying debts and remembering kindnesses. From Androcles, of course, originally. Can you see the lion in the painting?"

He didn't, at first; and then he did. There were many small details, a clutter of objects. As well as books, he could make out a hat, a porcelain jar, a little cat, a peacock. But there, in the background, almost unnoticed, in the shadowy nave behind Jerome, a silhouette coming over the tiles: lionlike but diminutive, the size of a lapdog. Limping, it would have been, sparing its sore foot. A shy annunciation.

"It's so small."

"Yes, well, Antonello had probably never seen a real lion. Very few people in Europe had. Often they come out looking like strange pug dogs in these old paintings."

"Looks like the saint hasn't noticed it yet."

"Of course, you're never expecting the lion, are you?" She touched the tip of her finger to the postcard. "Like something coming up in the rear-view mirror. Much closer than it appears."

Downstairs, he went through the door beyond the staircase, and immediately the smell tumbled him back twenty years: old leather, Gerard's tobacco. Death and chemicals. The passage was as he remembered it: dim, lined with the shadowy forms of animals on plinths; mounted heads reaching up to the ceiling; birds frozen in flight in glass cases. The display inspired less awe now – the trophies moth-eaten and not as big as remembered – but was somehow even more claustrophobic. Margaret had shifted everything from upstairs and from the entrance hall, cramming it in. The passage was wall-to-wall furred, feathered, clawed and winged. Bristling with the horns of a dozen different kinds of antelope. In one glass case was a tableau of a leaping caracal with a guinea fowl in its paws. The taxidermy was aged, the animals rigid and worn in patches. He could see where the cat's tawny fur had been neatly darned, like an old sock. He tried to imagine Margaret with needle and thread, tutting over a bullet hole. The floor, too, was carpeted in hides, gold and striped. Everything dusty now. For the first time, he considered how much labour this house would have been for the woman who used to work for the Carolissens. He could barely picture her: a quiet figure in the background of his childhood memories of the family, dusting, wiping, mopping their spills.

He paused at a small window. Green lawn and sunlight outside, and a ginger cat picking its way along a gutter. Con turned back to the passage with a red square glowing on his corneas. He pushed on blindly, rocking a duiker back on its pedestal, around a corner and down a short flight of stairs – the old house was eccentric in its construction. Birds seemed to predominate here, with flamingos and ibises inspecting his passage over their long bills.

The back door opened out onto the garden. A few trees had come down since he was last here, and the sky was more visible. There was the big plane tree, still with the wicker chair in its shade where Gerard liked to sit. The small path led down to the bottom of the garden as before. Mark's room looked small and shabby, just a kind of glassed-in garden shed, after all. Greenish moisture was trapped in the seams of the sliding doors. The key turned easily. Con stepped down into the musty room, his body remembering the step. He pulled back the curtain, for light.

A sad room, like a depressed student's – one fusty mattress on the floor, a wardrobe with its doors ripped off, exposing the shelves. No other furniture. Con let his eye travel over the pieces of paper stuck to the walls. They looked like pages from the book in Mark's rucksack: one showed a diagram of many concentric circles, densely annotated with curious symbols. More of that alchemy shit.

Surely the room hadn't been this small, this square? He remembered a long, generous space, luxurious even. He saw now that the room had been partitioned with a repurposed length of curtain. He pulled it open a few feet – behind, a secretive space. Sunlight entered, rebounding off clouded glass.

The panes, one cracked in two, had been removed from the old display case and were stacked in lethal dusty sheets against the wall. Now the case stood empty, its delicate lock tarnished from lack of use. Something in the dimness on the other side. With a sense of trespass, Con stepped through the frame where the glass had been, into the box of air and out the other side.

And gasped and stepped back, rearing away from the figure standing before him. He backed into the cabinet, which rocked and rattled against the stacked glass.

He remembered it: the small, dusty lion from that day years ago, when he first entered the Carolissen house. And Mark. Grinning, one slim leg slung over the creature's spine, rocking it back and forth. It gazed on him now with its mismatched eyes, one dark and patient still, the other stitched on like a monstrous teddy bear's. But more damage had been done. Terrible indignities. The fur was streaked with bilious green, with some dye that made the sparse mane knot together like seaweed. The creature's jaws were forced open around an object in its jaws – a bald old tennis ball.

Con held his breath. He did not want to inhale this madness. He'd been in rooms containing unhappiness before: it was not an unfamiliar atmosphere. Rooms like moonscapes, places where all life had been exhausted, all air consumed. This was different. Mark's room heaved with fervent unhappy life. The vapours on this planet were hot and moist and thronging.

He backed carefully away, through the empty case and the curtain and out of the room. Locked the door quietly but firmly.

Returning to the main house, he was greeted by Margaret halfway down the corridor. Once a tall woman, now she was stooped over her walking stick, face pale with pain. He returned the keys to her palm. She turned and guided him back, with evident difficulty, along the corridor past the staring glass eyes of the animals, holding the keys like a lamp to light their way, looking neither left nor right. He couldn't see her face but her back was rigid. She went straight to the front door and opened it wide.

They stood there blinking at each other like two people who have emerged from a deep cave into sunlight.

"Thank you, Constantine." She seemed eager now for him to go. Already she was creeping towards the foot of the stairs, one hand on the banister, ready to haul herself back to the cleanliness and order of the upper room. "I can manage, don't worry. I just go slowly. I'm a very old woman now, you know."

As he let himself out onto the stoep, he had the strongest feeling that he was leaving her behind in a place of danger. Menaced, somehow, by the creatures that husband and son had left under her roof, that perhaps even now were stirring from their pedestals, cracking their glass domes and inching towards the stairs.

baboon

Con was having trouble with this place: this city, its roads and corners and roundabouts. He used to walk everywhere as a teenager, cutting straight simple lines through the town. Pick a direction, go. These days his paths seemed crooked, curving, dead-ending and doubling back.

He was troubled also by strange mental absences and mistakes. Like this, now: the path to the hospital. Margaret had given him its name but he'd immediately forgotten – it was one of the new private places; and now he found himself automatically driving to the old state hospital below the mountain, like a homing bird.

He came alive to his mistake as he made the last turn into the parking area, but by then felt powerless to halt his drift into the past. He parked in a dank corner of the covered lot and sat for a moment with his hands on the wheel. People were walking in and out, from shade into sunlight. Women came on foot up from the main road, carrying plastic bags of food; a man stood with his head wrapped in bandages and a cigarette on his lips, squinting into the smoggy sun.

It was of course the place his mother came to die. In the last months of Lorraine's life he'd come to know it well, with its cracked windows and peeling plaster and patients shuffling forward in queues to collect their medication. Driving her to appointments, check-ups, x-rays, blood tests. It'd been a calm time between them, companionable almost, although he felt always her fatigue growing, as if she were something he carried that grew heavier and heavier as her physical form wasted. There was a quiet affection in the way she was with him then, the brusqueness gone. At times she'd lay a hand on his wrist or on his arm, in a way she'd never done before.

They'd spent a lot of time in the car in those last days, as they had when he was much younger. Except he was in the driving seat.

She'd sit quietly, small on the passenger side, as he lit a cigarette and one for her, despite doctor's orders. He'd drive her to the beach, or out into the countryside, until that started to be too tiring. On those long car trips, the light washed in clean and bright through the windscreen, southern hemisphere light, lighting every small fold and fade and wrinkle in his mother's skin, once so plump and oily. Often he would want to reach over and stroke back a strand of hair, straighten a hem. He missed her old unruliness. For the first time he saw the bravado that lay behind his mother's ramshackle life.

Mark's hospital, when he finally got himself there, was a much smaller place in the suburbs, with an entrance like the lobby of a boutique hotel and sunlit private rooms. You might reasonably imagine you were coming here for pampering, a spa treatment. There was barely a hint of sickness. But Con knew better. Under the scent of new carpet he could smell the rot and fear. He'd worked in a museum, after all. He recognised the odour of bodies in suspended animation.

Still, hard to believe that Mark was lying broken on just the other side of this wall, behind those watercolour poppies, seeping into the sheets. It had been easier to imagine his stricken body in the zoo, laid out on wet cement. Less of an obscenity, there.

Through a small square window, he got a glimpse of tubes and drips and pulsing monitors. In the closest bed was a shrouded form, the face obscured by breathing tubes. He stepped away again, stood leaning against the corridor wall.

A nurse came through the swing door and eyed him. Perhaps he looked ill himself, because she asked, "Are you okay?"

"I was coming to see Mark Carolissen."

"Well, it's not visiting time, but I suppose you can pop in quickly …"

"No, no, it's okay. I won't – I won't disturb him. I'll come back. Thanks."

Her expression hardened. "Do that," she said as he started down the corridor. "He doesn't get visitors."

Con stopped, surprised. "None?"

She held up her thumb and forefinger in an O. "Zero."

"Well, his mother … she's old, you know, she has bad legs, it's hard for her. And I've been out of the country." Oh Mark, he thought. Poor Mark. "Nobody else comes? Really?"

"Ag, there was one girl at the beginning. A little messy thing. Hair everywhere." She flicked a hand at her own forehead, as if chasing a fly. "She came in the beginning, but we had to tell her to go. She got too worked up; it was upsetting everybody else. Crying in the corridors, all sorts of nonsense. She wasn't really normal, you know?"

He nodded.

"And!" She rounded on him. Clearly this was something she'd been wanting to get off her chest for some time. "And unhygienic! With those feathers around her neck! You can't have that nonsense in high care!"

"Sure," he said. "But – sorry for asking – it's not like he's awake, is he?"

"No, he's not awake. But we always tell the people, it's good to talk to your loved ones. You never know what they can hear."

sheep

In London, years before, he'd seen Mark one day on the other side of a busy road. Swinging along with a head full of dreadlocks, wearing spectacles with big square frames; he looked buzzed, striding down the street like a prince. He'd spotted Con – then in a rather fastidious phase, all tucked-in shirt and polished shoes – and laughed like it was the funniest thing he'd ever seen. "What happened to you?" he yelled across the road.

Con walked on, eyes front. He was going to meet a girl that day, and the last thing he wanted was to be waylaid by the past. If you show nothing in your face, he told himself, if you refuse to recognise the moment, then it's the same as if it never happened.

But Mark was already reeling across the road towards him. Skin taut and battered-looking, eyes even bigger than Con recalled: some flesh lost from the face. Con felt instantly cautious, as one is in the presence of an animal sick or wounded. Mark looked wasted, but with an agile, wiry strength that lay in the bone, irreducible.

"Dude, hey!"

And Mark was leaning into him, gripping his elbow, then pulling in for a full, salty embrace.

His body was knotty and unfamiliar. He smelt the same though … almost. Just aged, grown salty and acid. All doused in a good obliterating dose of tobacco and the fruitiness of metabolised drink.

Con gripped his friend's upper arms and eased him gently back. Gave Mark a little shake. How strange, both men now. Pushing against each other as they had as kids, but they'd both grown stronger. They stood with their hands on each other's forearms, looking.

"Fucken malletjie," said Mark. "Let's get a dop."

"Sure, Mark, that'd be good." Already he felt himself adjusting to the old shape of their friendship, finding ways to fit this new Mark's face on top of the old.

"But not now," Mark said. "I gotta run. I'll text you. I live a bit far away, actually, but it's a lekker place. We can walk. You can tell me all about your life. Hey?"

The meeting place turned out to be a nondescript railway station some way out of London; a village surrounded by fields. Con wondered what Mark might be doing in such a place.

He was waiting on the platform. "You live around here?" Con asked after they'd greeted – cursory back-slaps, no hug.

"Ja, just over there …" Mark gestured towards a small street running down from the station. "But I thought it would be good if we got a walk in. Like old times?"

Con wanted to find a pub, sit down, ease things with a pint, but Mark was jittery, jiggling, wanting to be up and away. He wanted to walk. So they walked – across the fields, deep luminous green. Each meadow was much as the one before, four sides bordered variously by wooden fencing or a line of dark trees or a ditch or a path. Some had a few sheep arranged on them in slowly shifting configurations. Not another human soul in sight. It started to rain lightly, and at one point it felt as if tiny ice arrows were being shot at their cheeks, but they kept walking. Con watched the colours leaving Mark's face, and knew that his own face was growing white and numb. But Mark looked better this way: younger, cleaner. The earth smelt fresh, almost erasing the flat metallic smell of the cigarettes in his old friend's clothes and on his breath. Walking, walking. How many kilometres had the two of them crossed in each other's company? Leagues, countries, continents.

Mark with spectacles: no vanity about that now, it seemed. His hair was still very black, but the ratty dreads didn't seem clean. Long fingers, eyes still clear and a little vacant, just as Con remembered them. He smoked endlessly, one after the other, and Con accepted a cigarette too. Under an olive-green army jacket Mark was wearing a white vest with some kind of mandala printed on it. Scuffed jeans. Black boots. A style there, a loose angular ease, but wearing thin. Con noticed also how their heights had evened out. Press Mark's hair flat to his skull, take a slice off the thick soles of those boots, and Con might even be taller now.

"It's pretty here," said Con. "So many birds."

Mark made a spitting noise. "Nothing here," he said. "Nothing wild. This place was killed long ago. No bears, no wolves, no wild foxes even. All that's gone. Everything here is human."

They walked diagonally across a muddy field, climbed a wooden stile into a small copse where the ground was papered with damp copper leaves. In the next field, three wet sheep blundered out of their path. Con stopped trying to remember where they'd come from; his sense of direction was useless. The peril of growing up in a city with one tall mountain in its centre, drawing all compass needles.

As the day waned, the colours of the grass and leaves intensified and seemed to float a little way above the ground, a glowing mist. Mark's figure was flat against this rich background, a silhouette on green and copper. They didn't speak as they walked. Mark, ahead of him on the track, seemed to be sliding, careening away on some slippery surface that lay at a slight angle to the real surface of the world, transparent as ice. His blue eyes still beamed at Con, but there was a hard, clear layer separating them, a coldness. Perhaps they were both sliding, slipping; skaters reaching out to touch gloved fingertips as they spun by.

A stile. A low three-bar fence. Three different sheep, or perhaps the same. Con stopped short.

"Mark, we're going in circles."

"No shit. There's the station over there. We're heading for the pub." Then he laughed. "You always were kind of shit at the outdoorsy stuff, weren't you?"

In the pub, they sat next to a tiny window looking out onto the fields they'd traversed, which still glowed spectrally in the rainy light.

Mark stared out morosely. His mood had turned dark. "You'll stay here, won't you? It seems like your sort of place. England."

What did he mean? This flat greenness, where every field looked the same? His sort of place?

"Nothing there," Mark went on. "Dead. Couple of sheep. Everything gone."

"You've been living here too," Con said coldly.

Mark seemed to be regaining some chippiness. He flicked a dread, dense black from the wet, behind his ear in the old familiar way. "Not for long. I want to go back. I've had it with death. I've had enough of that in my life. Christ. No, I'm going home next week. My mom needs me. She's getting old, you know?"

Con felt rebuked. He and his own mother spoke only a little, these days. Every two weeks or so he'd call, and they'd have an uneasy chat. Behind her voice he'd hear the sounds of the old Woodstock house, echoes and cries. "New parrot?" he might ask, hearing an unfamiliar voice swearing in the background. "Or new guy?" That made her laugh. "This is getting expensive," he'd say quite soon, although he had a special package for cheap international calls. "Can't talk long."

"And look at you," Mark was saying. "You seem … dead. Like you're not even reacting to what I'm saying. Like something's missing." He snapped his fingers in Con's face.

Con was silent, numb.

Mark laughed. "You always were a bit of a cold fish. Could lie with a straight face, too. All that bullshit about your dad. And when Lizzy went …" He shook his head. "What a cold little fucker you were. Do you even remember Lizzy? My sister Lizzy?"

"I should go."

"No, no, wait, bru, I'm only kidding. Wait, I want to show you …" And then he was scrounging in his pocket, trying to pull something out, something that kept hitching on the fabric of his pocket, and for a mad moment Con was afraid it might be a knife.

At last Mark disentangled the object and placed it on the table between them. Con had the distinct sensation of letting his eyes float down upon the surface of the thing, so as not to sink too deep. But of course his gaze had to settle, by the sheer rules of gravity, and there: a piece of wood, whittled roughly into shape, dabbed with paint, this paint now largely worn away. A little lion, roaring. It was odd to see it again after all this time, backlit by the green grass of England. He reached for it, but Mark snatched it back, possessive.

"Lizzy loved this," said Mark. "I gave it to her. The Green Lion. Do you know what that is?"

Con said nothing, just watched his old friend's long fingers caressing the wood. Still the smooth oval nails, but hangnailed and bitten now. His own nails were far better cared for. All in all, better cared for, top to toe.

"It's this very, very ancient symbol. From alchemy. The Green Lion. Those old guys, like in medieval times, used it to make the Philosopher's Stone. Do you know what that is?"

Con just shook his head.

"It could bring things back to life. Cure diseases. When Lizzy went, she left it for me, like a sign, you know?"

His voice was lit and eager. Slipping away, slipping away on a sheet of ice, thought Con. Just now he'd wanted the lion – it was his after all; but now he was repulsed by the idea of it, the wood frayed and warm and damp from Mark's mad grip.

"A sign of what, Mark?" he asked tiredly.

For a moment, Mark seemed to regain himself. He laughed self-consciously. "Oh, you know. That Death is Not the End."

Con smiled. "I do remember Lizzy," he said. Although in truth, Con couldn't recall the child's face. Just a veil of black hair; the warm weight of a hand on his thigh; a white dress in the gloom. "She was beautiful," he said, and immediately that felt wrong: not what you said about a child, a little sister.

But Mark nodded, his eyes very still. "Yes," he said. "Yes, she will always be beautiful."

—

He didn't contact Mark again. Soon afterwards, he met Elyse, and she kept him occupied.

They met in London, when Con was working as a security guard in a palaeontology museum. He loved that about Europe: the art galleries, the obscure collections of swords or dolls or microscopes. In South Africa he'd never really bothered with that kind of thing, associating museums with tedious school outings. But up north he was overpowered by the vast accumulation of *things*. Ordinary and extraordinary objects, plucked from the maelstrom and kept forever, just exactly as they were, in these quiet, guarded rooms, varnished by the regard of a million eyes. Paintings, jewels, broken clay pipes or hand bones from the scene of some ancient calamity. All these objects, rescued from the milling entropy of time: such riches, a treasure hoard.

One day, some years into his stay and after a series of unsatisfactory menial jobs, he walked into a small museum devoted to dinosaur fossils; all clean bone and stone, things reduced to their sparest substructure. There were hardly any visitors. Con was alone when he wandered into a dim alcove where, all on its own in a gold-lit vitrine, lay an icon: *Archaeopteryx lithographica.* "Ancient wing, printed in stone." He'd never seen such delicate bones. The spotlighting was cleverly done: each claw was gilded; each slender rib thrown into relief. Shadows dappled the stone where feather-tips had touched the primal mud.

The placard said it may not have flown at all, just hopped and flapped. Not quite earth-bound, but not yet sensing in the sky a possible dimension. Mongrel, thought Con. Toothed and beaked, clawed and tailed and feathered. You could see it died a sorry death: feathers clogged, the sinews wresting back the neck. Time had purified the body, though. The antic pose – spread wings, bowed head – was stately, a dance saluting death. Con's own head tilted, hands at the glass. So much between them: every second of one hundred and fifty million years.

Shortly afterwards, he applied for a job there. The tranquillity suited him. The museum was a monochrome temple, consecrated to the ancient, the fleshless. The specimens were formally displayed in ways to discourage fanciful interpretation: ribs from various species lined up in order of size; skulls arrayed like iterations of some profound equation. He became one of those men sitting in chairs in the corner, deadpan, scowling at small children and reprimanding anyone who tried to touch. He loved to stay after hours, walking through the galleries of mounted bones, raised up in their classes and phyla, the cold wind of the millennia blowing through their rib cages. He came to know the collection very well.

Only once did flamboyance enter that ossuary. It was a travelling exhibition, something to do with crossovers between Art and Natural History. Photographs and video installations gesturing fuzzily to evolution, to species loss, to the history of the discipline. There were fabric sculptures, performance pieces, a few examples of ironically distorted taxidermy. A muddled assemblage that seemed designed expressly to annoy the museum scientists. They were hostile, protective of their specimens, and Con himself was suspicious of this intrusion into a space that had thus far been so calming.

Elyse was part of the crew setting up the exhibition. Con was aware of her as one is aware of warning colours in the wild: a sinewy form, clothed in red and black, twisting as she hung the big block-mounted photos or pasted on labels. She held pins between her teeth and used a stapler gun like a pro. When he first encountered her she was up on a stepladder, so she had to crane down to see him.

There was something sensually disobedient in her being there at all. He watched the smooth skin of her belly under the cut-off t-shirt; surely such luxe flesh had never been exposed in this building. He'd been too long in the land of old men, of old bones. And single for a little while now, too.

She seemed made of many component parts, artfully sewn together: a big-eyed, doll-like face balanced on a surprisingly tall frame. Her hair at that point was red, like the feathers of a macaw. Her skin seemed inhumanly textureless, pale as bone. When she hopped down off the ladder, she did it lithely, but also with an endearing wobble on landing. She put out a red-nailed hand to balance herself against a glass case containing Cretaceous fossils.

"Careful," he said.

The girl-creature looked him up and down. "You break, you buy?"

Her voice was richly projected, much too loud for a museum. And the accent threw him and stirred him: South African, a trace of Afrikaans. He felt at once that she could see straight through his camouflage – in this case, a bottle-green jacket and tie – and into the body within. He was struck by the absurdity of where they stood, among the fossils: Adam and Eve, an impossible Eden.

She walked away, with a dancing step and a smile over the shoulder, and Con in steady pursuit through the dim halls. He remembered this game. She led him right out of the front door of the museum and into the sunlight, and he felt like he'd woken from a long, dark sleep. She was just a girl, he saw, a tall, pretty young woman wearing too much make-up. But already it was all there, plain to see: her drama, her play, her confident ability to drag him to the light.

She laughed. "God, I'm glad to be out of there. All that dead stuff! Couldn't breathe!"

And Con smiled too, and allowed himself to topple into her.

Elyse was fun. She had a levity that was new to him, and took genuine delight in things that he knew nothing about: art, theatre, fashion. Very different to his mother's smoky cynical laughter, the dry banter of Mark's family. She would take him to see paintings, to the theatre.

He didn't get it.

"Look," she would say, gesturing passionately at an old man in a burgundy jacket going past, or a pair of turquoise shoes basking in a shop window. "Gorgeous! Just look!"

But he couldn't really see. He would stare at these things and think: but they are just things. Or not even. What was he supposed to make of those depthless planes of colour in the art gallery?

Once she took him to a display of children's art, and somehow that was even worse. The bright chalkings gave him a kind of surge behind the breastbone, the sense of being at the edge of a crevasse into which he must not look, a transport to which he must not submit. He turned away and leant his forehead against the wall.

Elyse came threading her way through the interleading rooms to find him at last, her face flushed with the pleasure of the work. She found him outside on the pavement.

"What is it? What's wrong?"

She touched his forehead and drew her hand away, brushing her fingers together in puzzlement. It was just a dusting of plaster from the chalky gallery wall.

"Didn't you like that show?" she asked later in a dim bar with drinks in front of them.

"Kids' stuff, I don't really get it."

"You're not interested in children?"

He felt he owed it to her to let this question reel across his mind, to examine each part of it carefully. Like holding a strip of old-fashioned camera film up to the light.

She tapped her fingernails against the side of her pint. "You don't like children."

"It just wasn't the greatest time of my life."

She gazed at him, recalibrating. Seeing in him for the first time something that perhaps could not be remade.

dassie

In the Sea Point bedroom, the duvet was straightened and turned back, waiting with its usual promise of dreams and nightmares. He sat heavily on the side of the bed and kicked off his scuffed shoes, flexing his toes in their socks and smelling the humble animal funk that came off them. Infiltrating Elyse's pale carpet, her gauzy curtains.

It was okay, though, really okay. He had learnt how to let these things leak out of him. Already the emotion that had welled in him at the sight of Margaret, at the sight of Mark's room, was ebbing. Moods slipped from him so quickly. He lay back on the bed and let his eyes fall closed. Elyse came into the room with her usual fluid stride. He knew what she would say before she said it. She'd want to know things from him: what had happened, how he felt. Surely all she needed to do was sniff the air to sense his weariness.

"So how did it go?" she asked, and he felt her weight on the bed. It was an ornate Victorian brass bed, too high and narrow for his comfort, but one of Elyse's essential items. Easier in fact for her to sit on its edge than for him; she was a tiny bit taller, with all the length in her legs.

"Okay," he said. "Weird."

"I meant the hospital."

"Oh. Ja. They wouldn't let me see him. High care, you know."

"Oh. And with the mother?"

Tiredly, he recounted his day. She was interested in the taxidermy; when he got to the part about the paint-stained lion model in Mark's room, she leant forward with her palms on her knees, excited. "Cool! So he is an artist."

"God, no. It's really … really crude. Not like what you're thinking."

But Elyse had a distant, speculative look in her eyes. Her gaze slipped sideways and she bounced herself off the bed, onto her feet. Con rocked in her wake.

"Well, I'd like to see it. We could even use things like that. The company. Dancers interacting with the trophies … Could be interesting. And I think it sounds like interesting work."

"Elyse, it's not *work*. It's morbid shit, crazy shit."

"Tell me when you go back to the hospital? I'll come with. Or maybe I can come round to the house sometime, check out these stuffed animals."

Such big eyes, so clear and round. They made him tired.

"What's up with you? I can't stand it when you go silent." She bent to pluck his socks from the floor. "Ugh. Fine. Maybe I'll just go see him by myself one of these days. Or give his mother a call. Now take off those clothes and give them to me."

Quite often, she would gather up his clothes and toss them into the washing machine or whisk them away to the dry cleaner. Sometimes, when items were particularly disreputable or worn, he wouldn't see them again. He didn't mind. Con wasn't attached to any of his outfits, which were all much the same; and every now and then she would buy him something new. Black jeans, shirts in black or grey. Things very like what he might buy for himself, but better than he could afford: cotton, not synthetics. Sometimes he even recognised the name on the label. Creased to perfection, wrapped in tissue paper. He liked the luxury, the mysterious renewal. My poor mother, he'd think, remembering: *re-use, recycle*, the mantra of his childhood. Elyse was having none of that. She was all about reinvent, replace. Retail.

Tiredly, he removed his trousers. He should never have mentioned the taxidermy. He should've known that would excite her.

A heavy body slammed into the cage with a sound like a car crash. Con reared up in the bed, trembling with the aftershock of the dream, receding even as he groped for its essence. Those golden eyes.

The room was wrong. No Elyse, again, and blue early-morning

light was coming through the window. But there was something else, some curious difference in the arrangement of light and shade.

He rolled himself off the edge of the bed, landing a little heavily – the height of it took him by surprise every time, even six weeks later – and blundered towards the bathroom. He showered, walked naked back into Elyse's bedroom and flicked on the light. Immediately he saw what the change was. The wardrobe mirror was not giving up its usual dawn reflection. It was covered by something. Elyse had been and gone, it seemed, in the course of his dead sleep, and she'd left some things arranged for him in an instructive tableau.

Mark's uniform hung there, square-shouldered and straight-limbed on a wooden hanger. It had been cleaned and pressed. Elyse had treated it with the same careful attention she gave her own garments. She'd even laid out Con's last good pair of black leather shoes under the hanging uniform, polished to a shine. He stood there dumbly for a moment, trying to read the scene. What did she mean by it? It was a uniform. Clothes to work in.

Con stepped forward and touched the cool sleeve. Safari-style short-sleeved jacket, long matching trousers with a dapper line of braid down the outside leg. Bright brass buttons. The lapel pin was polished, brand new.

Elyse had been thorough. Underwear was laid out on the chair next to the wardrobe. Clean pair of boxers, folded white T-shirt, dark socks in a ball. Like a dutiful five-year-old he put them on. The jacket and trousers were nylon, but felt cool and crisp against his skin. Buttons chill as he slid them into their holes. He squared his shoulders. The effect was surprisingly sleek, as if Mark had tailored the thing to fit more closely to his body – and to Con's. The size was perfect. Mark had been taller by half a head when they were boys; clearly, Con had caught up. As uniforms go, it wasn't too humiliating.

Con smiled to remember how Mark was always customising his school uniform: a safety pin there, the shoes scuffed just so.

His personal appearance was very precise, but seemed off-hand. Con had tried to emulate his friend's casual elegance but had never achieved it. He never knew when to push up a cuff or when to let it trail. Although they'd done their best to ruin their school uniforms, had defaced them at every opportunity, secretly Con was glad of his. Partly because his own clothes were cheap and a little sad, but also because he wanted simple rules to follow. Mark was always setting other, more stringent standards, with signals ever subtler: the hem just so, the particular kind of beads worn at the neck under the school collar, the hair falling exactly right. Con had had to be a very watchful child to pick up on the constant tweaks to the secret dress code.

Con liked the little lion's-eye brooch: the rich gold against the brown, the buttercup of light the metal cast on the underside of his jaw in the mirror. It gave some colour to his face, as the eyeliner had given life to his eyes.

Outside the Lion House, Con sat in the shade as the sunlight came creeping along the road, glinting on the bars of the fence. God, he'd surprised himself with longing for this mountain. Its shape against the sky, wherever you were in the city; a steady magnetic pole. Only now did he realise how his compass-needle heart had wavered and spun, all those years overseas.

On the flight home he'd let Europe go, all its rich pictures dropping out of his mind and through the window of the plane as it hung above the plains of central Africa, the lights down there so few and small. All the treasures of Europe, the paintings and the buildings, the museums and galleries, he let them go. He watched them spinning, tiny as postage stamps, into the vast Saharan night.

By morning, and Cape Town, his mind was empty, waiting. And there below, tipped beneath the silver wing and circling closer, was the shape to fill it, richly green and grey: the long pointer of the peninsula, the pedestal of the mountain. Fissured, fecund, ringed by the city but cupping its secrets high above the city's eyes. So different to the vast, life-repelling slopes of the Alps, which had filled him with exhilarated dread when he looked down on their crowns from his first ever aeroplane, crossing north.

When he'd left Cape Town, nineteen years old and desperate to get out, it had been a smoggy day, dreary and windblown, the air salted and sanded and the mountain a blue-tissue silhouette. But now it looked lush, greener than he remembered. Perhaps kicking all the people off the mountain had helped with that, after all.

Looking up at it, he let his head fall back against the fence, and half-slumbered, breathing in the deep green scent of the mountain. The air seemed full of birdcall: doves, starlings. So this is what he missed each morning, drowsing late in Elyse's sheets. He opened his eyes at the sound of steps approaching.

It was the woman with the steel-grey plait, Amina, making her way up the walk. As she moved out from under the trees, her face was soft and unguarded, the expression shifting as shadows flowed across it like thoughts. When she caught sight of him, though, she stopped still and her face hardened; she put her hand up to guard her eyes from the flash of sun off the metal sign. He was disappointed by her stony expression; he'd had a smile ready, a little joke. After Elyse's accusing absence, he wanted a small moment of human contact. Con felt suddenly uncertain of his purpose here.

She walked past him without a word, but with a wary, apprais-ing look. At the gate, fiddling with the key, she glanced over her shoulder.

"We're not open today," she said as the lock surrendered in her hands.

Perhaps she needed a moment to place him. More likely – and this occurred to him too late – she was simply nervous of a man here so early, with no one else about, his body concealed by a long coat. He made his face pleasant and unthreatening, made sure his hands were in view. "It's me," he said. "You remember – I came the other day ... Con Marais. I came for Mark's things."

The gate swung open. Her hands fell to her sides. "Oh god, what's happened? Is he ...?"

"No, no, he's fine. I mean, not fine, but – no change. I wanted to ask you about something else."

She watched his face a moment longer. "Come in," she said, pushing through the gate and leaving it open behind her.

Con followed her in and down to the building where they'd first met. This time she let him come inside the office, gesturing at a chair. It was pokey, just space enough for a computer station, a fax machine and a couple of chairs. The wastebasket overflowed and there were books and pamphlets stacked on the floor.

"You'll have to excuse the mess," said Amina. "We're cutting down on cleaning shifts. As I mentioned before, we're short-staffed. So." She put her handbag down on her desk and sat provisionally on the edge of her rolling chair, looking as if she would far rather be attending to her morning rituals – the inevitable coffee, perhaps the cigarette, the switching on of the computer with its encouraging click and glow – and would get back to these just as soon as she'd rid herself of him. She gripped the edge of the table with both hands, and he was reminded of something – the pilot of a boat, grasping the tiller, preparing to cast off. "How can I help you?"

Con had a little speech prepared for this moment, something ingratiating. He'd imagined himself sheepish. Running a hand through his hair with a wry smile. The director would've been surprised, wary of course, but ultimately grateful and delighted. She would've taken his hand to shake, mock-formal.

But all that seemed foolish now. This was no time for charm. Amina seemed impatient, and the facts of the matter were best laid simply on the table.

So he just opened his coat to show her the brown uniform underneath, the shirt and trousers that fitted him so well. It wasn't meant to be a dramatic gesture, just a demonstration of the situation, the offer on the table. But it came out feeling teasing.

Her eyes widened, and then she laughed for the first time. Casting herself off from the edge of the table, she propelled her rolling chair back against the cupboard with what was, after all, a rather gratifying smack, almost jubilant, and he knew that another small seduction had been contrived.

"Well," she said, "I'm not going to look a gift horse in the mouth. But I hope you understand that we can't really pay you."

It didn't take long for Amina to show him around the property. Apart from the lion den, there were a few other small enclosures where less spectacular animals were kept, or would be in future. "Aviary," said Amina, gesturing with her chin at the airy cage. "Although for some reason the birds aren't so popular. People go to Bird World; things are more colourful there."

Indeed, all he could see were a couple of guinea fowl pecking in the dust around the bottom of the cage, and higher up some small-headed, drab shapes lined up on their roosts like unwilling trapeze artists.

"We had squirrel monkeys once. The kids liked them, but they're not indigenous, so …" She tapped a ringed finger sharply against the bars – producing what seemed to Con to be a spiteful ding that travelled through the metal and made the roosting birds shuffle their feathers.

"Dassies," she said shortly, moving along to a low odorous cage set with artificial rocks. There were a dozen of the scruffy little animals in there, chewing on leaves and scowling up at their visitors.

They'd come up against a tall new wall. "And that's pretty much it," said Amina. "The grounds of the old zoo carry on beyond here, but they're in ruins."

This he remembered. The tiny, cruel monkey cages built to resemble circus wagons, the cracked cement pools, the iron bars cocooned in morning glory and blackjacks. He'd come here with his mother as a child, but even then the old zoo was in decline, melancholy and inexplicable, with animals hidden or ailing or invisible in cage after cage. He remembered the magnetic dread of the lion's den – a pit where a few moth-eaten African lions lounged. Later, after the place closed down, the cages were left standing like an abandoned city, doors swung open. Parts of the zoo were built over to make parking spaces for the university; some of the old cages were occupied by vagrants.

"We hope to expand," said Amina. "We'd like to absorb the quagga enclosures, have some of them in an area where the public can get close. The dassies are fun for now, but ultimately we'll keep our focus on extinctions. The quaggas, the black-maned lions. Like everywhere these days, the focus is on species loss, but we've got something different. We can give it a positive spin: animals brought back from death, you know? If we ever manage to breed, there'll be space for cubs … But this whole business has been very bad for fundraising, as you can imagine." She frowned. Mouth-twitch. "Sorry, that sounds bad."

"I know what you mean."

She led him back into the area closed to the public: the grassed corridor, the cold prefab shed, the offices. When he glimpsed the dark archways leading through to the lion den, he braced himself in anticipation. But Amina turned aside before they got that far.

"I wouldn't hang around down there," she said. "She's bad with new people. People who smell different."

He wondered what he smelt of. Elyse's cigarettes, Elyse's perfume? With a last glance at the dark space – in which nothing moved today – he followed Amina inside.

She led him into a long room with a row of lockers down one end near the bathrooms, and at the other an arrangement of plastic chairs and tables and a couple of whiteboards. Wide windows ran the length of the room, but the view was of nothing but a sandstone wall.

"This is the staffroom," said Amina, "and this is the staff. What's left of it."

There were only two people there. A young woman in her early twenties – small, with busy dark fingers poking from the rolled-up sleeves of a too-big uniform – was sitting consulting her phone at a trestle table. Pouring himself a cup of coffee from an urn at the end of the room was the bald, constantly smiling man Con had encountered sluicing out the lion cage two days before.

"People, this is Con Marais; he's the new volunteer," said Amina. "He'll be doing a few other things around the place too, filling in, until we get the new hires. Con, this is Thandiswa, she's our nature conservation student from the university." The girl smiled and gave him a fingertip wave. "We have a few more volunteers; they generally come in later. And Elmien; she's on the gate. Canteen staff come in later. Isak you've met." The man raised his mug at Con, teeth glimmering.

Everyone was in uniform, which added a stagey element to proceedings. His own, he saw, was in the best nick, and worn the most formally. The other three had on running shoes, different-coloured т-shirts under their jackets. Coats were unbuttoned and sleeves rolled up. The staff seemed a little shy, not quite easy in his company or each other's; Con supposed they were all still slightly in shock after the accident. He wondered how much longer they were planning to stick around in this clearly unnerving job. But then Thandiswa gave him a wink.

Amina pointed at the lockers. "Coffee and tea over there, self-evident. Staff meetings once a week." Then she was on the move again, leading him across a narrow passage back into her own office, and then into an even smaller cubicle at the back, just big enough for a chair and a PC. "There you go," she said. "This is where Mark worked."

"Oh." He looked for something personal, but the workspace was clean. A glass ashtray, a jar of pens. A couple of books, propped up by a decorative bookend. His gaze slid away from this object, then flicked back, troubled.

"You'll need to start with the emails – there'll be hundreds of unopened ones in there, I can just tell. Sort them out, weed out the crap. Anything that looks like it has to do with funding, anything that comes from the Department, forward it to me. If it's something that just requires a pretty answer, write a pretty answer. Get rid of journalists."

"Oh. Okay."

"What, not quite what you had in mind?"

"No, no, that's fantastic …"

"Once you get the email wrangled, we'll talk about other things that need doing. The staff rosters are in chaos, with all the people who've left."

"Right. Right."

She smiled at him. "I know you were thinking you'd be working with her. The lioness. I know that's what you're here for."

Was it? "I had hoped to see her."

"Everybody loves the lions," she said. "But maybe not just yet, okay? She needs to get used to you. She can probably smell you, right now."

Elyse liked to argue on the balcony, in front of passers-by. Perhaps it was because the flat seemed very small when things were tense between them; perhaps she just liked an audience. She would perch on the balcony rail and brace one naked foot against the wall, curving her back; her feet were very clean, long and high-arched. Toenails polished blood or black. It was a fighting posture that heightened the drama of the scene and filled him every time with a thrill of vertigo.

That evening, Elyse had taken one look at him in the doorway and immediately led him outside, a toreador stalking into the ring. She spun around in the small space of the balcony and smacked him with a look: coldly puzzled. More than ever her head seemed mismatched with her body, a cool mask twitching up and down to take him in, her big eyes lidded. She smelt of lilacs.

"So what the hell is this? You look like a postman. Or some kind of policeman from, I don't know, the sixties."

He straightened his collar and clicked the heels of his shined-up shoes.

"Seriously. What is that?" She leant in, pointing her nose at his little gold badge.

"I'm working at the Lion House."

She searched his face for the joke.

"What? I thought you'd be pleased; I've got a job. Wasn't that the idea?"

"What do you mean, the idea?"

"You put the clothes out. For me. The uniform. I thought you were making a suggestion."

She tapped a cigarette out of the pack and lit it, taking her time, each movement very deliberate. "No, Con. No. Actually that wasn't *the idea*. Actually, I just thought you might take the goddamn morbid thing back to the place it came from, like a normal person. Apparently I was wrong. It wasn't some secret fucking coded message. God, if I actually wanted you to go work in that place, where your friend has just been *ripped limb from limb*, you don't think I'd just tell you so?"

Con had no answer to that.

She tapped her ash off the edge of the balcony and gave her head a disbelieving shake. "What are they paying you?"

"I'm a … volunteer."

"Hah! Volunteer zookeeper? Jesus fucking Christ, Con, no, that's not what I had in mind."

"I might get a raise soon. Or at least, paid."

"I can't decide if you are unbelievably full of bullshit. Or if you really are that strange."

He knew this phase, in relationships. The charm, he could tell, was wearing off him. He gave her his smile and she assessed it. At length she softened; he could see it in the way she gave her head a little shake, a little nod, not quite a smile. She held out the pack of cigarettes. He sighed and accepted one, although he rarely smoked these days. Might as well get what he could, while it was still on offer.

"Well, I suppose it is quite cute," she said, inhaling. She leant forward and felt the shiny material of the collar, with the keen eye of one who knew her costumery. She tapped the lion badge with a hard nail. Strong beautiful nails, Elyse had, silver today. "What have they got you doing, anyway?"

"Lion tamer."

That got a laugh, a snort of tobacco smoke. "What, with a chair and a whip?"

"I have to get in there with a trident and a net. Then they release the animals."

She regarded him steadily for a moment or two, then pulled her long arm out from under her elbow – she'd been holding it tensely trapped there – and held out a thumb. Thumbs-up, thumbs-down, the hand slowly swivelled. Thumbs-up.

He leant forward and took her fist in his hand and kissed the cool stem of her thumb, pressing the nail into his lips. "*Morituri te salutant.*"

"What?"

"Nothing."

"No, what did you say?"

"Shh." Always, always so many words with Elyse.

But she pulled away, with a light, deliberate scratch of that nail on his lower lip.

"Wait," he said. "I got a present for you." He hadn't, actually, had any intention of giving it to her, but now he'd drawn it out of his pocket and was holding it on his palm. It was the bookend from Mark's shelf in the office. Which wasn't a bookend at all.

She picked up the little wooden lion as if she'd rather not touch it, with the tips of her fingernails. "That's sweet," she said doubtfully. The toy was delicately carved, characterful, with a snub muzzle and a big Afro mane that had once been green and gold; the paint had worn off almost completely. "Is this from the gift shop or what? It looks … used."

It was all wrong for Elyse, of course: she had nothing like it, nothing old or tatty or sentimental, no souvenirs. Soon enough, the house would spit it out, like flesh expels a thorn.

II. THE FENCE

The Pointers to the Southern Cross were formerly men, and at the same time lions. One of them became a star, because a girl looked at him; and the other lion also became a star. They now stand silent, not far from the lionesses, who sit silent.

– ‖KABBO, as told to Lucy Lloyd, 1871 (summary)

virus

Con didn't have many memories from early childhood. Those he had were a few bright coins gleaming in shadow, lost behind cupboards, slipped into cracks between floorboards. The problem was that all his memories were made in his mother's house, which though small was a convoluted space, folded like a human brain.

The first thing to know about Lorraine was that she never threw anything away. Animals, old bills, boyfriends – she kept them close. At any point in Con's childhood, there might be four or five stray cats in the house, two rusted motorbikes in the back garden with morning glory growing through their spokes, a guy off the street drinking a glass of water at the kitchen table. Strangers in the bathroom, the bedroom, smoking joints on the stoep. Odd lots, bits and pieces, like chipped cups and sugar bowls from a dozen different tea sets. They washed up in the little brown house by no volition of their own, but through some natural law of flotsam and jetsam. Lorraine attracted junk.

In fact, she trafficked in the stuff; she kept stalls at three or four weekly markets around Cape Town, and went to all the auctions, and the rest of the time worked shifts in an antique shop in town. She never had cash, but she always had old clothes to barter, knick-knacks to swap. She wasn't ashamed to peel promising items off the pavement and bring them home. Mismatched furniture stacked together, chair legs in the air, cushions and tall birdcages and pieces of washing machines and porcelain doves and oil paintings with dinged gilt frames. The house was full, full, full: a dense matrix of *stuff*.

As a young child, the clutter had given Con a reassuring sense of abundance. They had so much! Every corner was packed; there were no blank spaces, as in other people's homes. It was only later, when he was a teenager newly infatuated with sparseness, that he wanted to throw things out. He went through a period of trying to clean things around him, scrubbing a small neat track from his bedroom to the kitchen to the bathroom. At one point he even bought Windolene, sulphuric acid to pour down the blocked drain, dust-cloths. He tried. He was constantly tidying his room, and then coming home from school to find she'd moved new shit in there, pushed under his bed or leaning in a corner: a cat box, a set of Christmas lights.

"Just for now, until we find a place for it," she'd say. Or, holding up a chipped garage-sale teapot: "Amazing, isn't it? *Anyone* might have owned this. And if we hadn't saved it, all those stories would just be lost."

The objects were dumb to him, unspeaking. They could only hint at strangers' inscrutable lives.

The truth was, Lorraine wasn't really one for memories either; she lived fervently in the present. Her impulse for hauling home all this stuff, Con eventually decided, was to fill the holes where memories should be, or perhaps where bad ones had been re-moved. These absences were distributed around the house like unexpected air pockets; Lorraine tried to stop them up with threadbare carpets and hamster cages. Sometimes the whole edifice felt precarious, as if in fact one giant sinkhole yawned beneath their property, although from the outside, the roof and walls seemed quite intact. It was a clearly defined, neat-edged hole. They took their supper and breakfast at its crumbling rim, but every now and then their gaze would flick to the side and catch a glimpse of something unspeakable in the rubble at the bottom: a hand, a finger, a mouth still moving.

On certain days, his mother held herself tensely, with no sudden movements, like someone waiting for the ground to fall beneath her feet. He knew then that the next day, or the one after that, she would arrive home with something big to soothe herself: a fake-walnut dresser with a cracked back, a three-legged puppy.

She pretty much left him to forage through the home for things he needed. Like clothes and school supplies. The house was a rich hunting ground. There were plenty of toys lying about, often in the boxes of miscellaneous goods that came from the auctions his mother obsessively attended.

The first toy Con loved, when he was a little kid, was the soldier. He never had a name. The figure was hard, moulded plastic with a removable drab-green uniform and plastic bandolier. The soldier's face was angular and hard, with pale-blue eyes and a neat cap of gloss-black hair, painted on. You could take the clothes off and underneath he was aggressively pink, with minimally suggested pectorals, no navel and a bulge of undefined crotch. Con liked to run his fingers over the smooth bumps and hollows, wondering at the differences.

When he showed the plastic soldier to his mother she laughed. "Well, he's got a stick up his arse! Reminds me of someone." Patrick, her boyfriend of the time, gave a shout of complicit laughter. He was a part-time landscape gardener who sold bonsai out of the back of a bakkie at the Milnerton Market.

"Who? Who does it remind you of?" Con was always looking for clues. He'd already decided that the soldier's features had been his father's, that they would be his, too, when he was old.

"Never mind. I just wish you weren't playing with war toys, that's all."

"What must I play with, then?"

"We like animals, we like things in nature. Don't we?" She looked to Patrick for confirmation.

"Try this for size," he said, handing Con a piece of wood.

"Look, it's a horse," Lorraine said helpfully. "You can see the four legs and the head and the tail. Sort of."

It was unpainted, formless, barely shaped. "Who made it?"

"Nature made it. A tree made it."

"It doesn't have eyes." He saw with revulsion that it still had bark clinging to its underside, like a skin disease. It was just something she'd picked up on one of her walks in the forest with Patrick. "I hate it."

"God, Con. Sometimes I think you have no imagination at all."

But he did. He furiously imagined himself into the soldier's body, pink and black and blue. Although in truth his face was a gentle, irregular oval, his eyes brown like his mother's. Even his hair was wrong, curled and ill-disciplined. But perhaps things would change. Surely something different would hatch out of this misshapen egg of childhood.

To help things along, he once tried to change his hair. His mother used few cosmetics, and those she had were frustrating to him. The handcreams promised softness, but Con wanted one to make him tough. He found an oil that made his hair go dark and shiny, especially when he combed it back. But within minutes it started to dry, sticky and stiff, pulling at his scalp.

"What the hell are you doing?" asked his mother when she spotted him squaring his jaw in the bathroom mirror. She'd burst in without knocking as usual, a pile of cut-price beach towels in her arms. "Patrick! Come and look at this! Priceless!"

Con washed the crust of dried lotion out of his hair, the warm water dissolving him like their laughter. In later years he wondered if the liquid had perhaps been something hilariously terrible, like spermicide.

In revenge, he took the stupid eyeless not-horse down to the bottom of the garden and snapped off its stupid not-legs. It broke easily, the wood half-rotted. The remaining knobbed stump looked a bit like a rifle, and he ran around with that in the garden for a while, shooting the cat with it. He killed the cat several times, clean shots. His father, he decided, hadn't been a soldier after all. He'd been a hunter.

Then he took the cat inside and fed it all of the disgusting homemade yoghurt that Patrick had been culturing in the fridge, which Con found completely gross but which the cat seemed to love.

He didn't let Patrick get to him; the man wouldn't be around for long. They all went away, eventually. It's not that there were fights or dramatic break-ups; more that the boyfriends seemed to wear out fast, as used goods do. There were often overlaps, with one guy hovering in line while the previous incumbent was still gathering his shoes from under the bed. And sometimes you might find an ex on the sofa weeks after formal eviction.

Weird thing was, he knew his mother didn't really like people, on the whole; she barely spoke to them. Con understood. For as long as he could remember, he'd daydreamt himself into a world without people, without conversation. Even as an adolescent, he still liked to page through his favourite children's book, one with dinosaurs, where in each watercolour landscape, lush with swamps and volcanoes, there wasn't a solitary human soul. Con knew without having to speak about it that he and his mother would inhabit such a world with similar relief. Lorraine having a smoke in the shade of a giant fern, way on the other side of the Jurassic meadow. And over the hill, near but not present, perhaps his father lived. Polishing his weapons.

Still, she seemed to like having people around the table, talking shit and drinking while she smoked at one end, ciggie after ciggie, watching the men with a look of sly amusement that she sometimes shared, wordlessly, with her son.

The hollowness at the heart of things, Con knew instinctively, had to do with his dad. Constantine senior: that's where the name came from, and this was just about all Con knew about his father. Lorraine didn't like to talk about it, and was disconcertingly vague about the details of the man's life and death.

"He got sick, very sick," she'd told him when he was small. "There was nothing they could do."

"What kind of sick?"

"What? Oh, well … it was some kind of disease. A virus."

"What's a virus?"

"Questions, Con …!" She sighed. "Well, it's a teeny, tiny, *teeny* animal …" She held her finger and thumb up, a fraction apart. "They get into your blood and make you sick. Terrible thing. And that's what got your father in the end, I'm afraid."

It was extremely troubling. Animals the size of fleas, and they were *inside*. Worrying to discover that animals could turn against you. In Lorraine's house, pets were safe recipients of demonstrative love. When things got difficult, for example now with this conversation, it was best to break away to feed a rabbit or let a goldfish nibble the fingertips.

When his mother seemed to run out of facts about his father, Con turned to the house for clues. There were certain objects that vibrated with dad-ness – a particular black leather jacket, a chessboard, a book on polar exploration – and Con was sure they'd been his. Lorraine, when confronted, would usually confirm this, although she seemed curiously cool towards his finds.

The fact that nothing was ever thrown away meant that there was archaeology to be done, stratigraphies to be revealed. Except, instead of digging down, Con's explorations went up: as he grew taller, more and more levels became accessible to him. High shelves in the house lowered themselves benevolently to his reach. Treasures there, and puzzles, and moments of fright, and a great deal of dust. He touched each new landmark with his fingertips: the doorknobs, the lintels. The tops of bookcases, upper shelves. These waystations were markers for his memories; they were how he was aware of growing. His own height was the one thing that changed in a methodical manner in that house, which otherwise altered in only accidental ways.

One afternoon when Con was eleven, he came downstairs to find Lorraine and Clive, the boyfriend of that period, sorting mushrooms at the kitchen table. Clive was very much like Patrick, but older, with a gritty jaw and silver hair down his back. He called himself an "urban forager". Lorraine had brought him home from an organic fete a few weeks before. Since then they'd taken to going for walks in the forest, gathering not only oddly shaped sticks but wild foods, not something Lorraine had ever shown the slightest interest in before. The mushrooms were yellow and multi-branched, and Con looked at them with suspicion.

"It's amazing what you can find up there," explained Lorraine.

Clive pulled the bunches of fleshy fungus from a damp plastic bag. Con reached over to take one, but Clive extended a long arm, like a greying chimpanzee's, and slapped his fingers away.

"Ow!" Con yelled, louder than was necessary.

"Don't take what's not yours," said Clive.

Con gaped at his mother, outraged. Private property was not a concept that had ever been much recognised in Lorraine's house.

She screwed up her mouth at him in wordless apology. "Just don't, love," she said. "It's not a good idea."

"Well, I suppose he could try a little one," muttered Clive.

"No, he bloody couldn't," said Lorraine. "Love, go outside for a minute, just until we finish in here. These mushrooms aren't for little boys."

He screeched his chair away from the table and stomped to the kitchen door, flinging it open and then shut behind him. The door rebounded off its jamb, tearing from the hinge. Con leapt aside just in time as the door fell right out of the frame and slammed into the concrete step. A stunned moment, and then hilarity for Clive and Lorraine.

The door was wide open for weeks, covered only in a bit of tarpaulin. Any broken thing stayed half-mended, propped up, bodged together with gaffer tape and string. His mother didn't or couldn't fix stuff, and the boyfriends – who might reasonably have been expected to change a lightbulb here, whack a nail in there – never did a thing. Breakages were another way of marking time: a slow clock of dissolution. The clock's hands would stick in one position for years, and then all at once, after some spectacular collapse of a wall or floorboard, swing halfway round the clock face.

It wasn't that there were no tools for repairs. Outside, currently being used as a rabbit-hutch roof, there was a large piece of plyboard, gridded with holes, on which were the spray-painted outlines of saws, hammers and other tools. Some of the shapes were mysterious: bumped and spurred and ridged. As a younger kid he'd imagined they represented lost torture implements, weaponry. But now he knew better, there being something similar in the woodwork room at school, with each tool suspended perfectly in front of its own negative space. Con had no way of knowing who had originally set up the board and meticulously sprayed the outlines. But he could guess.

"Where are they?" he asked his mother, pointing at the cryptic blue shapes.

"Hmm? Have the cats got the rabbits again?" Lorraine squinted at the hutch.

"The tools."

"Oh … they're around," she said. "I'm sure they are. There's a toolbox, I think … haven't seen it for ages though. Who knows? Black tin box?"

Con closed his eyes and let the picture come to him. Black tin box. Although Lorraine's house held no history, one could, with careful effort, build and keep some memories of one's own. Indeed, life here frequently felt like playing a very elaborate, years-long, multi-dimensional game of Memory; a slippery one, where the objects moved around behind your back. But, yes: he'd seen something, somewhere, sometime. A patch of black tin … Up high.

It was put away on the second-highest shelf in the kitchen behind a collection of empty coffee tins. A large black box with thin looped handles on either end. Before, he'd been too small to do more than touch it with his fingertips, but now he could grip one handle and pull it off the shelf. It was much heavier than he'd realised, and at once he could feel that this wasn't his mother's possession; it was tight and weighty, everything shipshape and squared away. He eased it out and for a moment swayed on the narrow top of the stepladder, then found his footing, the burden hugged to his chest. The box impressed him; it had been packed by someone with an understanding of balance and control, and he absorbed these lessons as he took its weight in his arms. Steadfastly he stepped backwards, spine straight, calves straining, unseeing down one, two, three steps, bringing his feet together at the bottom and swivelling.

"You'll mash your toes," said his mother, drinking tea at the kitchen table. He ignored her and carried the box outside, laying it down at the foot of the back steps. Lorraine watched him through the open door.

The toolbox had metal catches, and when they were undone the top cracked open into two halves. Inside, compartments packed with gleaming objects, black and silver. Handles of wood, and of red or amber plastic, showing the rub and wear of use, of a man's hands, as if they had just been put away. When he tugged at the trays, they magically concertinaed into cantilevered segments, like the mouthparts of a robotic insect. More partitioned trays filled with shiny screws and discs and rings and rods.

"What is this one?" he asked, holding up a c-shaped curve of metal, with knobs. "What does it do?"

Lorraine shook her head, the rim of her teacup motionless.

"And this?" A rod with a hexagonal socket on the end.

"No idea, Connie. I was never good at this stuff."

"So these were Dad's." He was laying out the tools on the concrete.

With a determined sigh, she put down the cup, hauled herself to her feet and came to sit on the step above him. "Yup."

Clive wandered over from where he was aimlessly piling pieces of scrap wood. He reached down and picked up a saw. "Well, this one's for cutting, obviously." Clive rested the blade playfully on the top of Con's head. Con ducked under the teeth, so it chopped the skin at the back of his neck, more painfully perhaps than Clive had intended. Lorraine laughed.

"Put it down," said Con. "You too, Mom." She was fiddling with a wing nut; he could see it was going to come off and spindle away into the grass.

And she did put it down; she wasn't really easy with the things. Together, mother and son, they sat and looked at the tools that lay between them – glamorous, they were, with their weight, their cold and mysterious functions – and Con felt their mutual helplessness.

Hopeless, hopeless, he thought, we're all hopeless. Looking with annoyance at Clive, who was now smashing – none too efficiently – the pieces of the broken door across his knee. Clive liked a bonfire.

Con messed around a bit with the tools at the bottom of the garden, twisting the knurled knobs, pressing the tips of the drill-bits into pieces of wood. It was no good, he couldn't fix or make a thing, couldn't even think of things he might want to make. The tools were inert in his hands, and now it was starting to drizzle. The stray tortoiseshell cat came loping up to him and pressed its bony back against him. He scratched its back with a chisel, then poked it a bit too hard. The old cat leapt away from him into the rain.

When he went back into the house, he was soaked. His mother was sitting at the kitchen table, cat in lap. The parakeet chided. The cat, a forgiving creature, came over to him purring, butting its head up under his wet chin, and he stroked it gently. Outside, the rain came down steadily; the tools lay rusting in the woodpile.

"What did he do with those tools? My dad."

"Well … he made things, didn't he?"

"Like what?"

His mother looked at him thoughtfully, stroking the tabletop. Then she gave it a smack. "Here. For one thing, he made this, right here. Look how solid it still is. That was your dad."

And it was; it was a fine table, one of the only free-standing pieces of furniture in the house that didn't need a folded-up piece of cardboard under one leg. Con ran his fingertips lightly over the surface. Scarred by a thousand knife-cuts, but sturdy. "What else?"

"Oh, you know," said Lorraine, her gaze wandering. "Bits and pieces."

"Like what?"

"Well." She thought for a moment. "He made a Noah's Ark once, with all the animals. Two of each. They fitted inside this wooden boat with a red roof you could take off. It was very clever."

"Oh." A toy. For a little kid. But still … "Where is it now?"

"Oh, I don't know, it's around here somewhere. I didn't throw it away, that's for sure. You should have a look for it."

And he did, surreptitiously. It was a little embarrassing, to be so interested in a kid's plaything. At any rate, he never did find the Ark, lost in the flood. But he wasn't too disappointed. He'd gained important pieces of evidence: his father was a practical man, a man with tools. This, Con might learn to be. Dad was also an animal lover, or else why would he choose to build an ark? The pets, in their mysterious ways, were clues to his father's heart. The parakeets and the dogs and goldfish and occasional guinea pig were holders of this secret behind their small, wise eyes. Hunters love animals too; they know them better than anyone.

Only one of Noah's escaped animals ever surfaced – in the jaws of a new puppy. Con wrestled it away and took it up to his room. The puppy, who was very young, hadn't done too much damage, leaving only milk-tooth needle-holes in the wood. It was a jaunty little lion, intricately patterned in green and gold like a carousel ride, the mane painted with gold lines radiating from the face, legs braced and head pulled back and mouth open in a doll-sized roar. He knew at once that it had come from the missing Noah's Ark. He didn't tell Lorraine.

He kept the lion under his pillow. At night as he lay in bed he reached out a hand and felt its smooth flank. Sometimes he talked to it, or made him buck and canter across the sheet. Often he just lay and stared at him: a secret animal, one part of a puzzle. In his dreams, the miniature lost animals marched two by two along the veins of his father's forearm.

He carried the lion with him long after he'd grown too old for such things. It grew battered in the bottom of his canvas school satchel, down under the weight of the textbooks, the green and gold wearing off its corners.

—

In Elyse's bedroom, the lion smiled at him in the blue dark. It had ended up on the dresser, for now. He could tell Elyse was awake too. They didn't often talk like this, together in the dark. Elyse's performance work was often exhausting, and sleep came for her quick and deep.

"So aren't you afraid?" she asked.

"What do you mean?"

"Of the lion. I mean, how does it feel? Working there, where Mark was?"

He didn't like the way it had changed from "your friend" to "Mark" – as if he was now a friend to her too, an intimate. "Lioness," he said. "Actually I haven't even seen her yet."

"Still, don't you feel vulnerable? I mean, it's a bit weird, putting yourself in his shoes like that."

Shhh, he thought into the night. *Shhh.* "I haven't really thought about it," he said at last.

"Liar."

And then, a little later, still wide awake: "I think it's weird."

He turned his back on Elyse in the dark, although he could sense her buzzing dissatisfaction. If he touched her now they'd be awake all night. He wanted to be silent, the better to bring on sleep, the sooner to wake and go back to work.

He woke quite early in the morning, calm and energetic. He hadn't dreamt. He thought about the day ahead and the road he would walk to work, and had the strangest feeling that his dreams had emigrated from the sleeping hours to manifest in the world before him.

rooikat

Con was twelve when they first started talking about the fence.
The first section wasn't controversial. It was right up at the top,
out of sight from the bottom of the mountain, fencing off a
section for the tourists around the cable-car station and the little
paths that ringed it. The Department of Parks and Tourism said
it was for security: there'd been too many problems, too many
visitors mugged, too many people walking off the cliffs in the
mist.

Con saw it for the first time when they were taken up in the
cable car on a school outing. In revolving gondolas, the class of
forty kids and four teachers ascended into the cloud. Con stood
apart in the metal pod, watching the cliff-face reel past. He'd made
no particular friends. He was a quiet child, never approaching
others, although there were certain people he liked to watch.

At the top, the mist hid the famous view. Everything was grey:
rocks, sky, plants even. After the obligatory lecture on denuded
fynbos and climate change – easy to believe up on the bleak
plateau, populated, it seemed, only by the silver and orange
plaques of ancient lichen – the pupils were allowed to wander. A
hundred metres from the cable station, the new fence stopped
them short. They ranged along its length like prisoners.

"Trapped!" said a voice next to him, and he turned to see Mark
grinning.

Mark was a tall, slender boy, with a long face and long hands
and a fall of black fringe over one eye. He had a quick humour and
already the teachers all liked him. Girls, too. By the second week
of school, he was offering to finish a popular girl's needlework
homework. He was that kind of boy; he could knit an angora scarf
and it would be cool and funny, not naff. The colours were the
school colours but funked up, just a little off – purple instead of
maroon, sky blue instead of navy. The girl kept that scarf around

her neck for weeks, although the days were hot. The knitting was good, too – the stitches chunkily rounded. Fluid and attractive, like his handwriting, like his drawings in art class. A good artist, that's what everybody said about Mark. He was that boy, the one that the older girls took under their wing and fed cake at lunch. He'd never paid Con the slightest attention.

Mark wasn't wearing quite the right pants, not the grey flannels that the school prescribed, but trousers made out of some silkier, slightly darker fabric. Anyone else would have got detention for it. Con's own flannels were second-hand, baggy and hemmed at the bottom.

The two boys looked through the bars at the valley beyond. A small wind struck up and made the fence moan like a harp; they could hear the noise starting in the dip below and running along the struts.

"See anything?" asked Mark. "I heard there were gangs living up here. They kidnapped some girl and kept her on the mountain for a week or something. Then they left her body hanging on the fence."

Con noticed that Mark was squinting just a little as he peered through the bars. Short-sighted? Perhaps that's how he maintained that distant, dreaming look. His olive skin was paler in the mist, the dark hair swept back off his brow, the eyes a blank watercolour blue. There was a scent coming off the other boy, organic but clean, like peppermint. Con became aware, for the first time in his life, of his own sweat. He was standing downwind at least, catching Mark's breeze. Con was surprised by a quick spurt of saliva at the back of his jaw; he didn't trust himself to open his mouth. Picturing something gross and uncontrolled emerging: a gush of spit, an idiot blather.

"I could climb over here," said Mark. But Con could see that it wasn't so easy. The poles were tall, like game-fence poles, with razor serrations running along the top.

"I don't know," he said, "maybe it's electrified."

"You reckon?" said Mark.

"Could be."

Con remembered a story one of Lorraine's old boyfriends had told him, of how someone got electrocuted by a downed power cable, and how his hands flexed around the wire and locked him to the killing current. Con turned his hand around and laid the backs of his fingers very lightly on the metal. There was no shock, but the cold surprised him and he pulled back quickly.

"Was there? Was there a shock?" asked Mark, delighted.

He hesitated, then rolled a dice. "Tiny one."

"What'd it feel like?"

"Lekker," he said. "A rush."

Mark gave a shout of laughter. "Fuck, you're a headcase! You're a crazy dude!" He turned to the fence, and Con held his breath.

"Get away from that bloody fence!" shouted their teacher from a distance, and Con saw the momentary relief in the other boy's eyes.

On their way down, he stood next to Mark, pressed up against him in the crowded gondola. Mark was talking animatedly to two of the more popular girls. The mist had thickened and obscured the rockface, and everyone had turned away from the curved windows except Con. He was looking out, watching the shapes curl in the vapour, occasionally snatching a glimpse of grey stone or dull-green bush. Halfway down, a patch cleared for a second or two, and Con found himself staring, without surprise, directly into the eyes of a small reddish cat with long black wisps at the tips of its ears. It was perched there like one of his mother's tabbies, paws tucked neatly together beneath it, alert and calm and vivid against the grey rock. He held its gaze for one second, two, before the veil of cloud was drawn over it again and the cable car sank towards the road.

Mark turned towards him, throwing a damp blazered arm around his shoulders. Scents of musk and rain. "This guy!" he yelled jubilantly, wrestling Con into the centre of the car. "This guy is a complete malletjie. He gives himself shocks for fun!"

—

"I saw a cat on the top of the mountain," Con said that evening. Clive – who'd stuck around longer than most – was cooking something disgusting on the stovetop: waterlily bredie, the plants skimmed off the soapy surface of the Liesbeek River.

"Shame," said his mother, not too interested. "Someone's pussycat."

"No, it was wild. Big. Sort of goldy."

Clive raised his furry brows. "Rooikat?"

"Don't be stupid," said Lorraine. "It was obviously a pet cat. Some poor little runaway."

"I *saw* it."

Lorraine was almost pitying. "Connie. You know that's not possible. There hasn't been a rooikat up there for years."

"But I did see it," Con repeated softly. "It was beautiful."

human being

The fence was in the news: the Parks Department was extending it, proposing new areas of the mountain to close off, pushing through ordinances. There were plans to build a luxury lodge at the top, next to the reservoir. Talk of tender fraud, bribes paid and favours granted.

"Mushroom season, too," added Clive, indignant.

"They'll never close off the forest, surely?" said Lorraine. "They can't stop people going for walks."

Clive took them for recces in his battered Combi – up behind the houses at Camps Bay, at Constantia, at Kloof Nek – and they sat and watched the silver fence being looped around the mountain like a ribbon. Over the toes of Lion's Head, along its ribs, then skipping over the road to hem the edges of the Table's tablecloth.

"Bastards," said Clive.

The Department paid for adverts in the newspapers, broadcast half-hour TV specials, put up a Facebook page. They gave assurances: the public would always have access to most of the mountain, to the forests and the lower slopes above Kirstenbosch Gardens. Con read these things and became confused.

"They're doing it for conservation," he said. "Look." He showed his mother the website. They were going to do great things, up there on the sensitive tabletop. Stock it with antelope, zebra, baboons, breeding pairs of eagles, all kinds of rare and endangered creatures. The fence would keep all the animals safe from harm. Given massive species loss everywhere else, it was the only plan that made sense.

"And they'll still let people go up there," he assured her. "You'll just need to get a permit." He examined the smallprint in the sidebar. "And hire a guide."

His mother snorted in contempt. "A permit? To go up my mountain? A *guide*?"

It did seem improbable.

Then one day when Con came home from school he found six or seven of his mother's friends out in the backyard with a big pile of cardboard placards, painting out slogans. Clive, Clive's intensely tattooed sister, and a couple of new faces: Clive's hippie buddies.

Con's stomach tightened. Clive was always pressing his mother to take part in these things. Last time there were posters, it had been about shack clearances – or was it access to medication? – and his mother had tried to make him take a bundle of stickers to hand out at school. He'd left them on the counter at the corner shop instead.

Lorraine, who struggled with her weight despite currently eating nothing but berries and mushrooms, looked plump and damp with sweat next to her stringier companions. But also unusually vital. The curls of her hair were tied away from her face with a piece of colourful batik cloth, and she looked up at Con with bright eyes.

He knelt next to her and watched her working for a moment. She shouldn't be writing these, he thought; her handwriting was childish and uncontrolled. She didn't leave enough space on the board for all the letters. HANDS OFF started off boldly, ending with OUR MOUNTAIN written tiny and cramped against the right-hand edge.

"Have a go," she said, sliding a clean sheet of card towards him. "Fight for our rights."

Clive and his friends never seemed quite clear on what they really thought, or why. DON'T FENCE ME IN, said one banner; DON'T FENCE ME OUT, said another. Still, Con was impressed: they appeared to have bought a sheaf of clean cardboard, new paints even, nothing salvaged or second-hand.

As he worked, his mind was on two tracks. One listened to what the people were saying around him.

"Some people are making a killing," Clive's sister was explaining. "If you own fence land, the Department has to pay you out."

"But the shacks – Hout Bay, Woodstock, there by the quarry – they just slicing through it all. Taking the people's land."

"Just like old times, hey."

"Well, I just want to secure my herbs. My bark."

"Fascists."

The other part of Con's mind followed his own hand across the cardboard, tracing the letters in thick purple paint. He thought of Mark's handwriting, as even and rounded as knitted stitches, plain and pearl, and tried to make his hand move smoothly. But by the time he was done, he saw he'd written on a crooked slope, and that he'd left out a letter.

"But what about the animals?" he asked shyly.

"Con thinks it's nice that they're saving the animals," said his mother. He glared at her. "Explain to him, Clive."

Clive barked a laugh. "We'll never see those animals. They're going to sell permits to the rich fuckers. What good is an animal you never even see?"

"Besides, what do you care more about, the animals or the people?" said Clive's sister, jabbing at her poster with gobs of black.

His mother had paused over her inept slogans and now sat back on her haunches, staring at the lettering with a troubled frown. He felt an empathetic softening: like him, she often didn't know quite what to say.

Looking around, he saw that the whole group had produced similarly sloppy, illegible and unsatisfactory results. One sign was written in old-fashioned cursive. It was a mess.

The shacks up on the side of Lion's Head were made of corrugated iron and cardboard and cast-off bricks. They'd been there for a few months, spilling upwards from the Green Point quarry and along the spine of Signal Hill, organically colliding with the new fence as it marched around the shoulder of the mountain, just below the old gravel road. The building of the fence had been halted for some months by a court order, an unfinished segment standing useless; in that time the makeshift houses had found the metal and entwined it like ivy.

But that legal battle had been lost. New sections of the fence had been unloaded from trucks on the road above and laid flat on the ground, ready to be erected. The stacks were guarded night and day by uniformed security guards. The week before, men in overalls with shovels and pick-axes had descended on the shacks. Today was day two of the clearing operation, and the shack-dwellers had been joined by other protestors.

Lorraine and Clive and the others took some time unloading the posters from the Combi and from Lorraine's beaten-up old Mazda. By the time their group had trudged up from the parking lot with their banners and posters, the protestors and the demolition crew had squared off. The shack-dwellers, massed above the unfinished fence, were standing in a light rain. Every now and then a section of the crowd would start up with an old freedom song, others joining in, call and response. The clearance crew waited in a cluster to one side, some still sitting in the backs of their trucks or leaning against the bulldozer; and on the road above the fence were the cops, with riot helmets, Perspex shields, batons. Guns.

The protest was swelling. People arrived all at once, with an angry purposeful energy. These new arrivals had better banners, printed with logos of housing organisations and trade unions, and they were chanting strongly in unison and singing through megaphones and toyi-toying; many wore T-shirts from more venerable struggles. To one side, further up towards Lion's Head, another, much smaller posse of protestors was standing, holding signs – neatly laser-printed – that said SAVE OUR MOUNTAIN and PROTECT OUR ANIMALS. This lot were mostly white, and they had no songs. There were a couple of photographers, a TV crew. Con could feel Lorraine's tension, the bumbling indecision of Clive and his crew. Their hand-painted banners trembled in their hands.

Something else about the arrangement of forces bothered Con: he could see quite clearly that, given the line of the fence, there was no place for the police to go except through the protestors. The nicely behaved bunch above them seemed to realise the problem at the same time. They started to edge up the gravel path, looking over their shoulders. There was no way down in that direction; they'd have to hike all the way around the base of Lion's Head to get out. Lorraine turned with a worried frown, and groped for Con's hand, but he saw her coming and dodged. "Con …" she said. But more and more people were coming up from behind, and suddenly the press around Con was tightening, and then the top of Lorraine's head vanished behind the heads of the others and he didn't see her again.

An electronically amplified voice crackled across the megaphone chants: a policeman commanding the crowd. Con couldn't make out the words. There was a low rumble in response – so many voices together, he could feel it resonate in his chest. A couple of angry yells from the back.

Then, movement: a sharp surge backwards as if all of them had been slapped at once. He felt the wave of pressure moving through the crowd. Somebody screamed. Hands and bodies pressed up against him, and for a moment he felt his feet lifting, but then his toes caught the ground again. He tried to wriggle backwards but the tides weren't running that way; now they were surging forward. With no volition, he found himself passed sideways through the crowd and ejected, right up against the intact portion of the fence. His face was pushed against the bars. Trapped, he stared for a moment into the face of a person on the other side. The man was sitting on a plastic chair in front of a tin shack – he looked like he'd drawn it up to watch the action, like a spectator at a soccer game. His eyes widened, and Con wondered what he saw. There was a muffled stuttering sound from the front, and the crowd pulled back again like a poked jellyfish and gave a moan of distress. A body slammed against his shoulder and he was again pushed hard up against the fence. This time he felt his cheek mashed against the bar, harder and harder until he feared the bone would break.

Then the man leant forward and reached through the bars and grabbed Con's shoulder and pulled – and with a wrench to the neck somehow his head was through, and the man kept pulling and the whole of Con's body followed, the bars raking his chest and his groin, until he was there, on the other side of the fence. Behind him there were screams and dogs barking, but the man didn't allow him to look around or pause or speak; instead, he gave him a shove in the back. "Go, go on!"

And Con could hardly disobey, because already he was running, legs swinging out in front of him to keep up with his falling body as he clattered down the slope through the shacks, and then through the bush and down towards the little car park where his mother's car sat askew, unused placards still stacked in the back window. The Combi, he saw, was already gone. Behind him, heavy percussive bangs seemed to crack the air.

He crawled into the Mazda – nobody had bothered to lock the doors – and pushed down all the knobs and sat very still on the back seat, sinking into the smell of cardboard and poster paint. Peeking out the front window, halfway up the hill he could see the line of the fence shaking and rocking as people were forced against it, until eventually a section of it came down and a group of marchers streamed through the gap, cops in pursuit. They swarmed down the hill and around the car, rocking it lightly with their hands as they passed. Con crouched down and pulled some of the spare posters over his head.

He was only roused by his mother's hands slapping against the glass and the sound of her calling his name – faintly, as if through a reverse megaphone. He looked up and saw a smear of blood on the glass, and Lorraine's face, distorted with panic. He reached forward and pulled up the toggle on the driver's door and she came blundering in, breath rasping, bringing cold air and a feral smell of crushed fynbos and burning.

She cranked the engine and turned the car around with a squeal. Con peered out the back window and saw Clive running behind them; he'd dropped his banner and was shouting and waving, but Lorraine didn't pause or look back. She accelerated away and down off the mountain and onto the road home.

As they drove, Con surreptitiously examined her hands and face for a wound, but the skin was unmarked. Which was more shocking than anything: the palm-smear on the side window was a stranger's blood.

At home, when they saw what had happened on the TV – the homes flattened, the rubber bullets, a man with his arm torn by a police dog, a woman crushed against the fence – his mother wept. "They were shooting people," she kept saying. "My god, Con. Those were *people* getting hurt. A human being got *shot*."

After that, Clive did not come around any more and there were no more marches for Lorraine and Con. A few months later, when things had died down in the press, the fence-building recommenced, completing a circlet around the base of Lion's Head. Later, the houses came back too, following the line of the fence all the way round and meeting again under the jaw of the lion.

The stack of rejected posters stayed in the lounge for a while, and then later was moved to the spare bedroom. One ended up lining the budgie cage.

With Clive and his crew gone, the house resumed its silence. It was comforting, the quiet. They were not themselves big talkers, Lorraine and her son, not wordy at all. In another time, another place, they might have been quite happily illiterate, using a few small coins of language for everyday transactions, leaving the weightier denominations unspent. He once heard a teacher say, "Why use a fifty-cent word when a five-cent one will do?", and it had made him laugh. He hadn't known the saying but it expressed a familiar calculus. Lorraine hoarded small change in her purse, collecting coins from behind the couch cushions, and would produce the exact amount necessary for a particular transaction; so, too, she saved up her words. She would mull over something for a long time before expressing it; and then it was always a spare statement, straight to the point: "That fucking tosser", for example, regarding an ex-boyfriend.

To meet Mark was to enter a world of easy speech. "Howzit, hey, I saw you on TV!" Mark said to him at school two days after the protest, grabbing Con's sleeve in the stairwell as they passed. He offered the greeting like a handful of nuts. Con nodded cautiously.

"That was you, right? At that what's-it-called, demonstration?"

Demonstration, what kind of word was that – a TV word. Something out of their textbooks, from history. He could hear Clive saying it: demo. "I guess it was me," he said, emboldened.

"Cool," said Mark. "That's very cool, I wish I'd been there." He paused. "I would've gone too but my dad would explode. Dude, is that blood?" Mark ducked and touched the scab on Con's leg. "Did they, like, *hit* you?"

Mark's finger was a chill pencil, but Con stiffened his leg and didn't flinch away. He had a long scratch down his shin, impossible to hide in the shorts of their school uniform. "It's nothing," he said.

"Maybe I'll come with next time there's something like that. Like a march?"

"Sure," he said, copying Mark's nonchalance. "But … there's no point now. They're going to put the fence up."

"Oh, right. Well, you should come to my house then." Mark nodded, then leant forward and tugged at Con's shirt, pulling it out of his pants. This time Con couldn't help himself, his stomach contracting in fright at the touch. "There," said Mark. "That looks better. Not so stiff." And then Mark gave him a sudden brilliant smile, flipping his fringe behind his ear with his little finger. Long fingers. Small ears. Almost pretty.

Con kept his shirt flapping out of his pants for the rest of the day. It felt strange, free but unsettling, as if he was half-naked or his fly was down. They were punished for things like this, uniform infractions – at least everyone else was. Mark got away with it. Walking home, Con tucked his shirt in tight and smooth across his belly. Then pulled it out again.

chicken

Con's office work was deathly dull, alternating between tedium and unease. There was an avalanche of old emails to go through, mostly trivial, but some referring more ominously to funding problems, urgent meetings, requests for budget reports. These he passed on to Amina. There was nothing in the inbox relating to Mark personally. But he was present.

Con imagined that when his workmates looked at him, they pictured Mark's body hovering in the air behind his head. Bleeding, sleeping the sleep of the dead. They approached Con with concern, as a mourner, and avoided saying Mark's name out loud.

"Give him my love!" Elmien would call from behind her ticketing counter as Con left for the day. Or, "How is he getting on?" from Amina, hushed and respectful.

"Fine, good, slow progress," he would reply, with a tight smile to indicate it was painful to elaborate.

They all assumed, of course, that Con was regularly visiting Mark in hospital. But this he'd found impossible to do, the ward thrusting him back like a repelling magnet. It was just that he couldn't think himself into that room, couldn't hold his mind's eye steady on that form swathed in – sheets? Bandages like a cartoon mummy? Tubes dribbling queasy-coloured fluids in and out? The thoughts bounced him brusquely back to the now, to the tasks of the day.

Thandiswa was in the Lion House staffroom early most mornings, with her books and notes and a cup of tea, her too-big uniform sleeves rolled up to her elbows. It was a good place to study, apparently, quieter than her college residence. But she didn't seem to mind Con's disruption, always looking up from her notes with a smile when he arrived. She made him laugh. They had coffee together in the mornings, and sometimes she shared her sandwiches. At lunchtime they sat together on the slope behind the parking lot, up against the fence, looking out across the Flats to the Helderberg. Behind them was a gate in the fence. Thandiswa amused herself by fiddling with the Department lock, trying to find the magic combination.

"Six six six?" he suggested.

"Too short. One day I'll get it."

To the left and the right, the fence followed the contour, the trees kept clear for a few feet on either side, although green shoots and saplings were constantly invading the no-man's-land. Con had grown more used to the fence now, and was happy to rest his spine against the bars while he chewed on a cheese-and-tomato sandwich and listened to Thandiswa make her plans.

Thandiswa's family was from the Eastern Cape; there was no money and no deep family roots in Cape Town. She'd come to the university on a scholarship, had no particular plans to stay. At first it reassured him to think that he wasn't the only scrabbler and scraper, the only drifter. But of course he was wrong about that: to get as far as Thandiswa had come required something a lot more steely and directed than he could ever summon up. She already held down another part-time job with a tour company, she told him, and had detailed plans for the future.

"When I graduate, I'm going to go to one of the really fancy game farms, upcountry near Kruger. Work my way up to management."

"Good for you."

On the whiteboard in the staffroom, there was always an agenda: Amina seemed to like them. Usually there were two or three ordinary things, to do with funding or feeding schedules, but one morning there was a longer list, written in red:

- *Regular lions*
- *Cheetahs??*

"What's all this?" Con asked as he poured a cup of coffee.

"No, I don't know. Amina was having a meeting with the money guys." Thandiswa pulled an exaggerated wince. "Trouble."

"Money trouble?"

"Well, obviously. This place is going down the tubes. Without the lions, it's nothing. They need to find some way of making money out of it."

- *Animatronics?*
- *Cloning*
- *Theatre / Arts*
- *Safaris????*

"Animatronics? What, are we turning into Jurassic Park now? And safaris, what's that about – game drives through the aviary?"

"You'd be surprised. There's people who would love to do that. Take pot-shots at an endangered species."

He snorted. "Yeah, right. That's what I volunteered for."

Thandiswa was watching him thoughtfully. "Why are you here, actually?" she asked. "Love? Or money?"

He was saved from having to say more. A long grumble carried through the bricks of the building. A whiff of lion odour too: meat and dung, a smell like a growl. Con's body twitched in sympathy.

"Ooh, she wants you," said Thandiswa.

"For breakfast, maybe."

Thandiswa smiled. "Watch out with that lion, hey? Don't get too caught up in the whole thing."

"What do you mean?"

"I'm just saying. Your friend was a weird one. A bit intense. You know? The animals pick up on it."

Con just laughed and shook his head. At a loss for words, he turned his attention to his lapel badge, pinning it straighter.

"Ja," she continued. "Mark got all involved, did extra work. Made some posters for the education section. You should check when you're down there next. He was quite artistic."

"Yes, I know."

"Ancient symbols and stuff. A bit hippy dippy if you ask me. Amina wasn't so happy. And the funders wanted something more upbeat. But, you know, volunteers. You can't really complain. He had schoolkids in, did workshops and everything." She shook her head. "To be honest, I always just assumed he was some kind of charity case. I mean, sorry, sorry, I know he was your buddy and all. But he was a bit ... mad, you know? I thought maybe his mother was a donor or something. He was always going on about the animals. Like he was half in love with those lions. He liked to sit and watch them. Just staring, for ages. He had a funny girlfriend too. Some people are just crazy about animals."

"Aren't you? I thought you had to be, in this line of work."

She turned upon him a lucid gaze of sanity. "Animals are animals. I love them, yes. But me, I am a human being." She said it with such calm certainty, as if with long-held knowledge, that he had to smile.

"You can't let yourself get too involved, in this game," she carried on. "It gets too sad. You can't get too attached to this one, that one. Or too ... mystical. I'm a conservationist. I want to find ways to do what we can with what we have left. Maybe there will be nothing left. I'm okay with imagining that. But I want to see it coming."

"Mark wasn't okay with it?"

"No. Mark wanted to drag each and every animal back from the brink. When Amina started talking about cutting the funding, he behaved like someone had died. He wasn't stable. Him and his friends."

"Mark had friends?"

"Sure. Weirdos. They used to come around here all the time. You know – animal wackjobs."

Later that day, Isak appeared at the door of the office in his overalls, raising a rubber-gloved hand in greeting. Con was growing accustomed to his perpetual grin. "Can I borrow you for a bit?" Isak said.

It seemed it had been decided: Con was ready. His scent had now circulated sufficiently, passed through the leaky prefab and out, between the bars of the lion cage and into Sekhmet's discerning nostrils. She'd given her assent.

Con followed the bald man back to the shed where Dmitri's body had lain in state. Isak went into the cold room at the back and came out with a steel bucket. He let it drop with a clang onto the cement between them, a splash of blood slopping up the inside and over the edge.

"She likes it fresh," he said. Con saw a mess of innards, a couple of plucked chickens. "Come, I'll show you."

The bars where the lioness had so frightened Con were only the outermost wall of her castle. One great, archaic-looking key opened that up, and Con and Isak passed into the dark, musky space where her chew-bones lay. Con looked around flinchingly.

Isak laughed. "Don't worry, she's in her bedroom now," he said. "This is just where she eats when it's raining." He stooped to negotiate a further narrow corridor. This ended at the door to the real cage, which was sturdier, a modern steel grid, with another heavy lock. The inner cage was dark, but through the mesh Con could make out, on the other side, a barred patch of green-tinged daylight.

"She's sleeping – can you hear?"

Con cocked his head. Yes, there it was: an inhale, a long, gravelly exhale. His heart responded instantly, like a springbok leaping away. He snorted through his nose, half a laugh at his own alarm.

"So. We need to get her out onto the grass, so we can go in her bedroom and clean out the shit, change the straw. That's how it works." Isak pointed at the lock. "Obviously, never ever open this unless she's out in the yard. Never ever ever."

Con nodded. He understood. The cage was a series of holding pens, and if you were in one, the animal had to be in the other. It made him think of astronauts, airlocks. He saw that to share air with a lioness could be fatal.

"Other lions, you know, they're not so bad," Isak was saying. "They're quite easy to train, actually. You can scratch their heads.

Fuck like bunnies, too, mostly. More cubs than you can keep." He laughed. "These ones, not a chance."

Con looked at him with interest. "You've worked with lions before?"

The old man nodded. "I was a circus man," he said, with a sudden flourish in his voice. "Long ago now. When it was legal. I had good lions then."

Con smiled. Whip and chair and flaming hoop. He could see it now: Isak's gleaming ringmaster smile.

"So now obviously we have to get her out into the yard so we can get in, hose out the cage. Change the straw, etcetera, etcetera. We feed her outside, too. Saves clean-up. So."

Busily, Isak led him back the way they'd come, locking up behind them, and showed him a narrow-runged ladder built into the exterior stonework.

"Take this," he said, shoving the bucket into Con's hands and starting to heave himself up the rungs. Con followed cautiously, bucket in one hand. The rungs were thin beneath his shoes. Again he thought of astronauts: spacesuited men clinging to fragile spars on the side of their ship, in danger of floating away at the slightest jolt. The shoes are wrong, he thought to himself. I should have moonboots, or at least a pair of steel-toed workboots like Isak's. How did the old man manage this every morning? Especially challenging were the shakes in Con's legs, just like that first day when the lioness had startled him so badly. It was some kind of reflex response to her presence. He picked his way up the ladder, paying close attention, and came out onto the battlements of the lion den.

He and Isak stood on the narrow walkway that ran along the top of the wall, encircling the enclosure and meeting the metal roof of the information centre. There was a small retaining wall, not high enough to be very reassuring. A gorgeous panoramic view of the mountain, and out towards the city. But all Con's attention was focussed on the stones under his feet, and the animal that lay below.

Set into the wall was a crank handle. Isak slapped it with a wiry hand. "So this contraption here. Winch. Operates the door" – he pointed – "down there."

Con peered over the edge, leaning out, thinking of Elyse's fighting stance on the balcony. He could just see the metal portcullis set into the wall, suspended by chains, a neat black square of shadow in the stonework. On the far side he could see the glass observation window. Just as he was looking away, a movement in the glass caught his eye. Two pale palms were pressed against the other side of the viewing pane, as if someone were cupping the dusty glass. The watcher's face was hidden. Could it be Elmien from the ticket office, cleaning the glass? But Elmien's hands were pillowy, while these were small, like pincers. They seemed trapped there. After a moment, and a futile scrubbing motion, they withdrew.

"You get her out into the yard, then you slam this shut so she can't get back in. She's eating her lunch, you go back down and sweep out the bedroom. Close the bedroom, sweep the lounge, out again, lock up, get back up here, open up again. Leave it open, she goes in and out as she fancies. Right?"

"Right."

"Okay. So. Come give it a try."

Con came forward and cranked the handle. It was stiff and heavy; again, he was surprised that Isak was able to manage it. It all seemed rather old-fashioned and low-tech; he turned the wheel three times, four. Peering out over the edge, he saw that the hatch had opened only ten centimetres. Isak reached forward and with great ease and rapidity cranked the hatch all the way up. Then he gave a musical whistle, three ascending notes. There was no response.

"Funny," he said. "Usually she's out running. She must smell you. She doesn't like new things, new people." He clattered the bunch of keys against the metal crank: still nothing. Shaking his head, he reached into the bucket and brought out a raw chicken.

"She likes it bloody," Isak observed, and slung the chicken down. The pink carcass landed on the grass and lay there.

Eventually, Isak tipped the rest of the contents of the bucket after it, but there was still no movement from the dark doorway. He shook his head. "Okay, let's give her a bit of time to think about it." He settled himself on the wall and started rolling a cigarette. "You go on down. She doesn't like you yet. I'll sit with her. Take this with you." Without warning, Isak tossed the aluminium bucket through the air. Con caught it awkwardly at his feet with two hands and a clang. A spot of blood sprang from the bucket and landed on his cheek. "And listen, the thing is …"

"Ja?"

"The thing is this: you must be careful with that cat, okay?"

Con nodded.

"I mean it. Always keep the bars between you. Don't stick your hand through; she'll grab it. Don't turn your back on her."

"I get it."

"I'm telling you: don't turn your back."

Later that afternoon he went down to the education centre to look at the posters. Mark's contribution was in the corner, away from the other boards about species loss and extinctions. Hand-painted, nicely framed, and actually quite beautiful: a good way with line and colour, after all. A large green lion standing up on its hind legs like a dog doing a trick. A golden sun caught in its jaws, bleeding golden blood. The lion's coat and mane were mossy green. Con recognised the image: it was copied off the cover of the little alchemical book that Mark had had in his rucksack. Something out of an old illustrated manuscript. Beneath the image was a block of text, done in careful calligraphy that mimicked an ancient text:

> *The Philosopher's Stone,* lapis philosophorum, *was the goal of medieval alchemy. This mystical substance could transmute base metals into gold. It could rejuvenate, revive withered plants, create golems. It could make the dead rise.*

The Great Work of creating lapis philosophorum *involved complex steps and substances, named, in the language of magic, after animals: ravens, dragons, toads. Vitriol – the "Green Lion" – was used to dissolve gold. Thus:* The Green Lion Devours the Sun.

> All hail to the noble Companie
> Of true Students in holy Alchemie,
> Whose noble practise doth hem teach
> To vaile their secrets with mistie speech;
> For no man lives that ever hath seen
> Upon foure feete a Lyon coloured greene
> And yet full quickly can he run,
> And soone can overtake the Sun:
> He bringeth him to more perfection,
> Than ever he had by Natures direccion.

And then something else clicked into place. That messed-up stuffed lion, smeared green, the ball in its teeth. Devouring the sun. Perhaps Mark had not meant to make a horror, after all; perhaps it had been done in hope.

Oh Mark, thought Con with a sigh. He touched the painting lightly. Vitriol was sulphuric acid. Drain cleaner.

parrot

He used to think of Elyse as something of London, as London-made. But back in Cape Town, he immediately saw that she fitted much better in this city than he ever had or could. She whipped them around town in her car, she knew where the smartest restaurants were, she changed lanes with a spin of the wheel; and she paid for everything. There was money here, and it didn't come from acting. Someone must have bought that brand-new car for her, and also the flat.

"My dad," she shrugged. No wonder she seemed so light and cheerful: a well-tethered balloon.

"Your family live here in Cape Town?"

"Sure. Old Cape family. We even have a graveyard." She gestured vaguely towards the mountain. Generally, she preferred to look out in the other direction, to the sea. "Up there by Rhodes Mem."

"Who? When was this? Was it a farm?"

She looked at him a little funnily. "I'm not so interested in that old stuff. Gone is gone, hey. Bad old days."

And he was left marvelling. At someone with a story, and who casts it so lightly aside.

If he was honest, these revelations added spice. He felt when he took her wrists tightly in his hands – which she liked him to do – that he was linking himself to a thin but very strong gold chain that held him fast: to a past, to a place.

Gold chains were also expensive, of course. Even Elyse's scent was expensive, delicate but strong. He loved it; loved tasting gold on her lips, gold gilding the inside of his mouth where her cool little tongue flickered. She liked to kiss as well as fight outside, on the balcony with nothing but the sea behind her, and to bend her limber back so it looked like she might slip right off the edge. He held her wrists together; he held on tight.

From time to time, he pretended to be looking for proper work.

He bought a second-hand laptop and took it to bars and restaurants and sat tooling around the net, reading the classifieds. He found a site that sold second-hand taxidermied specimens; it seemed there was a market. And sometimes he went to see Margaret. They sat upstairs in her little white room, or down in the garden if the weather was nice. He showed her the taxidermy website on his screen and she leant in, puzzled, as if she'd never seen a computer before.

"Oh, I just don't know," she said. "I should ask Mark."

Mark. Mark slept on.

Con started to drive Margaret to the hospital, in Gerard's old Mercedes. But he still couldn't make himself go in. He let her go up to the high-care ward alone, waiting in the miserable pastel lobby where they sold teddy bears and bad coffee and fruit baskets. He tapped away at his wonky laptop, bringing up bright image after bright image, keeping his eyes on the screen.

Afterwards, in the car, Margaret was usually pensive. Sunlight through the windscreen would pass across her delicate face, and her bleached eyes did not flinch away from it. The sad light reminded him of doing just this with his own mother: driving her around, thinking of death and hurt and healing.

Sometimes, though, after these visits, Margaret would seem seized by a curious glee. She would insist – girlish, almost flirtatious – that they go for an outing. Once or twice she asked him to take her to art exhibitions: botanical art, old Cape classics on auction. Magnolia blooms, farmhouses, Karoo vistas. He was surprised by her enthusiasm. He thought again of paintings he'd seen in London, the meat and fowl and fish laid out in those rich and easeful old Dutch still lifes. The artworks here seemed dull and twee in comparison. But Margaret observed them keenly, bringing her old eyes close to the paint.

Other times, she'd want tea, a toasted sandwich or a scone somewhere nice. "Kirstenbosch!" she might exclaim.

But no, not there. He didn't want to go there. "The Rhodes Memorial tea room," he suggested. He wasn't sure why. It was a kind of test.

ie peered up at him, almost shy. The rims of her eyelids were , tender-looking, the lashes sparse. "Yes, let's," she said.

They drove past the lion den without comment, parked and picked their way to one of the tables on the lower terrace. Con had strong memories of this place: in the restaurant, there used to be a grey parrot in a cage which repeated what it heard, and a tame bat-eared fox that would dart between the tables like a little cat. Looking out once again at the city with the mountain behind them, Con considered how this place was a needle that his life kept threading back through, over and over, double-stitching. Down there, just above the highway, was where he and Mark had set up the tent that time. His mother used to come mushrooming in the trees above, fenced off now of course. Hallucinations forever out of reach. His thoughts, too, looping back and back again through the eye of the needle.

Now he let his eyes slip down the path next to the quagga enclosure, wondering idly about Elyse's family graveyard. He could see no sign of any built thing, and it seemed unlikely. Could she have been lying, mystifying? Just another breezy bit of theatre.

He always made sure Margaret had something to eat on these excursions, filled with some vague concern about keeping her fed, about restoring vigour that might have been drained by the hospital fluorescents. And indeed, after a sandwich and particularly a glass of wine or two, there was more colour in her cheeks and brightness in her eyes. And she would break the silence and start to talk.

He'd tried to feed Lorraine sometimes, as an adolescent: simple things, scrambled eggs, bacon, things that could be cooked all together in a pan, but that had a richness his childish mind turned to fat well-being. She'd always been trying to lose weight, never been able to resist. It was the same kind of food he'd made for her when she was ill at the end, when it was too late to worry about health or weight or vitamins, and all he could offer her was taste: as sharp or sweet or salty as possible, to pierce her fading senses.

Watching Margaret cut her sandwiches into tiny triangles, he'd ask the dutiful questions – the ones Amina always asked him, "So how was Mark today?"

"Blinked his eyes," she might say, or, "Less puffy in the face."

"Good, good," he'd answer. "Getting there."

"Did Mark carry on with his art?" he asked one day in a garden-centre tea room, the rain outside a solid grey wall.

"His art?"

"Well … he always said he was keen to go to art school. Didn't he? What did he do after school?" He realised he hadn't actually asked Mark about his life that strange day walking through the English fields.

"Oh … no. No, he didn't do that. We had to take him out of school, you know. He was very troubled, after Elizabeth. He worked a bit in things like, oh, set building, set painting. This and that."

This and that, thought Con. Security guard, museum attendant.

"Not a strong boy, you know," Margaret continued. "Not as strong as you. He couldn't hang on to anything."

Con watched as two women came towards them through the spindly tables and chairs, slow but resolute, smiles set, careful not to trip. Margaret stiffened slightly in her chair. The women were softer than her, their features puffed and powdered, in a way that made Margaret's features seem starved, deprived. These women, you could see, had had ample love and little heartache, had been allowed to spread into comfortable age. Clearing the obstacles, they bustled forward with cries of pleasure.

"Why, Margaret!"

"Hello, dear Kay." Half-rising to her feet to receive a powdery kiss.

"You remember my sister Tamara?"

Tamara raised jolly eyebrows at Con. "And this must be … is it? Looking so handsome!"

Kay put a soft hand on his shoulder and withdrew it again quickly. "So so *good* to see you!" She turned back to Margaret. "He *is* looking handsome, Margaret!" And there was a tremor of something – disbelief? – in her voice.

"Oh …" said Margaret with a vague denying gesture of the hand. Con smiled on gamely through the awkwardness.

"Well," said Kay, cooling, "we don't mean to barge in. We were just on our way."

"It's lovely to see you, dear," said Margaret. "Do come by for tea sometime."

"Will do."

And the women retreated, Kay turning back to say brightly, "Goodbye!" Then they were gone, soft sister hands on each other's wrists, bundling out of the door which was too narrow for the two of them, into the rain. Margaret watched them go, then returned her gaze to her half-eaten sandwich.

"I'm sorry about that," she said.

He laughed awkwardly. "We don't look that much alike, do we? Mark and I?"

"No, no you don't." A bite, a chew, a swallow. "As I was saying, after Lizzy … well, he just fell apart. He was even a little … violent at times." She looked up at Con. "But you would know that too, I think. There was that time with Elizabeth, when she got hit in the face. And other times." Con pressed his fingers together. "And then there was the medication. He put on a lot of weight at one point. Then he couldn't live alone, so he was with me. I looked after him on my own. I was so glad when he seemed to get interested in this volunteering thing. The lions. So *stupid* of me."

Mark felt a cold weight travel down his gullet. The strangest feeling. When they were children, Mark had always been the strong one, the light one. But their destinies had been swapped. Somehow, when he'd walked out of Mark's house that last time as a teenager, growing hard, he'd taken with him some of Mark's resilience, and had left behind in Mark's body some of his own sad dust and weight.

"I'm so sorry," he said.

He saw now what Mark's accident must have been like for

Margaret: not a sudden catastrophic punctuation, but rather one more dire subtraction. His childhood, his happiness, his mind and now his body, taken away from him piece by piece as if by animals gnawing on a carcass; leaving her to sew him up again as best she might, with a piece of twine and thick needle and her sad attention.

"I'm sorry," Con said again.

His own loss had been faster. When Lorraine went at last it was quick and silent, as if she had finally run out of all patience: with words, with him, with the world, with her own past and any possible future. She spent only a day and a night in hospital before taking her leave. In dying, her mouth set into a shape that he saw had always been waiting there: one of sour disappointment. Then, the sad, fumbling visit to the morgue. The packet of gritty ashes.

"My mother is dead," he said to Elyse on Skype, and watched with some amazement as these words turned a key in her face and opened, for the first time, the tiny locks to her tears. Con wanted nothing more than to go to her then.

First, though, he needed to clean out Lorraine's brown house, as he'd always wanted to do. Everything went, every last magazine and vinyl record and fur coat and sideboard. A thousand precious, worthless, broken objects, a hundred thousand stories of people he'd never known and would never know. In among them, some things that were genuinely his, some things that were genuinely his mother's. He dusted them off, but then mostly let them drop back into the rubble.

As for what were his father's things, who could say? He was still half-looking for the Noah's Ark: the red roof, the wooden hull, packed with every animal, two by two. Saved from the flood! But he knew that boat had long since sailed. He wondered if the Ark had ever existed, or if it was some foundering memory from Lorraine's own lost childhood. As he worked, the idea of his father became smaller and smaller, reduced at last to one small screwdriver in Con's pocket. One useful thing.

He put all the throwaway stuff in black plastic bags and stacked them in the driveway. As he worked through the day and into the night, he became aware that people coming past were picking up items, carrying them off, leaving only the most tattered and obscure. The remainder he burnt, or binned, or, in a satisfying continuation of the cycling and recycling of his mother's life, hauled to the charity shop down the road. Eventually, even the house was folded back into itself, leaving no waste or excess: its modest sale price, he discovered, just covered his mother's debts.

One way, Con thought, to make an empty-earth fantasy come true. Start with your own home, empty every room. Lonely, though, to be the last man left alive.

The time with his dying mother had been unclear, like a bank of smog passing over the city. He'd wanted higher ground, some bright outcrop above the murk. Which was much how Elyse's Sea Point home appeared to him on first sight. It was a sparkling Atlantic day and her flat was a fancy one, tall and white, the penthouse, too. Its balcony faced out to the blue of the sea and away from the hunched shape of the mountain, tangled as it was with rocks and thorns and memories.

It was getting dark as he made his way to her door. He looked up and saw window shutters showing cracks of welcoming light, and thought that it looked like an advent calendar, its little doors waiting for him to lever them open onto something warm and precious.

There was a lift, but in his nervous energy he took the stairs anyway. And when she opened the door, she smiled and enfolded him in arms as long and cool as lily stalks. She smelt of lilies too, and him in his black bat-clothes stinking of death and grief and cigarettes and the long walk here.

But she was still smiling, and let her forefingers trail down the front of his white shirt, circling both nipples lightly through the cloth.

"You'll have to undress," she said, and he wasn't sure if it was lust or fastidiousness speaking, but at that point he didn't care. He unbuttoned his clothes and kicked them away and entered the atmosphere of her house, which was warm and dense with perfume, steaming him clean.

And he felt so renewed, so full of light and optimism, that one bright morning soon afterwards he found himself dialling an old familiar number. One he could never forget, like the chorus of a favourite pop song. Smiling quietly, even, anticipating Mark's voice on the other end, his old friend's surprise. But it was Margaret who answered, and her voice was beyond all astonishment.

quagga

Con set himself to cleaning the den observation window. He rinsed out the blood-bucket and filled it with water, tossing in a stiffened rag, and brought it all into the paddock through a small, seldom-used gate hidden behind a boulder.

As he swiped a circle in the dust with the damp rag, he remembered: waking up in Mark's bedroom, a lifetime ago, the curtains wide open as usual. Rolling over to see a woman on the other side of the sliding doors, in a maid's uniform with a yellow dust-cloth in hand, cleaning the glass in just this way. Mortified, scrambling to pull the sheet over his fourteen-year-old nakedness as Mark slept on. Lettie, he remembered now.

He became aware of the small hairs on his neck rising. He turned and squinted across the grass at the portcullis, but it was closed and there were no eyes watching him from the gloom. He washed the whole window thoroughly, all the way into the corners, stopping only when he heard Isak's keys clanging on the bars behind him.

Inside the dim education centre, he took his place on the bench in front of the observation window. The same scene, reversed: through the cleaned glass he could see the grass yard, the bushes, and on the opposite side of the enclosure, the opening grille: a black trap in the artifice. Here came the chickens, sailing down from Isak's unseen hand. The carcasses bounced and spattered. A tangle of cow innards exploded onto the grass, startlingly red. After several minutes, a big black-and-white crow alighted to peck at the flesh for a few moments before being startled off by some unheard noise or unseen movement. No lion. He realised he was holding his breath, and let it out in a slow stream.

Only then did he become aware of a figure beside him, a slim shadow alighting on the other end of the wooden bench. His gaze was skewed sideways by its odd gravity. The figure – sheathed in some kind of voluminous fabric from head to toe – leant forward slightly, a tangle of mousy hair obscuring its face. He knew immediately that this was the owner of the pale hands he'd noticed the day before, pressing at the glass. Now they were little white fists, bunched together at her breast. He could feel the tension vibrating from her body.

A moist heaving had entered the silence of the room. The figure on the end of the bench was shaking, with the stricken rhythm of a person in silent tears. Con felt in his pocket for the clean serviette left over from his lunch break, and leant over to offer it. He felt her tremble in the dimness like a moth, and then touch his fingers as she took the tissue with a gasp of gratitude. After a moment she blew her nose, rather loudly.

"Is she still there?" A soft, husky voice. The dimness of the room inspired most people to a hushed whisper, as if in church, but this person was barely audible.

"Who?"

"Sekhmet, is she still okay?"

"Yes, she's fine," he said. "She's just a bit shaken up. She has a new zookeeper and she's sort of shy of him."

He became conscious of the stranger's intense interest: she'd turned to stare. She had large dark eyes that picked him over carefully. Now she slid along the bench towards him, a little too close. "You work here?"

"Yes."

"Did you know Mark?"

"Yes, I did."

"You are like him," she said. "Very much like him." She turned her face away towards the glass.

He laughed, discomfited. She was sitting close enough now that in her shining eyes he could see the light of the window reflected, a pale rectangle. In that tiny inverted frame, something flickered. The girl sat back sharply, and Con followed her gaze.

Sekhmet was there.

She stood side-on in the centre of the space, great head lowered and turned towards them. Her eyes twin moons. It was the first time he'd seen her like this. The whole of her, entire, unshadowed, close.

The lioness was even bigger than he'd grasped: her head would be up to his chin. Her body was barrel-shaped, densely muscled. Eyes pale, as was her coat – torn and healed in spots like a prizefighter's, but shining like silk in the early sun. The flesh hard-packed beneath the taut skin. A long, brutish muzzle, lightly bearded. The broad, convex arch of the nose ending in a pad of a surprising tea-rose pink, kittenish, the curlicues of the nostrils picked out in black. A whorl of fur above each eye; black tears dripping from the inner corners; black lips. The tail, black-tipped.

The lioness swung her head away and ambled over to sniff at the red lumps of chicken in the middle of the enclosure. She made herself comfortable, lying down to her meal, holding the meat between her paws as if it were still liable to get away. It took mere minutes to crunch it down. Con watched her jaws moving, cracking bones. Then she was back on her feet and pacing towards the gate of the inner den, without another glance at her keeper.

Behind them, he heard the staff-only door pull open, and a bar of sunlight fell into the room. In a concealing instinct, he was quickly on his feet and walking towards the door, just as Amina held it open for three burly men in suits to enter.

"Con," said Amina, her still face communicating little but her body tight with tension. "These gentlemen are here to have a look around. We were hoping to catch feeding time."

"Just missed it."

"Ah. That's a pity." Amina, still holding the door open, peered blindly into the gloom, and seemed to lose heart. "Well. No point then."

He glanced over his shoulder. The viewing bench was empty again, the window devoid of life.

The men came inside anyway, the three of them filling the space with jostling dark-suited shoulders.

"Gentlemen, this is Mr Con Marais. Our new Head of Large Mammal Management."

Con shook hands with each of the officials in turn. He recognised their names from email correspondence: Mr Meyer, from the Parks Department. Mr Godoba, from a higher tier of government. Mr Nelson-Pick, a representative of a large financial institution. The Department, he knew, was on the verge of cutting funding; the bank was considering not renewing their sponsorship. Like fish to a lure, the men drifted towards the educational posters down the other end of the hall, each in its pool of spotlighting. Amina gave him an obscurely commanding look, and he trotted over to stand next to the visitors in an accommodating way.

The Department man turned to him. "Tell us about these special lions, then," he said. Was there mockery in his tone, or simply humour? He was an older man, grey-haired, with a fold of fat at the back of his neck and a soft, confiding voice.

Con found himself speaking, fluently and persuasively, about *Panthera leo melanochaitus*. How magnificent the original lions had been, how famously large and ferocious. The thick dark manes that grew over their shoulders, down their chests and along their bellies; their tails tipped with a black whisk and the fronts of their toes that, in a delicate touch, were tufted and pale.

He showed the visitors the expressive ink drawing by Rembrandt of the reclining Cape lion. He invited them to examine the photo of the last known true Cape lion in captivity, a dim black-and-white shot from 1860 of a sick-looking animal in a tiny cement cage in the Jardin des Plantes in Paris. Also a photo of the gracile young mounted pair in the Stuttgart zoo, the male and the female side by side, their straw-coloured backs lined up; and the robust, full-maned male in the Natural History Museum in London, posed on a tussock against an aquamarine sky, jaw dropped to show its black lips.

He talked about the quagga, how white-rumped specimens – on view on the slopes just next door! – had been successfully bred back from the brink using zebra populations. Amina's line: species loss, with a positive spin.

As he spoke, he felt more than saw a shadow slipping out the half-open door behind the men's backs. The girl, caught in a sliver of light, raised the tear-crumpled paper napkin to him in a curious greeting – not really a wave; it was more like the gesture of a discreet but determined bidder at an auction. And then she was gone. He found himself blushing. Something about the face turned into the light when she slipped away … the crushed napkin, the tear-moist, tear-warm fingertips in the dimness. It had been a long time since Con had blushed for anything.

"The Nazis did something similar," pink-faced Mr Nelson-Pick remarked brightly. "With the aurochs – you know, the wild cattle. Interesting parallels. Nationalist politics, and so on. They thought they were suitably Aryan animals."

Con just raised his eyebrows. It seemed a needlessly hostile remark.

"So tell me, Mr Marais …"

Con turned his attention to the older man. Mr Godoba. He hadn't expected direct questions.

"Why should we care about these demons?"

Con shook his head and laughed politely. "Demons?"

"Demons. People used to believe that, you know, lions were demons. In the old days, they attacked many people, terrified villages. Even now, up north, these lions kill. They were destroyed, here in the Cape, because they were killing people, children. Why on earth would we want them back?"

Con just kept shaking his head and smiling. He wasn't prepared for this kind of conversation. His charm didn't extend this far. "Because they're precious," he said. "Because once something is extinct, it's lost forever. You can't bring it back."

"But is that not precisely what you are trying to do here, with this project? Bring back something that is rightly dead and gone?"

The other suits were rounding on him too now: "And what about cloning?" Mr Meyer said. "With modern genetics, we can recreate animals from scratch, surely? No need for this old-fashioned hit-and-miss approach."

"You know, there are people who say this whole thing is a waste of time and resources, with all the important existing species we're losing …"

"They're doing amazing things with mammoth DNA!"

"… that there never was a separate black-maned species in the first place, that anything we breed now will just be a funny-looking lion. That they're nothing special."

Con kept smiling, but he let his gaze float beyond the suits and settle on a dim corner of the room. There, he noticed, was the last of the educational posters, the one he hadn't bothered to show the visitors. Mark's alchemical illustration: a green lion rampant, yellow sun clenched in its jaws.

"Well, gentlemen," he said mildly, "I'm no geneticist. But Sekhmet seems special to me."

"Head of Large Mammal Management? Quickest promotion I've ever had."

"Ja, well. Keep this up and you'll be sitting in my seat."

They were back at the Rhodes Memorial restaurant. Amina had asked him to join her for a drink after work, and after a long day he'd been happy to oblige. Elyse was having a rehearsal at the apartment later – their usual practice space was being repainted – and Con had no desire to hurry home. "We're doing fables," she'd told him. "Dog in a manger, that stuff. Just with African animals, you know? It's fun."

Con had been irritated: the flat was far too small for that kind of thing. But of course it wasn't his decision.

Amina smiled at him across the table, but she was looking strained, and her age was showing. Strands were escaping from her plait, which seemed greyer than before. It had been a trying week for her, flying to meetings with funders, with the Department. "Seriously, thank you for that. You should be dealing with these guys. You're very persuasive when you talk about the project. Calm, rational. I get a bit … emotional. So thanks."

"It's no problem. I don't think I handled it that well."

She clenched her hands together, gold rings pinching her fingers.

The atmosphere of the place had changed since the old days; now it was oriented to a drinking crowd, mostly students from the university below. But it was still pretty up here. From the bar one could look down and see the cars speeding home along De Waal Drive, and sometimes even a quagga or two romping alongside the wildebeest on the slopes above the highway. There was one below them now, standing very still, its stripy zebra half staring out to sea and its pale rump mooning the drinkers at the bar.

"Bloody quaggas," said Amina. "Get all the good press."

On the terrace above, he could see the last remaining Lion House volunteers, Thandiswa among them, sitting at a table with a couple of other people. He'd noticed that the volunteers liked to keep their jackets on after hours, roguishly unbuttoned. The uniforms, brass buttons glinting, attracted attention. Members of the public often came over to ask questions about the lions; even more so after the accident. There were some up there now, hanging on the staff's words. One visitor clasped a coffee cup demurely in her lap like a begging bowl. Thandiswa caught Con's eye over their heads and gave him a cheerful wave.

He'd rather be up there with her. Down at this table, Amina's perpetual tension was evident, the side of her mouth twitching again. She raised a finger and the student waitress came at a scurry.

She ordered a beer for him and a Coke Light for herself. "You like this place?"

"Rhodes Mem? Sure. I remember it from when I was a teenager. We used to come here at night. Someone said there were Satanists here. Midnight masses, animal sacrifices."

"We?"

Him and Mark, actually, but he didn't feel like telling those stories right now. "Friends," he answered a little shortly. "It was bullshit of course. I think they had Christian prayer meetings here at one time; that was as supernatural as things got."

When the beer arrived, he sipped it cautiously and waited for item one. This was Amina who'd asked him here for a drink, and he assumed there was an agenda.

"So. You like that lion?"

"I do. If she ever lets me catch more than a glimpse of her."

"Oh, don't worry, she'll come around, I can tell. It's like my cats at home: they like the boys."

"So she liked Mark?"

Amina smiled. "She liked him very much." Her face fell for a moment, and then she sighed and raised her drink. "To Mark."

"To Mark," he repeated. And it seemed right: the first heartfelt and straightforward tribute he'd given his friend in all these weeks. At the same time, his mind skated guiltily over Mark's indistinct image and away, as if his body lay beneath ice.

Above them, a small group of people had gathered around one of the bronze lions, halfway up the steps – the same group who'd been chatting to Thandiswa earlier. An adolescent girl in a sparkly top was straddling the sculpture while another five or six people sat at its base. You often saw kids messing around up there, but this lot seemed out of place, and strangely mismatched. A middle-aged couple who looked like awkward visitors from out of town; a young man in preppy jeans and a polo shirt; an older grannyish woman, conservatively dressed; a couple of others in flowing, homespun clothes. He couldn't identify them, but something in their self-conscious alliance reminded him uneasily of his mother and her friends, back in the day. They had a wary, watchful look to them.

"Who's that lot?"

Amina looked up at them, a little sourly. "Zoo groupies," she said. "They exist. Haven't they bothered you before? Animal nutters."

"What do you mean, like animal rights people?"

"Something like that … but also … not. They're not

environmentalists, exactly, more just nutters. Sometimes I think they're plotting to free the lions, sometimes I think they're planning to jump in the cage with them. Every zoo gets a few jumpers, you know? It seems like the fewer wild animals there are in the world, the weirder people get about them. You haven't seen anyone odd hanging around, have you? People messing with the cages?"

He shook his head, but saw again those two pale hands, pressed against the glass. "I'll keep an eye out."

"The point is," – Amina returned to her running order – "you obviously fit in well here. You know how to handle the animals, you can talk to people." Her hands groped the wooden tabletop, as if for a pen. "But also, obviously, you've come to us at a weird time. The funders are unsettled, they want a new business plan." She worried a splinter with a fingernail. "The Department wants it to be educational, but also good PR. The funders want some return on investment. One dead lion, one invisible lioness and a couple of dassies isn't cracking it. They want cubs. I've been talking to these people all week. They have some different ideas for the place."

"Such as?"

"Well. Obviously we need a male lion. And having spent the last five years of my life scouring zoos and game farms for black-maned lions, I know one isn't just going to walk through our door. At least not a real one. So. We have options."

She held out her fingers and clasped them one by one in the opposite palm as she made her points. "One. We take a regular lion and dye its mane black. Two. We say, to hell with it, here are some regular lions for you to look at. Or maybe some nice white ones – people like those. Cheetahs, even. But there are other places that do that, better than we can here."

"So … dassies."

"Hah. Ja. Three. We turn this more into a general educational place for kids. We have talks, lectures, theatre performances. Just to keep things going. Four."

"Let me guess. Cloning."

"Not practical. Vastly expensive. And, anyway, we don't have a perfect black-maned lion to reproduce: the whole point is that we wanted to breed the traits back. Guess again."

"Animatronics."

She laughed. "Well, actually, yes. They can do amazing things with robots these days. They move, they roar. I've seen some very scary T. Rex displays with robots."

Con sipped his beer slowly. Without the real lion at the heart of the place, what was the point? "What would happen to her, to Sekhmet?"

"Maybe donate her to a zoo or something. There's a sanctuary for old circus lions, did you know that? Out by Paarl. Or …" She shrugged.

"Or what?"

"She's no good if she doesn't reproduce. And she cost us a helluva lot. Some of these operations will pay good money for a special animal."

Con was recalling the whiteboard. "What kind of operations? Safaris? Game-watching?"

Amina looked away.

"Amina. You wouldn't …"

"What?"

"*Hunting?*"

"All I'm saying is, people would pay a lot, you know …"

"Pay for what? To be the person to kill the last black-maned lion in the world? Jesus."

Amina held up her hands. "Okay, okay, don't get worked up. That is, like, Plan Zed, okay? You know I love that lion."

He found he was actually biting his tongue, painfully. He looked away from her. The light was dimming and they'd put on some kind of cocktail-bar jazz with a schick-schick beat that was getting on his nerves. The restaurant was transforming into an evening zone, a bar.

"Anyway, let's not worry about that now. As I say, Plan Zed. I just wanted to give you a heads-up, as they say. This job … it might not be here for long. There's pressure from the top."

"Ja, I got that. Well. Thanks for letting me know."

"Another beer?"

"I don't think so."

He left her staring into her drink, an unhappy smirk flickering on and off at the side of her mouth.

white-eye

From the lowest terrace, a path led down through the quagga enclosures. Despite the highway below and the memorial above, it was possible to feel, here, that one was out on the mountain, walking through pleasant green meadows. Con felt the relief of solitude.

This was short-lived. Soon enough he saw, on the path below, a ragged group of individuals heading down. He recognised them as the odd bunch from the memorial. They were moving slowly, but Con hung back, not wanting to interact. His session with Amina had left him feeling talked-out and tired. It suited him to dawdle, anyway: he had no wish to go home to Elyse just yet.

He let his gaze wander to the side, into the trees. And there – was it? – yes, something there, hidden and overgrown: the suggestion of white walls.

He waded through the thigh-high bush and found a small rectangular kraal of whitewashed bricks. He edged round to the threshold, and once inside he had no choice but to step from slab to slab, as the weeds were grown thick between the stones. Dutch inscriptions, some too worn to read; and many small unnamed infant headstones. He found Elyse's surname on a stone set for a couple: Johanna Maria and Hermanus Jacobus.

He smiled; it was true: Elyse was rooted here. The golden chain of family was real. Not his chain, though. He wasn't linked. Con picked his way back to the path and slowly on down.

Just before the road, the party below him paused and consulted and then split up. One figure carried on towards the bridge going over the highway, while the remaining three headed towards the university. The solitary figure was one of the ones wearing flowing clothes – some kind of poncho maybe. When she started over the highway bridge, he followed: he might wander down to Main Road and catch a taxi.

But the girl stopped in the middle of the bridge's span, above the road divider. Below, the sparse cars heading into town sheared past the clogged rush-hour traffic going in the other direction. She put her hands on the railing and for a dislocated moment he thought she was going to jump: there was drama in the pose. But no. It seemed she was simply waiting for him.

Con reached the bottom of the slope, crossed the verge and climbed the steps to the bridge – committed now, no way to change direction. She turned to look at him. As he had half-known, it was the girl from the lion den, the girl who'd cried. Inevitable. The vanes of the old Dutch mill on the other side of the road rotated gently, and he felt he was being brought to the apex of the bridge by some relentless mechanism.

As he came towards her, he saw that she was holding something cupped in her palms – a bird? – as if about to release it into the air. Not a good place for such a gesture: the winds were busy up here. He hung back, waiting for the delicate moment to be past. But the girl looked up at him instead, and immediately tucked whatever it was she was holding – and he doubted now that it was a living creature – back into the folds of her garment.

Even in the luminous early-evening light, lit from all angles and floating in the sky, she seemed an unclear figure to him. The impression of someone dim, uncertainly outlined, tentatively and provisionally drawn, remained. Sketchy, was the word that came to mind. Her hair was blowing across her face and her hands were busy dragging at the strands, as ineffectually as they'd pressed at glass or crumpled tissue paper. Her clothes were made of some flyaway stuff that concealed her shape, and of an indefinable shade: the colour of dust and moths and mice. He'd instantly forgotten her face the last time, and he knew he would instantly forget it again. The setting, so dramatic, seemed to call for some more forceful character to play it – someone like Elyse, whose clean features and striking eyes would be used to great effect here on the windblown bridge, with the traffic below and the city laid out behind. This insubstantial girl seemed in danger of blowing off the edge of the bridge and away with barely a whisper of complaint. Con wanted to reach out and comb back her hair, neaten her up somehow.

The traffic was loud below them, and she seemed content to stand in silence with him for a while; and he was quite happy, too, to be suspended there without words.

"Hello," she said, and for half a moment he felt disappointed: this ordinary piece of speech.

"Hi. I met you in the Lion House."

"Yes, thanks for the tissue." She laughed. Her teeth were small and uneven. She held out a little hand, fingers and fingernails all small and uneven too. "My name's Mossie."

"Mossie?"

"You know, like the bird. And you're the lion man."

"Head of Large Mammal Management." He said it with a smile, although she wouldn't get the joke. "My name's Con. So – how did you know Mark?"

She gave an ambiguous flex of the shoulders. For a moment he saw the shape of her real body under her capacious garment, the swell of a breast. "Where are you headed?" she asked. "Do you want a lift? I'm going to town."

Her car was parked just on the other side of the bridge's span: a tiny little Fiat, much abused. It sagged on its toy wheels at the weight of two bodies. She piloted it down to Main Road, and then around and back onto the highway, past the mill with the whale bones embedded in the grass around it like bollards. She was silent, seemingly lost in thought as she drove.

He was surprised by the intensity of the traffic. In recent times, he'd become dislocated from the everyday rhythms of work, of waking and commuting, the tides of the city. He watched the people in their cars – now edging ahead, now dropping back according to the mysterious physics of rush hour.

He too spoke only a little, just "left here" and "right here" once they got to the city, as was needed. When they came up below the apartment in Sea Point, she sat for a moment with her hands on the wheel, letting the engine idle. The silence continued between them. It was peaceful. Soon he would have to go up and deal with Elyse again, her questions, her vivid and provoking self.

He could see that she was home: the lights were on, and the lit windows seemed to sparkle with all the complexities and puzzlements of human life. Shadows moved up there: the silhouettes of animal-headed beings, gods with extended necks or several arms, swaying to silent rhythms.

Shit. He'd forgotten: the rehearsal. He'd hoped to skip it entirely.

The space inside the little car felt much simpler, free of difficult meaning. They could, right now, drive far away from here, out to some country road. He and the strange girl sat looking up at the lights like two jackals gazing on a campfire.

"We're having a little thing for him, you know?" she said.

"A thing?"

"A whatsit – not a memorial," – she gulped a laugh – "because he's still alive, obviously. But like a … a show of support. You should come."

"Sure, when is it? Nobody mentioned it to me."

"It's for his friends, just his friends. Not anybody else from the Lion House." She looked at him sternly.

"Sure."

She leant across him – that thrusting shoulder again, indicating a hidden body. A pale hand snaked out of the poncho and jerked open the glove compartment. She took out a piece of paper and scribbled on its back with a gnawed ballpoint. She wrote strenuously, the pen-grip whitening her knuckle, her whole torso moving slightly back and forth in sympathy with the words. The exertion kindled a warm, musty scent from her body. As she wrote, something swung loose from the neck of her garment. A pendant of fur, or feathers … a rabbit's-foot charm? He looked more closely and saw what it was: the body of a bird, folded in on itself but the feathers still bright. A white-eye. The kind of finch that came to eat the flowers in the tree outside Elyse's balcony. For a moment, he wondered if it came from Gerard's collection.

Seeing the direction of his eye, the woman stopped writing and tucked the feathered secret inside the folds of her clothes again. She handed him the paper with a sideways look.

"Thank you." He slipped it into a pocket. The seatbelt trapped him: "I can't …" He groped at the catch.

"Here," she said, leaning over to release it with a stab of the thumb. As she did so, she kissed him quickly on the mouth and pulled away. The seatbelt slithered up over his shoulder and freed him.

"Right," Con said. His face felt a little affronted. It had been an odd kiss, close-mouthed, aggressive. He was, he realised, a little disappointed. "I'm late, I better run. My girlfriend …" He wrenched open the door and struggled out.

Her face was obscure, as if she had sunk under a shallow depth of silty water. He nodded goodbye; she gave a reproachful nod back and pulled away, her exhaust racketing into the evening.

He stood in the road for a little while, passing the key-bunch from hand to hand and looking up at the flat's windows.

Con didn't dislike Elyse's crowd. Many of them were witty and generous people. Musa, Elyse's co-director in the small theatre group, was particularly friendly towards him, often trying to draw him out. But somehow the theatrical world still put him on edge. He'd made the mistake of trying to explain this once to Elyse. She'd looked at him as if he were monstrous. "How can you not like theatre? It's storytelling, it's what people *do*. Don't you get that?"

"Yeah," he said, not wanting a fight. "It's not the acting on stage that bothers me, so much. It's just … sometimes it seems like they never stop."

"Just because you struggle in social situations doesn't mean other people have to tone it down," Elyse had snapped. "Sometimes I think you have some kind of problem. With people. With communication."

"I communicate fine."

"I'm not talking about small talk. I know you can do that. Anyone can do that."

"No, they can't," he'd said, faintly offended. He was good with small talk. It had taken a fair bit of work to learn how to do that, and he didn't like the way she dismissed it.

Con let himself quietly into the flat, but instead of heading for the lounge, he cut through the kitchen to the balcony. Here he could sit and watch through the glass. He'd been there a while before any of them noticed him: he saw one or two people glance his way, and Musa smiled and raised a friendly hand. Elyse, too, was conscious of his presence, he could tell by the slight vibration in her profile even as she turned her face away. She was irritated; she'd want him to go in, say hi, be normal. But Con felt resistant. He just couldn't bring himself to sit with these people and try to move his mouth and hands as they did. He'd done too much of that today already.

He marvelled at them, though. Just bodies, just flesh and blood, but look what shapes they could make! Even Elyse's annoyance was wonderful to watch. Their throats moved up and down – such beautiful actorly projection, diction – although he could hear nothing through the glass. He might as well still be in the car, driving, commuters sliding past him in their separate lives.

They were all good-looking people, lithe, dressed casually in tracksuit pants and t-shirts for rehearsal. They were acting something out now, practising moves: bending, curving, rocking. Every now and then someone would pick up a prop, a mask, and slip it on for a few steps before laying it down again. Elyse wore a mask with a long beak. Con noted Musa's hands on her hips; they seemed to fit snugly there.

Music came on. Something rhythmic and drum-heavy. Four people in the room got to their feet and started moving together in a line. All four wore masks, feathered things that covered the tops of their faces, transforming them into a line of birds, flapping and pirouetting. Their movements suggested the leaps and skitters and flutters of animal motion, but imagined by people who didn't really know animals outside of storybooks, who'd never been close. The melody was damped by the glass and only the deep beat came through, shivering the doors slightly with each thump. Now they were singing, mouths opening and closing like fledglings'. Con turned his face away to laugh.

The balcony – the tiles on the floor, the pot plant, the ashtray holding a stubbed-out joint – filled him with nostalgic fondness. Already he felt that soon he'd be leaving all of this. For something to do, he lit one of Elyse's cigarettes and smoked it evenly, trying but failing to resist the rhythm of the music. Hand rising to his mouth and falling on the drumbeat, smoke rippling from his mouth in lieu of melody.

The guests left early, before ten, and he supposed that was his fault too: his glowering presence on the balcony must have soured the vibe. Elyse vanished from his field of vision for a moment, and then suddenly the airlock was broken and the glass door slid open, letting out the sounds of the last people leaving, chatting. Her mask was perched on top of her head, but as she came out onto the balcony and sat opposite him, she pulled it back down over her face like a visor, eyeing him through a slit. He smiled, but had no way to tell if she was smiling back. Why was she always doing this, always putting materials between them? Masks, for god's sake.

"What are you, a bird of paradise?"

"Some kind of stork, I think." She observed him. "You're smoking."

"So it seems."

"Me too." She held out two fingers for a smoke.

"Only if you take that off. I don't want you going up in flames."

She sighed and pushed up the mask, reaching to take the cigarette from him and leaning in again to have it lit. She was flushed from the dance, and the mask had left light lines around her eyes and across her cheeks where the elastic had pulled it close.

"So what happens with the stork?"

"Oh, you know, it's a stork and a crow. Different bowls for water. The stork can't drink from the shallow bowl, the crow can't drink from the deep one, etcetera. The moral is, to each their own. I think. So. Where were you?"

"Just work. I had a meeting with Amina."

"Oh." She tapped the end of the cigarette into the pot plant, and it seemed she was about to accuse him of something: betrayal, infidelity. And he would've felt justly accused, although he'd never cheated on her, as he had before on others.

But instead she said, "I thought you might have gone to the hospital."

It took a moment for him to know what she meant. He'd not been thinking of Mark. Clearly the man had been on Elyse's mind, winking and beckoning.

"He's still in hospital, right?" she continued. "Your friend."

"So I understand."

"You understand? You haven't actually gone to see him, have you?"

"I've taken his mother a few times. Hey, I'm not even family."

"That's fucking shocking, Con." She stared at him. She'd had to take off one hostile mask in order to reveal this other, even colder one below. He tried to match her look with a blank one of his own, but he couldn't manage it. He leant forward, touched her exposed stomach. Warm, as always, and damp with sweat. He felt it flinch away from his fingers.

Impatient with this, he slid his hands further up her torso and tried to kiss her. He felt like only nakedness would allow them to see each other now. But she was too fast for him. Somehow the mask was on again: the hard wire of the beak dug into his nose, his lips found feathers. He worked his fingers under the edge of the mask and tugged it away from her face – too roughly; then grappled with the rest of her armour, hurting his hands on all the catches and latches.

At last she softened, allowed her clothes to fall. But it felt to Con like there was no end to her layers; that for every skin peeled another lay beneath, and under that a hide of a different colour, spotted, striped. However deeply he plumbed her body, he would never again get down to that softest skin.

The next day it rained heavily, and Elyse offered him her car. He knew what she meant by this. If he had the car, he could visit the hospital.

After work, Elmien asked him for a lift to the train, and Isak came too. But when Elmien heaved herself out of the back seat at the station, Isak stayed put. "Ja, you can take me home," he said.

Con was a little surprised – he'd assumed Isak lived far out, on the Flats probably – but tried not to show it. He was prepared to take him anywhere. But the older man pointed him along the highway to town, Con's usual route. Soon he realised where they were going. Through town, to Kloof Nek, up to the houses on the side of Lion's Head.

The old pointy-headed lion was still there, one eyebrow made from a crooked pine tree. The slope was looking bushy and green; there'd been no fires on the mountain for several summers, he'd read. The houses below – an extension of the old shack camp in the quarry – had been made respectable, with running water and electricity: no more open fires or paraffin stoves knocked over. From a distance, the fence-line was clearly demarcated. Above, it was bush; below, clustered roofs. The dwellings now ran the entire length of the fence, completely ringing Lion's Head and the old mosque on its shoulders and enveloping Signal Hill.

Con slowed the car as they came up to the Nek.

"It's okay," said Isak. "It's not dangerous. The people all know me here."

"No, it's not that. It's just, I haven't been up close for years. It looks different."

It was very different. What had been a collection of shacks back when he was growing up, a place to score dope or after-hours booze if you were a reckless suburban teen, had transformed into something like a small town. There was a row of tiny identical two-room government houses painted pale blue; behind that, a bigger double-storey block with laundry hanging out of the windows, and some free-standing houses. The place was built up. He could barely see the fence.

"You know Leeukop?" asked Isak.

"I came here …" He turned to Isak. "Were you here? When they were building the fence? And pulling down the houses?"

"I wasn't in Cape Town then; I was up north in those days."

"It was a long time ago." Con felt oddly shy, now, to mention it. "There was a demonstration … People got hurt."

Isak shrugged. "There's no one living here from those days, when it was just shacks. They chased that lot away. These people here now – we all came when they put the proper houses up. I came when I got the zoo job, got my papers for the Department house. I don't know what happened to the old people."

The top of Lion's Head poked up from the backs of the houses. People could still go up there, he'd heard; once a month, at full moon, there was a guided walk. But it wasn't really popular these days. The sight of the Department houses below spoilt the atmosphere.

"I'm just up here," said Isak, nodding them up a steep track. It started out tar, but by the time it dead-ended at the fence it was sand. Isak's small house was on the left, built up right against the barrier. Thick bush, covered in tiny yellow flowers, poked through the bars as if slyly trying to grab things from the world of humans. An old tyre, a child's push-cart, a piece of tarpaulin. Isak's house seemed to turn away from the fence. The stoep was on the other side of the house, and the only window on the alleyway was covered with a net curtain that looked like it never moved.

"You ever see animals, on the other side?" Con asked. "Like those big ones they talk about? Are there really eland up here?"

Isak shook his head, laughed shortly. "Animals? I get enough of that kind of thing at work," he said. He got out and leant against the passenger door. "Thanks, man," he said. "Oh, here …" He tossed a jingling handful through the window. Con caught it, surprised by the spiky weight.

"Ow," he said. "What's this?"

"All yours."

"What do you mean?"

"I chucked it in this morning. Resigned. Bloody lions." And he hopped backwards away from the car, raising his hand in salute. "Watch out for the wildebeest on your way down!"

Con stared at the keys in his hand. Each seemed enormous, antique, and there were a ridiculous number of them: one for each of the many gates behind which Sekhmet was jailed. He wanted to protest, but Isak had already vanished into his house. Con carefully clipped his own house key onto the bunch and stashed it in the cubbyhole, as you would a loaded gun.

Doing a five-point turn out of the cul-de-sac, Con nosed the car up close to the narrow section of visible fence. There were things piled up against this side of the bars: old car doors, pieces of wood, a rusty washing machine, blocking out the view of the mountain. Leant up against the fence the way you'd barricade a door.

III. EDEN

I dreamed of a lion which talked
of lions which talked to their fellow-lions.
I heard them, I saw them: in my dream they were black.
Their paws were just like the paws of real lions.

– STEPHEN WATSON, version of ‖KABBO's account, from
"‖Kabbo Tells Me His Dream", 1991

mouse

"You want to *sleep* there? But why?"

"Mom."

"Why can't you sleep here?"

"We do our homework together," Con repeated dully. "We've got a project. We'll finish late. It's easier for me to sleep there."

She observed him over the scarred table. He ran his fingers along the familiar knife tracks, pressing his fingertips into the grooves.

"Well, why doesn't he come here sometimes?" she grumbled, and he knew he'd won. "Too fancy for us, your friends."

Where would we put them? he wanted to ask her. Every bed is taken in this house, every corner crammed. Having seen Mark's home, he was struck by the claustrophobia of his own, its meanness. For the first time he understood that Lorraine's wealth of things wasn't wealth at all. The empty acreage of the Carolissen property showed him what money could truly buy.

Mark was the only child he knew who lived in his own entire building, a kind of separate cabin. His family lived on the other side of the large garden; you could barely see their house through the trees. In fact, the first few times Con went around there, it seemed Mark had no parents at all. There was a mother and father of course, a sister too; but they were hard to imagine. Mark appeared to have raised himself, directing his own development, just like he tailored his own school uniform.

Mark's room was almost empty. There was a mattress, a wardrobe, some posters, a stereo. One side was entirely taken up by a sliding patio door, covered by a thin white curtain that let in the light from a streetlamp on the other side of the wall. Even Mark's technique for entering the property was excitingly rudimentary: toe in the gap in the brick wall, grab a branch, launch yourself over into the leaves, fall out of them on the other side … Con never thought to enter by the front door.

The first night he stayed over there, Con was pulling his balled-up school trousers out of his rucksack when the wooden lion fell to the ground with a clatter. Mark caught it and spun it on his fingertips. "What is it? What's that in its mouth?"

"It's nothing. Just something my dad made. Some dumb toy or something." Con's cheeks were flaming.

"It's cool. It's artistic. He's artistic, your dad?"

"I suppose."

But Mark was nodding as if at some significant confirmation. "I must do some sculpture. Woodcarving, ja."

Mark had already told Con his plans: to go to London after school, to be an artist. It was completely plausible. Mark was already an artist in everything he did. The way he tucked the hair behind his ear, the loops of his signature, the curve of his mouth, the angle of his lush eyebrows. All strokes in a harmonious calligraphy.

"Let's put him here," said Mark, reaching up to hook the lion by his tail to the edge of the lampshade. "That looks kiff."

Con was flushed with pleasure. Lying on his back, staring up at the swinging animal, he watched its magnified shadows dance around the room. The shapes were playful: the lion forming, dissolving, reforming in distorted silhouette, pouncing and rushing and pulling back across the ceiling. He didn't say, You can have it if you like it; there was no need.

"You're so lucky," Mark murmured later, after they'd switched off the light and lay waiting for sleep. "You're so lucky to have a dad who can do this kind of shit. Does he teach you?"

"Well, actually. He's not … he's dead."

"Oh, oh man. Serious? Sorry!"

"It's okay, it was a while ago."

"So how …?"

Con was a little drunk with confiding. "It was the animals," he said, and laughed.

He could feel Mark's interest immediately beside him, electric. "Animals? Jees! Like wild animals?"

Another pause. Con could taste the dark. When the lights were off, words were less your own; nobody could see your mouth make them. Con couldn't say whose words these were, scrolling above the bed, black ink on black fabric. "Sure," he said. "It was a hunting accident. In the Arctic. The wolves came for him."

"Fuuuck!" Mark thrashed the duvet excitedly off the bed.

Con retrieved the bedclothes. "He had six bullets. But there were eleven wolves," he continued. "They couldn't reach his body until the summer thaw."

"Hectic."

The next morning, Con woke from a dream of his mother, or perhaps Mark's mother, wrapping something slippery around his body, his face, his groin. Long wet leaves. It was early.

Mark had pulled the covers completely over his head, leaving his long toes poking out at the bottom of the duvet. Even Mark's toenails were shapely, long ovals without ridges. They gleamed in the blue early-morning light, as if polished. Con put his face close to his friend's feet, then drew back, embarrassed.

The garden tapped its leaves against the glass. In his tracksuit pants, Con quietly slid open and closed the glass doors. His skin prickled in the cool, but he didn't want to cover himself; the cold was sharp, freeing him from the constriction of the dream.

It was like stepping into another dream altogether. The strangeness of walking through an unfamiliar garden, almost naked. The volume of the birdsong was startling. Here was a path. The moss was chill and moist on his soles.

And here was a body curled up in the grass. A peaceful sight: a child of about six or seven, so snugly nested in the grass that it didn't even strike him as strange. After a moment, when she didn't move, he saw that she was sleeping, her breath even and regular. She was dressed in fuzzy lime pyjamas. Black hair straggled over her cheek, mouth open. Curled up like a mouse.

He crouched down next to the little girl. Her eyelashes were fine strokes of ink. Hands wrapped together near her mouth. Con had never paid much attention to the fact that Mark had a sister – but here she was, up close, alive; a miniature, more delicate version of Mark himself.

He sat and watched the child, feeling the damp come up through the seat of his pants. She stirred and rolled, her hand coming down warm and limp on his knee and her face nuzzling his leg. He stiffened, a small jolt of imprecise panic coursing through him at this sleepy trust. I could be anyone, he thought.

As if lifting a porcelain bowl, he took her head in his hands – the ticking pulse, the delicate bone! – shifted his leg and laid her head carefully down on her own folded hands. She looked wrong, though, skew, as if he'd broken something. He stood up, the cold seeping through to his buttocks and the places where her warm head and hand had lain.

Paleness through the branches solidified into the body of a house, lemon-coloured, its windows glowing a deeper yolky yellow. It was as if it had been invisible before, a house in a fairytale that springs into existence at the seeker's approach. As it emerged from behind the trees, and Mark's glass door behind him, Con felt observed.

He stepped over the dewed grass and peered in through a window. Inside, two figures moved as clearly as on a television screen. A man was reading a newspaper at a kitchen table; behind him, a tall woman swayed at a counter, as if to music. Mark's parents, must be. Except they seemed old, much older than Con's own mother. A certain gravity in their movements. The next things he noticed were the animal heads looming down on them from above, as if nibbling at their greying crowns. A zebra, some great heavy-headed antelope that Con couldn't name. At first the couple seemed fragile and bowed beneath the weight of the mounted animals. But then the woman glanced up and pinned him with a stare. She traversed the kitchen in seconds, mouth pursed in alarm. To his right, Con heard a door thrust open, saw a wedge of light cast onto the grass. His heart jolted like a thief's.

"Poor child!" said the woman, swooping down on him. "Come inside! Has Mark not offered you breakfast? It's freezing out here! Are you hungry? You must be starving."

"Good lord!" cried the man, in a richly thespian tone. "An intruder! He looks like he needs some feeding up, don't you think, Margaret? Come in!"

"Well now," said the woman. "Sit down, sit down! I'm Margaret and this is Gerard. And you must be Con."

He smiled, surprised that Mark had mentioned him at all.

The breakfast they gave him in the warm kitchen was enormous: two slippery eggs and a pile of bacon and three slices of toast. The older pair didn't touch the food themselves; they sat at the table and watched benevolently as he ate. Con perched on the edge of his seat, in alert discomfort. It was difficult to finish the big plate of food. Afterwards, he thanked them and stood up to take the plate to the kitchen, but Margaret stopped him: "Lettie will do that," she said. They seemed to want to talk to him. He fiddled with a teaspoon and returned their gaze.

For the first time in his life he was thinking of people over twenty-five: they are beautiful. Margaret had a long-limbed grace and fine features. Her colouring – pale eyes, faded hair – seemed a sign of a wise and tasteful restraint. Her hair was taken up in a bun, a style that belonged to someone older still. She must have been in her late forties, Gerard ten years older. He had a broad, owlish face set with emphatic features, his hair still mostly black, his profile only slightly blunted by time. Their age was glamorous to Con. Margaret had authority over his own mother, easily fifteen years younger. Lorraine – short and plump, with her oily skin, her full breasts beneath thin T-shirts, the sweaty ringlets at the back of her neck, the tumble of brown hair – seemed in comparison unformed, unrefined. Her lack of years was a kind of poverty, like their small home, their meagre meals, their spare conversation.

"Quiet little chap, isn't he?" said Gerard.

The "little" shrank him, deflated his belly around the mass of bacon and eggs.

"You haven't spoken at all," observed Margaret. "Tell us about yourself, Con."

He flushed, throat closing.

"For example, tell us about your name." She had a warmly commanding way of speaking. "Is it Conrad? Connor?"

He whispered his name.

"What?"

"Constantine," he said too loudly. Nobody at school knew his full name, which had belonged to his grandfather.

"Constantine! Well, how grand!"

He blushed, but she seemed genuinely pleased. Gerard said "Hah!" in a tone of happy surprise. "Emperor Constantine. Now there's a name. Much more imaginative than our lot."

The kitchen door swung open and Mark backed in, dressed, hair slicked back and damp from a shower, carrying the little girl across his chest.

"Oh, *Elizabeth*, not again!" said Margaret.

"She does it *all* the time. She's such a *pain*."

"Oh, come now, Mark. Be kind. She just wants to be near you."

"I know! She comes and hangs around me, she's waiting for me when I get up! It's impossible."

"It's just because your sister loves you," Margaret smiled, taking the sleepily bundled child onto her knee. The little girl's half-open eyes passed over Con without recognition. "This is our laat-lammetjie, Constantine. Lizzy."

He tried to avoid Mark's eyes, which no doubt would be full of evil delight at the sound of Con's silly full name. But when he looked up, he was surprised to find Mark appraising him quite seriously. Con tried a small smile, but it wasn't returned. There was a sulky, restive spirit in his friend this morning.

Now that the child was there, Con was struck by the wholeness of the family: mother, father, brother, sister. Full set, matching. They all shared pieces of each other: turn of the wrist, flare of the lips. One of those families where it's fun to play the heredity game, noting how the smile of the mother has recombined with the nose of the father, or vice versa, to create new and equally pleasing variations in the children. You could see Gerard in Mark's strong eyebrows, but the distance in the boy's eyes was from Margaret. Something tore a little inside Con to see it so clearly.

"And what do your parents do?" Gerard continued.

"His dad's a big-game hunter," said Mark, with a challenge in his voice. "He's not shocked by all your corpses."

"Mark refers to our historic family trophies," said Gerard dryly. "You've noticed them, I take it?"

Mark talked over him. "Come on, I'll show you." He gripped Con's shoulder and Con rose from the chair as if Mark's hand contained magnets. The skin on his chest goosebumped, and all at once he was embarrassed by its bareness.

"I just want to put on—"

"Okay, but I need to show you first."

Mark was irresistible. Con followed him out of the kitchen and along a corridor, under the watchful eyes of antelopes, eagles and foxes, down into a dim basement room. Inside, there was only one display case, a tall old-fashioned cabinet in dark wood with thin panes of antique glass, lightly bubbled. Mark closed the door of the room and then it was just the three of them: the two boys, and the lion staring directly at them through the glass.

"This is the oldest one we've got," said Mark. "My great-great-granddad killed it."

Con had never been so close to a wild animal before, and the proximity was enough to send the faintest instinctive jolt of fright down his spine. But this one wasn't very fierce. Although its pelt was patched in places – perhaps to conceal bullet holes – the lion was long beyond violence. His face was threadbare, his brown glass eyes like a lapdog's. A sparse mane. He was not much larger than a Labrador, and slender. "It's not as big as I thought," he said.

"It's a young one. One day I'm going to get an adult, a big male." Mark's voice was unusually avid. He was rustling in a drawer of a desk to one side, and came up with a tiny metal key. "Come on," he said, unlocking the cabinet and swinging back its tall door. When he stepped up, the sheets of glass shivered in their frames. Mark slung a leg over the lion's back and sat astride, grinning and flexing his bare toes, clicking his tongue. The lion continued to stare straight ahead.

"Come on," Mark said again. "It's fun."

Con hesitated, smiling uncertainly. He was embarrassed by the indignity: long-legged Mark straddling the animal like a little boy on a rocking horse. But he was about to join him when Gerard lurched into the room.

"Mark!" he barked. "Don't be bloody stupid! That thing is more than a hundred years old!"

Mark lost his grin. Con, head down, saw his friend's toes stiffen. Gerard strode across the room, reaching up to take his son by the front of the T-shirt. But he was moving quite slowly, controlled, the force concentrated in his grip as he pulled Mark off the lion. Mark seemed to cooperate in this. Con realised that they were both restraining themselves because of the peril of their situation: two people cautiously wrestling in a glass box, the tall panes rattling with every move.

As soon as they were out, Mark commenced struggling, and Gerard, still holding him by the scruff with one hand, brought the other hand up and gave his son a slap on the cheek. It couldn't have hurt much – Mark was wriggling, Gerard's arm cramped, the action clearly unpractised – but Mark flinched and Gerard dropped him in what seemed to be equal shock. Mark shoved his way out of the room, a red patch showing through the tan of his cheek.

After a moment's silence, Gerard turned back to the case and eased the tall door closed. Without looking at Con, he pulled the cuff of his cardigan over his knuckles and buffed Mark's fingerprints off the glass.

Con found him in the garden.

"Chatting with the old man, were you?" Mark asked coldly.

"Not really."

"Old fucker." His cheeks were still red in spots and his mouth looked bony and stretched, like the mouth of a fish. "What did he say to you?"

"Nothing. I came looking for you."

Mark laughed and flung a fist towards Con's chest. Con flinched away. "*Constantine*," he teased. "Don't be such a pussy." His eyes were very clear.

Mark jiggled his fist, then flipped his hand open like a conjurer. An amber marble was caught in the crease of his palm. Not a marble; it was flat on one side and had a dark spot in the middle. Mark smacked his hand to his own head, and the lion's glass eye stayed there, stuck to his brow. It glowed against his skin, gold-rimmed, dark in the centre.

stegosaurus

Mark's sour mood didn't last. Con visited often, and soon was staying over two or three times a week. He'd enter via the broken bricks to find Mark lying shirtless on the mattress, the shadow of leaves on his torso, a roll-up in his lips. Often he would be reading, or drawing in a sketchpad, which he'd put away as soon as Con arrived. Saturday night, preparing to go out: Mark levitating off the mattress, pulling down clothes for them both: Con in a string vest, Con in black jeans smelling of Mark's sweat and groin. A chain of metal links still warm from Mark's own chest. Mark was unselfconscious about undressing, even in front of that big glass window. His nipples, brown and perfectly circular on his chest.

"We must get your ear pierced," said Mark, reaching out to pinch Con's lobe between his fingernails. Pain, and the gold taste of beer on his teeth.

When it was time to go, they'd be over the wall and walking to town, to the clubs, to the bands. Walking was everything in those days: they were fourteen and tireless. Con understood, with a sense of exploding horizons, that nobody could stop this walking, that his feet could take him anywhere he wanted to be. Which was anywhere with Mark.

They were always the youngest people at the club. Most places didn't ask for ID in those days, but sometimes they'd be stuck outside on the pavement, hearing the music in snatches when the doors opened, watching the older punters come and go. More often, they got in. Mark had older friends, girls who would vouch for his age. He was the cool little dude, the mascot. And Con was his sidekick, the one who didn't need to speak. Once, a dark girl who looked about seventeen came up to where he was sitting on a wall and said to him, "Are you Mark's friend?" When he nodded, she leant in and gave him his first real kiss, tongue pushing nimbly into his startled mouth. She'd pulled away with a sweet palm to his cheek. Her skin shimmered with some kind of glitter balm that shone in the streetlight like dusted glass. Con hadn't had to say a word.

Inside, if they got in, Con kept by Mark's side. He knew that Mark's blindness wasn't just show: he really was very short-sighted, and stumbled from room to throbbing blacklit room without really seeing where he was going or who was coming up to hug him or ruffle his fringe or kiss him on the lips. Sometimes, when it was very dim, Con laid a hand on Mark's elbow, just there where he could feel the bone, and guided him, slightly left, slightly right. Sometimes away from someone, sometimes towards. And always, at the end of the night, he'd take his friend and direct him gently onto the safe side of the yellow line for the long trek home along the highway. They might hitchhike, but mostly they'd walk. It never seemed too long to them, or too cold. Mark would put an arm around Con's shoulders, his greater height assisting this arrangement. Con liked it best when Mark was a little drunk, when he seemed to relax from some unspoken tension. His friend became clumsier, kinder, with a spinning levity.

"Up there," he'd exclaim, waving a hand at the mountainside that started just a few steps away from the tar, enticingly formless in the dark. "Fucking *wild*. We're gonna sleep up there tonight, Con. Camp out."

"Not tonight," Con would smile. "Another time." Although he felt it too, the temptation to wheel around and head up into the sweet-smelling night.

Later, they'd strip down to their briefs and lie side by side on Mark's mattress, watching the leaves shift their weight against the glass doors, talking. Or rather, Con talked. A strange reversal was happening, at night in Mark's room. Mark, usually the chatty one, would fall silent as if in relief, while Con's tongue was liberated by the dark. Outside, the garden breathed lushly, pressing on the glass doors like a jungle, lapping up the carbon dioxide of so many glorious lies. It felt dangerous, luxurious. Con allowed himself, half-drunk and half-asleep, to speak recklessly, to say things without meaning them, without thinking them through, thoughts following in the wake of words.

Con talked about his father, the hunter. How he'd tracked flamingos in a microglider, following their migration routes down Africa. That time he went deep-sea diving in the deepest ocean trenches, through clouds of tiny phosphorescent organisms. How he'd taken Con camping in sub-zero conditions, on high-altitude mountain expeditions, on desert treks. Few of these stories were about actual hunting. They drew heavily on National Geographic specials. As the narratives progressed, his father became increasingly more enchanted with animals, less likely to kill them. Every now and then Con made an effort to introduce a skinning or a brutal goring, for authenticity.

Sometimes Mark would obtain a bottle of whisky and they'd sip from it, which helped the talking, and the stories. Often, later, Con would forget exactly what had been said. It did occur to him that Mark might not believe it all. But it didn't matter.

"Your father was such a *dude*! Hey, hey, Con, I was thinking. Maybe we could do that, sometime. Go somewhere new."

"New?"

"You know, camping. Like we said. You've got the gear, right? From your dad? You said."

And Con nodded. "Sure, sure I do."

"Camping on the mountain. Before they shut it all down. Somewhere far away from this nuthouse."

Con was filled with a deep, warm joy. He felt magnanimous: sure, he would organise it. Sure he had the gear.

When the talk ran dry and Mark fell asleep, Con would lie awake. He could hear Mark's breathing, smell the whisky and cigarettes on his breath, the musk of his skin. Sometimes he found the smell made him go hard; and, shyly, he pushed a hand down under the covers to hold himself. He didn't think Mark noticed, but, if he did, somehow that, too, would be okay.

He'd try to drift into the usual dream: the abandoned earth, the dinosaurs. But having Mark beside him made the fantasy less real, less satisfactory. Childish. The vision would have to be altered to accommodate. He tried to play a scene that was different, that allowed for two people, but it quickly grew too complicated. What would they talk about, just the pair of them, for all eternity? He closed his eyes and let himself be pulled away, into the old consoling loneliness.

The tent was a terrible old thing, a tangle of rigging and spikes and torn canvas. One flap had a dark stain down it. He sniffed it cautiously but it smelt only of mould. He'd found it, after much questing, inside a disused tumble-dryer out on the back stoep, under the desiccated corpse of an owl.

"Cool," said Lorraine, who was entertaining on the stoep. Her new boyfriend, paunchy and beleathered, rode with a gang of middle-aged Sunday bikers. "I never knew we had owls."

The rest of the archaic "gear" he managed to piece together from here and there in the house. He was gripped with shame. When he laid it all out in his bedroom, it looked like some abandoned campsite from the early seventies, where a hiker had maybe been murdered: a weird Oros-orange backback with a fixed external frame, blackened cooking pots, the stained and battered tent.

But, to his surprise and intense relief, when Mark arrived he regarded these grubby items with respect: "Old school!"

For Con it was unnerving to have Mark there, inside his own house, imperiously navigating the towers of Lorraine's stuff. Con was excruciatingly aware of the film of dust on everything, furring the dangling cords of the light fittings, of the cat hair drifting in the small breezes of the house's internal weather system. Mark flicked back his silky fringe, smiled.

It was a matter of getting Mark out of the house with minimal interaction with Lorraine and the gang. From the back garden came the frustrated roar of a motorbike engine refusing to catch. Con was keen to leave.

He stuffed the things into the rucksack hastily, not methodically as it was meant to be done. He knew he should've mapped it all out the night before, finding a logical slot or pocket for every item. But the camping gear had been in Lorraine's house for too long; it had picked up some of the house's sprawling disobedience. The sleeping bag wouldn't roll; the tent poles wouldn't lie down. The food was too weighty, there was no gas in the burner. In the end, he crammed the bag in quick, mortified thrusts and strapped it down as tight as he could, ratcheting the straps hard to stop the sleeping bag from exploding out the top. He hoisted the thing onto his back and tottered towards the front door. Mark made no move to help.

"Bye, Ma!" he yelled, scrambling to get the door open and closed behind them before Lorraine could spot him and start asking awkward questions. As usual, he'd told her they were doing homework at Mark's that night.

Out on the street, Mark turned to stroll backwards for a few steps, observing Con's progress. Con tried not to stagger. "That's a shitload of stuff," Mark said thoughtfully.

"Well, ja, it's the tent and everything," he gasped.

"Tent? What do we need a tent for?"

"For … sleeping. Unless you think we should just—"

"Sleeping?" Mark looked at him as if he were mad. "Anyway, we can't. I've got her with me." Mark flicked his fringe towards a small dark-headed figure sitting on the pavement a block down from the house. Elizabeth.

"You left her out here in the road?"

Mark shrugged.

She was playing with little stones on the ground, throwing and catching them in her palm, and as the boys approached – Con swaying, top-heavy – she looked up and gave a shy smile. "Hello, Con," she said, words light as pebbles.

Con was dumbfounded. "But – I mean – she's coming with us?"

"Ja." Mark was surly. "Bloody Margaret made me bring her. There's no one to look after her today."

They stood in an embarrassed circle, the boys with their burdens: Con with the foolish rucksack, chafing already at his shoulders; Mark with his sister. Only Elizabeth seemed unfettered, humming and tossing a stone in the air, higher and higher until it slung out of orbit and landed in the gutter. She was wearing a cotton dress with pink checks and a round white collar. Margaret seemed to favour oddly old-fashioned clothes for her daughter.

"How's that going to work?" The bag hung off Con's back, like a big man had grabbed him by the straps and was pulling him down. The thought of climbing a mountain made him feel nauseous. "I mean, if we've got her with us … we can't go far."

Mark looked relieved to hear it. "Ja, it's a drag," he said. "Where do you normally go? When you camp?"

Con's entire body had stiffened with the stress of keeping his back straight. "Well, the top. Usually."

Mark took something out of his jacket pocket. It was a wicked-looking catapult: a thick fork of peeled wood, elastic the colour of raw beef.

"What's that for?"

Mark showed Con a handful of ball bearings. "Birds. I thought I could take something down. Seeing as we're going to be in nature and all." He pinched a silver ball against the elastic, pulled back and sent it streaking into the neighbour's garden. Wings spanked the air as an unseen dove escaped.

A picture flashed in Con's mind: a hand smacking the car window, a smear of blood. "Don't be fucking stupid," he said. "You could kill someone."

Mark raised his eyebrows coolly at this new tone, and Con blushed. The most important thing was to keep moving, away from the house, before his mother shuffled out and laid eyes on them. He made a decision. "The forest's close," he said. "If we cross by the highway bridge."

"This is stupid," said Mark, chucking a green pine cone. "You can hear rush hour. This is not exactly, like, nature."

Con was putting up the tent anyway, stubborn, smacking the thin aluminium pegs into the ground with a rock. "You can't see the cars," he said shortly. "It's far enough."

The tent really was a pathetic old thing, and tiny, he saw now: not even big enough for two of them. But Elizabeth loved it. She crawled inside as soon as it was up and pressed her face against the fabric, laughing. "You can't see me!" the phantom squealed, appearing and disappearing.

The sun was dropping behind them, making shadow shapes on the side of the tent. Con made an animal with his hands, and opened its jaws and roared. Elizabeth screamed with pleasure. "We're on the mountain now, didn't you know there were lions and tigers up here?" He morphed his hands into something different, with a snapping mouth and a humped back.

"What's that!"

"It's a … stegosaurus." Con made his dino-shadow bigger, loomed over her, roaring, and she shrieked even louder.

Mark, meantime, was sulking in the trees. "Hey, malletjie!" he shouted, sending a pine cone stinging into Con's back.

They were too old for it really, but it was irresistible: the small green cones fitted into the hand like cool grenades, and Con felt infected by Elizabeth's laughter. Mark's throws were inaccurate but vicious. One stung Con right between his abused shoulders and he swallowed a girly shriek.

Mark lobbed a pine cone at the tent. Then another one, harder. The little girl, laughing still, pushed and pulled at the fabric, like she couldn't find the exit.

The cattie was lying on the needled ground. The handle fit snugly into one palm, the small dense nut of the green cone into the other. Mark sent off a high arcing shot into the fading blue above the treetops, beautiful. He laughed and spun around with another cone ready in his hand, and the elastic stretched, and the shot already aimed and gone before he could stop his own fluid release.

A hard *pwock*, and Elizabeth's bulge in the canvas disappeared abruptly. Con could hear her dropping on the ground inside, barely a rustle. A small green pine cone rolled down the slack slope of the tent and Con picked it up. He turned to see Mark standing there with his mouth open.

The tent was entirely still. Con thought, I will never be able to undo that zip. The thought of simply turning, walking away, leaving the stupid old tent and its suddenly sickening cargo right there, zipped up forever, was very strong.

But then the sound, a little whimper, not even a cry. Mark giggled, then stopped.

It was Con who went forward eventually, grappling briefly with the zip and letting out the struggling body, her top lip already blue and her nose bloody; but it was Mark she ran to. She took Mark's hand and turned to stare at Con, accusing, a line of blood down her lip, tears on her cheeks but not a sound. Brave, thought Con.

"I reckon that's it then. Fun time's over." He put the little girl up on his shoulders – Con could see it was a strain – and turned and started down the slope, slowly on the slick pine needles. "You coming?" Mark called.

"No, I don't think so," he said.

"Come on, man."

"No, I'd rather stay. You go on down."

Mark frowned; he reached up a hand to touch Elizabeth's cheek. The little girl had covered her eyes with her hands. "She's okay, you know?" he said. "Just a bit freaked."

A coolness had been collecting in Con's belly all day. Now the unaccustomed kindness in Mark's voice froze it solid. He shook his head.

"Okay, suit yourself," said Mark. "But this is stupid."

Con crept into the tent and listened to Mark's footsteps recede. Mark was clumsy out here, he noticed: smacking at branches, stumbling on roots. He opened a small length of the zip and pushed the cattie out, then zipped it up again. There were three perfectly round blobs of blood on the groundsheet. He lay down next to them. Leaf shadows shifted on the silky fabric. It was really a tent for a child.

He woke from a doze to the sound of something slapping the outside of the tent. And then the *zzzz* of a zip, slitting open a triangular crack of sky. It was not yet night. An arm parted the edges of the split. Con scrambled to his knees and the man yelped and jumped back. Con understood that he needed to show himself, show the man his youth and harmlessness. He came out on his knees into the cool light of evening, raising his hands.

The man was wearing a uniform. "What you doing here?" he asked. "Don't you know you can't be here? They're coming in the morning, going to put the fence in right along here. You can't be here. Little boy like you."

On the way home – walking, walking, always walking – he took things out of the bag one by one and threw them angrily into the gutter: the stove, the bags, the hard bread, the stupid heavy tuna can, the tent and, eventually, the decrepit old rucksack itself. Someone would pick it up, someone would be glad of it. Still, he half-expected to find it waiting for him when he got home, dragged back by his mother for recycling all over again.

He was afraid to see Mark's parents after that. But to his surprise, next time he phoned – letting it ring twice as he always did, then hanging up and phoning again so that Mark knew to pick up – it was Margaret's voice on the other end.

"Why, Constantine!" she exclaimed, and despite his apprehension, he felt himself flush with pleasure at the warmth in her voice, its pleasant modulation. In those two words alone there were valleys crossed, small summits attained. "Are you coming to visit us again? Next time, do come in the front door and pop your head in to say hello to Mark's poor old parents, why don't you?"

So it seemed they didn't know he was responsible for nearly braining their daughter. That moment was filled with such dread, he'd almost managed to disbelieve it himself.

Now, of course, he couldn't avoid going through the front gate on his next visit to the Carolissens.

The knocker was a heavy brass ring. He lifted it and let it fall, impressed with the weight of the thing. He was about to try again when a voice rose over the wall: "Give it a good push!"

He pressed a hand against the wood and it swung open. No hinge in his mother's house had ever been so well oiled. The small front garden was empty, but when he looked around the side, there was Gerard in a wicker chair under a large plane tree, smoking. He stood and gestured urgently with his pipe. "Constantine, thank god! I need a man with a steady hand and a strong disposition. This way!"

Con followed him through the door. A staircase wound up to the right and a corridor tunnelled into the house directly in front of him. The trophies were thickly clustered here, trooping even down the treads of the staircase, as if queuing to be let out of the front door. Con followed down the passage, pulling back from the spidery touch of a peacock's tail on the back of his arm.

Somehow they arrived, via an indirect route, back in the room with the vitrine, the long-suffering young lion. Its glass door was swung open and Gerard stood before it, fists bunched at his waist, eyes flicking over the lion's form.

"Right," he said, "I need you to get in there and do battle with that lion. *Morituri te salutant*!"

"What?"

"'We who are about to die salute you!' It's what the gladiators used to say before they fought. To the emperor. Which I suppose makes me Caesar. Fetch me the sewing kit, won't you?" He waved a hand at a desk in the corner.

Con brought a tin box and held it out at the door of the display case. Gerard fiddled in its depths, finding a reel of brown cotton and a needle. He tried to thread it, but his hands were unsteady. Eventually, Con put down the kit and took the needle from Gerard, threading it on the first try.

"Marvellous. Could you …?" Gerard gestured wearily at the lion.

Con saw now what was required. The cat had gone blind. The right-hand socket was missing its eye, and instead showed a tuft of pale stuffing that pushed between crude old stitches. Con stepped up into the box, needle in hand, negotiating his way around Gerard, who reversed carefully.

Con touched the puckered scar, then sunk the needle into the cat's face. But when it was all sewn up it still wasn't right; it looked like some grisly fetish, a shrunken head.

"That's so much worse than before," said Gerard from the sidelines, increasingly amused.

"Look – hold on." Con rooted around in the sewing box, fished out a big, round mother-of-pearl button and held it up.

"Give it a try, why not?" said Gerard.

But once he'd sewn it on, the pearl eye looked terrible, more blind than before. Con hopped down from the display case, ashamed.

"Good god!" said Gerard. "Hideous! Oh, don't look so worried; it's just a temporary measure. Sometimes you just have to make do." He considered Con. "Good with your hands, aren't you? Don't talk much, but handy. I'm glad Mark's got a practical friend."

Con smiled.

"You know, we've been thinking about going on a holiday," Gerard continued, as if this were a grave undertaking. "A family holiday. We would very much like it if you came along. Do you think your mother would agree to that?"

My mother? thought Con, confused. But he said: "I'm sure that would be fine. But, I mean, I'll ask her."

"We thought … somewhere outdoors. We think it will be good for Mark to be … outdoors. He was so excited about your camping trip the other day." Gerard seemed almost embarrassed. "Where's that bloody little key, then?"

"It's in the lock."

Gerard carefully swung the display-case door closed and turned the key in the fiddly lock.

"This was my great-grandfather's lion, you know?" he said. "Very fragile, very rare. There, you see?" He pointed through the glass, leaving his fingerprint there. "See the bullet hole? Just here." He touched his own chest. "Boom! He was a celebrated hunter. A great man, in many ways." Although Gerard's expression when he regarded the mutilated lion wasn't exactly appreciative. He looked queasy. Con felt a grudging sympathy for the man.

Gerard sighed. "Mark is very interested in this sort of thing. I'm afraid I haven't been much help to him, in that way. I've been so busy with my work. A legal practice … not much time for the outdoor life. And at my age … I was never able to be … well, to take him camping, that sort of thing. Teach him physical skills. That's really why we're so glad he's made a friend like you. With your background."

Later, Mark himself said nothing about the holiday. Con wondered if the plan had been kept from him, a secret. The thought excited him. It was as if Con could see the future, invisible to his friend. A landscape constructed for them, just waiting for them to walk into the scene.

IV. KEEPER

For a LION *roars* HIMSELF *compleat from head to tail.*

– CHRISTOPHER SMART, "Jubilate Agno", 1759–1763

elephant

Soon Con had established a routine. Each day he was at work early to do an hour or so of emailing and to listen for the lioness's first groans and rumbles. Then he'd go out to the refrigerated shed, where a bloody bucket had been set aside by the nightshift. It would be heavy with meat: a big beef bone, two whole plucked chickens. The corridor to the den would still be in shadow, cool and pungent.

He'd pause at the exterior bars, smelling, watching. Unlike Isak with his whistles and bangs, Con didn't have to make a sound. She knew he was there.

Movement in the shadowy back of the cage – nothing dramatic, just a kind of lolling, side to side. She could be very silent when she wanted to be, almost delicate. Then two large lemon-yellow eyes, pale moons, materialising in the gloom. The suggestion of a massive head, lowered from the shoulders. Bigger, much bigger than the lion statues at the memorial; she might take his whole skull in her mouth. A guttural rumble filled the air between them and vibrated through his flesh – in his throat, in his eyeballs, in his groin. His heart sped up, pumping a rich new mixture. He could feel his pupils expanding, the hairs standing up on his arms and the back of his neck. Not a purr: a lush, continuous growl.

"Hello, girl," he'd say, although he couldn't hear his own words; the lion's voice enveloped any other sound. It made the bars tremble like tuning forks. Beyond them, one layer of wire mesh, as thin as skin, separating the human from its ancient enemy. The animal on that side of the wire was designed to do one thing: demolish the animal on this, on his side. Con wasn't brave enough to touch the bars. He took out the big key and tapped it once on the metal: a formal click of greeting. Now, the next part of the game.

He hauled the bucket up to the ramparts and cranked open the gate, whistled softly through his teeth, and tossed the meat down into the arena. He didn't bother with the gloves these days, and his hands were red to the elbow and chilled by the time he'd cleaned out the pail. Above him on the slope he could hear the groan of the first tour bus pulling up. Although there was only one uncooperative lion left to pull the punters, still they came.

His communion with the lioness was unpredictable. Sometimes, he was allowed to glimpse only significant parts: a paw, a flank, an eye; as with the elephant in the fable, he could never see the whole. She'd wait for him to look away, then slip out and snag the meat, pulling it inside or into the shelter of a rock or bush. Often, though, she'd let him watch her eat through the observation window. Sometimes she'd lift her eyes momentarily from her bloody meal to meet his gaze through the glass.

Dreams no longer troubled his nights, although at times he felt awake and dreaming. Unwilling to go home, some evenings, he worked long past dark in his cubicle, conscious of how light streamed out of the office window, signalling beyond the fence. He'd read, or just switch off the computer and the lamp and sit blinking as the room settled. Sheets of paper on the desk glowed softly blue. When the moon was bright, he'd walk the grounds, letting himself quietly into the lion enclosure by the hidden side-gate. The walls of the den would loom above him, black against a blue-ink sky. He'd put one palm against the stone and feel his way around the curve, finding the iron grille, pulling back. The grass was soft and he'd stretch out on it, a few feet away from the bars. Inside, impenetrable darkness, smelling of straw and urine. It was warm here, as it would be at the mouth of a dragon's cave. He couldn't tell if she was close, or if she heard him breathing.

The shock of their first meeting hadn't subsided. Since that first day, when Sekhmet's slamming body sent a jolt through the cage bars and into his blood, Con had felt a kind of clarity. Walking home along the highway late at night, or sometimes after a drink at the restaurant, he felt sharply alert to light and shade, to things hidden, hiding, looking down from the dark mountain. The streetlamps burnt clear, like torches on a windless planet. Small sounds reached him from miles away: rustles, murmurs. He could smell the people dreaming in their homes below.

These days, it was frequently Con who came home to find Elyse asleep. Their schedules never coincided. He would slide in under the sheets, still cool and gilded from his moonlit walks, and press his nose to her shoulder, her armpit, her crotch, questing for scent, for something warm and animal. But here his senses were defeated. Snuffle though he might, he could trace nothing on her skin. Just the glassy odours of her perfumes, her waxen make-up and the astringent chemicals she used to take it off. She'd sleepily roll away from his seeking hands, rubbing her eyes and nose crossly, and muttering, "God, you *stink*." Con knew it; he smelt like a zoo. He just didn't notice it himself any more. "Go shower, *please*." Then he'd go and scrub himself in the shower and apply one of her ointments or scents – something designed, he supposed, to make her more appealing to him – before returning to bed.

But on one warm night he came home hot inside from a drink with Thandiswa; there was alcohol and lion-purring in his blood. Instead of joining Elyse, he went out onto the balcony to sit and smoke and listen to the faintly luminous ocean hushing and shifting.

When he reached into his pockets for his cigarettes, he brought out instead the folded piece of paper that Mossie had given him. It unfolded like origami to show, on one side, an address in the suburbs, a time and the date. Beneath this information was a picture – perhaps an old woodcut, colour added in – of a rampant green lion, clamping in its jaws a yellow sun. On the back of the leaflet was a kind of verse. It read:

> *Welcome to the Green Lion.*
> *In the wisdom of the alchemists*
> *"The Green Lion eats the sun":*
> *Vitriol dissolves gold*
> *In the Great Work*
> *Illness is healed*

Withered plants are revived
The dead brought back to life.
So do we seek to devour the energies
of the wild.

Con shook his head in irritation. Hippies. Animal nutters. The next Green Lion meeting, he saw without surprise, was the following evening. Underneath the picture, a handwritten phone number. *Call me*, said the scrawl next to it.

Mossie. Something inchoate, slippery, unfinished. She bothered him like a loose thread that needs to be snipped. A stack of papers that begs to be pushed straight. A little messy thing.

python

It was strange to use his cellphone, a present from Elyse, for anything other than texting her. On the line, Mossie sounded sleepy, then surprised, then almost embarrassingly delighted. He ended the call uneasily, with the sense of having bound himself.

She came to get him after work in her toy car, the engine muttering in anticipation, the girl herself buzzing with excitement and, confusingly, gratitude. She kept saying thank you.

The house they drove to was an ordinary one, a small bungalow out on the flatlands, too far from the mountain to be scenic, laid out under the fading sky of a hot summer evening. Con had never had reason to come to this area before. The streets were arranged in grids, the pattern occasionally broken by odd squares of threadbare grass – no playing fields, no parks, just sand tracks worn from corner to corner.

They parked at the top of a street choked with cars, not all with wheels, and walked down to the end. The semi-detached houses had tiny front gardens, some neat with roses, some cracked concrete. Seductive, this anonymous life, these interchangeable streets. He could sink in here, vanish quite easily, he thought. An appealing fantasy. But then someone leaning on a vibracrete wagon-wheel called out, "Looking for Cyril?", and Con had to smile and shake his head, and a small dog started barking at him frenetically through a wire fence, and he thought to himself, no, no, it would never do. People see each other here. There's more invisibility for me sitting in Elyse's posh Sea Point flat.

The house was small and a little run-down, the driveway taken up by a thirty-year-old car. The woman who opened the door was an ageing waif, with hair cut short to the skull, heavy mascara and the deeply lined face of a smoker. She smiled brilliantly. Her kiss to Mossie's cheek was cursory: her main interest was in Con.

"The lion man!"

"Uh, yes. That's me."

King of the beasts. Come in, they're all waiting. I'm Sandra, by the way."

He'd been worried that all the members of the Green Lion group would have taken quirky animal names, like Mossie.

Sandra led him down a short passageway, past a door with a pink-glitter fairy stuck to it and an array of framed pictures of Alsatians; through a dark lounge lumbered with couches, which turned into an open-plan kitchen with cat-food bowls below a chipboard counter crudely hammered together; and out through the back door into a yard where a collection of people waited, lit by candles and a braai and fire-drum made out of an old wheel rim. An ordinary backyard party.

"He's here," Sandra crowed.

There were greetings and introductions all round; Con soon lost track of all the names. He looked around for Mossie. She was squatting against the yard wall, almost out of the circle of light. She seemed to emanate a soft darkness. He went over to sit beside her, pulling up a plastic chair. This was where she came from, where she belonged: a dim corner, blurred with shade and smoke. She seemed prettier in the gloom, flicking her hair back to reveal a round but delicate-featured face. Her legs were crossed, her poncho pulled up to show plump calves in dark stockings, ankle boots. The lushness that he'd suspected under the clothes.

"What happens now?" he asked.

She just smiled at him over the tipped disc of the top of her beer can.

Sandra came to the back door and clapped her hands, and people stood up and shuffled inside. He followed them into the dark lounge. It flickered blue with movement from a big screen up against the wall. A wildlife video: painted dogs ran and skirmished through bushveld. There was the usual plummy voiceover. The gathered people – fifteen or twenty – sat arranged around the screen, bathed in the blue glow, half on the floor and half on sofas and armchairs. From what he could make out, they were all sorts: old and young, dark and pale. He saw a suited man, a headscarfed woman, a girl in running shoes. All rapt. Every now and then a sharply indrawn breath as something dramatic or acrobatic occurred onscreen – a torn throat, a narrow escape; occasionally someone would lift a hand towards the screen, as if wanting to touch. Con felt like the only one with his eyes open in a room full of people saying grace.

When the wild dogs had eaten their fill, someone leant forward and pressed some buttons. The image of a whale floated into view, suspended in shafts of sunlight in deep blue water. The air deepened, thickened; everyone held their breath as the mourning of giants reverberated through the tiny house.

Despite their concentration, Con sensed a pent-up impatience. They were waiting for something to happen. When Sandra paused the whales in their weightless frolic and turned up the lights, clasping her thin hands together, he assumed she was about to say a few words about Mark.

But no. She unclasped her hands and held them up and away from each other in a gesture of ritual celebration, or thanksgiving. "She is ready for you!" she said, with a ringmasterly flourish. "Please, if we can have you coming in one by one? Or two by two! We don't want to scare our guest by crowding around." She laughed gaily, but nobody else joined in. People were occupied with shuffling, pulling their jackets around themselves, the ones on the floor getting their feet up under them preparatory to standing, like giraffes. They kept each other in view, angling subtly for position. By "the guest", did she mean him?

A man and a woman picked their way through the dark bodies on the floor towards the bedroom door. All heads followed their progress; the door opened a crack. The chosen two disappeared into the darkness beyond and the door snapped shut. With an exhalation, the heads turned back to the screen and another clip started up: some kind of mountain cat emerging from a den, followed by cubs. There was a new restive energy in the room; Con could tell that though eyes were on the screen, hearts were behind the closed door.

When it opened again, ten minutes later, there was a positive jostling among the crowd. One tall man lumbered to his feet and cantered towards the door. But Sandra raised a hand to hold him back until the previous couple had emerged. They seemed joyful, their faces lit with wonder as they drifted through the seated people, through the kitchen and outside. In the light of the braai coals, Con could see them standing shoulder to shoulder, spreading their hands to the warmth, holders of a secret revelation.

Mossie was next to him, leaning against the wall. Her dark eyes seemed to hold him, but when he tried to snag the gaze it slid away like soap in a bathtub. Con felt a wave of impatience. He thought of Elyse's neat cap of hair, her direct look, her collectedness. No guile in her. Artifice, but no guile.

"Lion Man!"

He didn't react until Sandra's hand was on his shoulder. Then he turned, startled, towards her voice.

"You," she said. "Our special guest."

"And me," said the tall man, wading his way across the room again and slapping his hand on the door.

"Gentle, Bryan."

The man, chastised, folded his hands on his belly. After a moment Sandra nodded, and the man twisted the doorknob and ducked his head under the lintel into the darkness.

Con followed cautiously. The door closed behind him with barely a click.

It was a little girl's room. There were posters on the wall of youthful pop stars, a messy clothing rack. Everything was in shades of mauve and lavender. There was a narrow bed against one wall, and against another a large empty fishtank. In the middle of the floor, cross-legged, sat a young girl, twelve or thirteen years old. Around her neck and arms were twisted the loops of an enormous snake. It was patterned cream and yellow, candle-wax pale against the girl's dark skin, matching her lacy nightgown. The girl was downy, with soft hairs on her upper lip, a long fall of shiny black hair down her back. Con couldn't see the animal's head, just the bands of its body embracing the girl. It seemed asleep, but as soon as she looked up it stirred, slightly shifting its coils.

Next to him, Con sensed the tall man easing himself to his knees on the carpet. But it was Con's eyes that the young girl met.

"You can come," she whispered, lifting her chin. She held out her manacled wrists. The animal looked heavy. Con could see it cinching a little tighter.

If only to be more on her level, Con went down on his knees too.

"You can touch it," she said in a soft voice. "Go on."

Con didn't really want to, but he reached out a hand, laying two fingers on its scales. Smooth, the same temperature as the air. As he knelt there, awkwardly leaning forward, the head of the snake appeared soundlessly in the crook of the girl's neck. Although Con didn't move, he felt his heart lurch. For three beats, four, he held the girl's eyes as the snake's head weaved closer, back.

Then there was a sharp rap on the door and the tableau broke, each of them falling back. Sandra poked her head through the door. "Okay?"

The girl rose, moving carefully to her knees and then standing, hoisting the looped snake. "She's had enough," she said, and carried her burden to the fishtank.

Bryan struggled out of his trance and to his feet. "Hey …"

"Sorry, we can't push our guest," said Sandra.

She had one hand on Con's shoulder and another on Bryan's, guiding the two men out of the room. Just before the door closed on them, Con turned for a last look. The girl was leaning over, hair and arms draped into the fishtank, hiding her face. The pale snake, uncoiling, gleamed like butter. Then the door closed and Con was blinded by the sudden dark.

The first thing he made out in the dimness was the gleam of Sandra's teeth. "My granddaughter," she smiled at him. "She's beautiful, hey?"

He nodded, smiled. "She's very pretty." In the background, onscreen, bears fished salmon from an icy northern stream; but everyone's eyes were on him. "So now?"

"Ag, now we watch some more programmes. Then we have a nice braai, and discussion."

In the car on the way back, Con was quiet for a long time, shaking his head every now and then.

"What? You didn't like it?" There was a smile in Mossie's voice, but also tension.

Con shifted in his seat. "You told me the meeting was for Mark. To support him."

The usual shrug. "I said something to get you to come. I wanted you to see it."

"See what? You get together ... to watch wildlife movies."

"And we have our special guests."

"Snakes."

"Oh, no. Bryan actually has a horse. We go out to his small-holding sometimes. Other people have less to offer, but they try. Maryke has nice fish. Just pets, if that's all we can manage. Cats, dogs. Even a hamster, once. The snake is always exciting, but she gets stressed. It's not all small things, you know. We went to an elephant park, but we had to save up for that. I mean, it's hard. There are so few really wild things left, now."

"And that's it? It's a club for people who *like animals*?" He couldn't say what he'd expected; what he had half-desired. Rituals, ceremony. Alchemy.

"It helps the people. To have that contact, yeah. You can understand that, can't you? I know you can." She held up a hand, as if to stroke something in the air. "To have the animal there. To touch it. Every person in that room – it helps them. It is something outside themselves. Their human lives."

He thought of touching the snake. The quickening shock of it. Its cold eyes.

"And Mark was part of this?"

"Of course. Mark was the one who gave us our name, and everything."

"Green Lion. That bullshit."

"It's not bullshit." Hair hid her eyes as she ducked her chin. "There's … *energy* we get from wild animals. That's what Mark said." The way she said his name: a luminous syllable.

"Energy. Jesus."

"Some kind of charge," she continued, stubborn. "And because there are so few wild creatures left now, we have to find different ways of getting that contact."

He was filled with impatience, driven this way and that by a crazy girl. He twisted in his seatbelt, turning to look at the road vanishing behind them, above it the dark mountain. The fence came down close to the road here; he could see its silver barrier.

Her glance kept touching his face, like a piece of soft cloth or a dead leaf. She murmured something.

"What?" Why was her voice always so soft? Why did his ears fill with cotton wool when she spoke to him? He'd been spoilt with Elyse's perfect elocution, her trained projection. Listening was much harder work with this woman.

"Mark had access."

"To what?"

"To them. To Dmitri and Sekhmet. He was going to let me meet them. He said he would."

Con laughed, looking out of the window. "What, like a petting zoo?"

A flinching silence.

"Christ!" He stared at her. "You're not kidding. What, did you think they'd let you touch them? Scratch their chins?"

"Maybe." Her voice was barely a whisper.

"Mark petted the lions," he snapped. "And look what happened to him." Something else occurred to him: "That's what this is all about, isn't it? You thought you'd found a new lion guy, right? You can fucking forget it."

Mossie clutched the steering wheel. She was silent after that, driving with her eyes fixed ahead on the road. He rested his head against the window and closed his eyes.

He felt the car turning, slowing; the engine died. They couldn't be home yet.

"Listen," she said.

He could hear the movement of dark leaves. Old pines waved their drooping branches in the breeze, brushing their needles across the top of the car.

"Con."

He opened his eyes. It had got darker. They were in the parking lot of the zoo. On one side, the world was dark and steeply climbing; on the other, the slope pitched down towards the sodium lights of the Lion House.

"Take me in," she said. "Take me to her."

"I can't," he said. "I can't do that. I don't have the keys with me anyway."

"You lie!" It was almost a sob. Was she crying again?

"She would kill you," he said, more gently.

"Mark would've done it. Mark was going to." Her wet cheek caught the light from below and for a moment she looked like a much younger girl, almost a child, the skin smoothed out. "But he didn't." She shook her head, angry. "He went alone. Do you see?"

For the first time he really did: the man walking towards the lion. The lion rising to its feet.

Disconcertingly, she was laughing now. "You *are* like him," she said. "Actually he hated it too. Those people at the meetings – he said they didn't get it. He said they were just looking for comfort."

"Nothing wrong with comfort."

"He wasn't into it. He was interested in …" She paused. "He was interested in death. You know about his sister, right?"

"Yes."

She seemed chatty now, swabbing her eyes, the little bird awakened. Talk of Mark, he thought. It rouses her.

"He wanted to let that lion go, free it. And he wanted to … he wanted to be gone too. He thought he would be done, then." She nodded, bright-eyed. "We used to come here together, you know? Come and watch the lions. They were looking for volunteers then. A lot of the people who work here, you know, they've had losses. Things taken from them. It helps people, working with the animals."

"You too?"

She glanced at him. "Me too. But I didn't get the gig. They took him, not me. People like Mark get the gigs, you know? They wouldn't let me come near. But I kept an eye on him. I knew. I knew he was fragile. I got … look." She pulled something from her purse. A zoo season ticket, frayed and softened from much handling. "I was here as much as I could be. And I used to come and wait for him here, in the evenings after work. Right here under this tree. The night it happened …" Carefully she stowed the ticket again, zipped closed the purse. "I was supposed to be with him, you know?"

He knew.

"And now Mark is … stuck in that place. Have you seen him? In the hospital? They won't let me go, any more. Not family, some crap like that." Now her restless hand went to her neck, feeling for the bird that hung there like a necklace. "And I look at her too, at Sekhmet. And it seems so sad. All alone here. No mate. No others like her, anywhere at all."

And for a moment Con saw her as a figure wandering in a sculpture garden of frozen figures: Mark, the lions. Unable to move them or even be seen by them, a ghost in a world of solid things. He felt for her. And was also starting to feel a little dangerous around her, like he'd be allowed to say anything, do anything.

"Were you … involved with him?"

"You mean fucking?" She gave him a sly smile. It shocked him a little.

"Yes."

She shook her head impatiently, as if this was of no great import. "He was going to take me in. To the lion," she said with some fire.

"He would never have. Unless he wanted to kill you."

A shrug. "I just wanted to get close, that's all. Like everyone." She laughed.

"But you didn't. Why not?"

"Because, big fucking lions? I was afraid." She laughed again, then quickly sobered. "Also, I wanted him to be safe. I wanted him to stay where he was, and the lion too. This is a zoo; it's a place where things are supposed to be kept safe. Locked up. Not allowed out."

This time, when she dropped him off at the flat, the kiss lasted longer.

Afterwards, it was her laugh he remembered, even as he entwined himself in Elyse's long limbs. The little gust of warm musk breath, the snag of a baby tooth. Tender flesh under her chin, the excitement of hard on soft.

You mean fucking, he heard Mossie's voice again, with its sharp little grin.

swan

The next day he couldn't stop himself from falling asleep at his desk. He came home straight from work and slumbered for an hour in the evening light, until he was woken with a shake. No fool, Elyse.

"Come," she said. "We're going."

He squinted; she was very bright in the lamplight. White and tall, a swan rapping at him with her beak. "What? Where?"

"To the hospital. Up-up. It's time."

He pushed himself back quite violently in the bed. "Give me a break."

She folded her arms across her breasts. "It's outrageous that you haven't been to see him."

He'd never seen her so pale or so prim. White tunic dress, pearly stockings, beige lace-up shoes with a blocky heel. Her hair was up and she even had a cardigan draped over her shoulders like a nurse's cape. He wanted to throw something at her. A bit of meanness, like mud.

He laughed. "Fuck that. You go play Nurse Betty dress-up if you want. I'm not into it."

And to his astonishment and immediate shame, he saw her blush, although it was hard to make out under the thick foundation. She left the room quickly and he understood: it was unconscious; she hadn't realised that she'd dressed for the role. He heard her leaving through the front door.

He dressed and followed her downstairs to the car. When he let himself in on the passenger side, he was amazed to find her dabbing at her eyes.

"It's just," she said, recovering admirably, tipping the last moisture out of the corner of her eye with a fingertip, mascara unmarred, "I'm trying so hard to get what's going on with you. I just wish you would *speak*. You used to speak to me so – beautifully."

He opened his mouth, effectively struck dumb. He could only shake his head slightly back at her.

"Con!" It came out as a high-pitched yelp, and they sat for a moment in its echoes. When she spoke again her voice was level: "This thing with Mark, it's the one time I've seen you … actually *emotional* about something …"

Was I? he thought. "Emotional" didn't quite cover it. At the same time thinking, as another tiny diamond formed in the corner of her eye: I am so sorry.

"… or, or having some kind of actual bond with anyone. You know?"

He nodded stiffly.

"But I want to see it," she continued, "that's just it, I would very much like to see, actually, what you are like when you are with someone that you, ah, care for."

Breaking just a little at the last. *Love* wasn't a word they used between them.

This was followed by another silence, both of them eyes front. Con held his breath, then let it out at last with a groan. Without looking at her, he reached over and put his hand over hers, knotted on the steering wheel. Her knuckles hard as marbles. "We can go, okay?"

She drew a long breath in through her nose, still looking away.

"Let's go right now," he said.

She flicked his hand off hers, then found the gearstick. Bucked a little too fast away from the kerb, roaring in first gear. Con felt he was being rushed to hospital on his own account: for doctors to probe some terrible ailment, some mortal deficiency.

"So do you know which one he's in?" she asked, in a small voice, five minutes into the journey.

He said the name of the hospital. Elyse turned the car around without a word and they continued in silence in the opposite direction. He felt further respect at that: in the drama of the moment, she'd driven off furiously in any old direction. She'd always been better at these gestures than he was, at shouting or weeping.

Her foot tapped the accelerator, the engine whined, and the car strained towards their destination, even as Con pressed himself back into the seat. He shut his eyes, but Mark's blue gaze sought him out even there, behind the lids.

Five minutes to go before visiting time. Con took a chair in the waiting area, among several other disconsolate well-wishers. They all sat in silence, as if composing last farewells. Elyse paced up and down, stopping to peer in through the little window set into the door of room 38B – Mark's, according to the matron. It was the same nurse as before, the angry one. Today she appeared to be silently controlling a seething rage, switching her glare back and forth between Elyse and Con as she sat at her station. After a while he turned to meet her belligerence with a bland expression. She dipped her head, then lifted it again for combat.

"You came before," she said, "but you didn't visit."

"Yeah," he said. "So how is he?"

She shook her head, disgusted. "His arm is very bad. He opens his eyes. Talking is hard."

This was a surprise. "So … he's out of the coma? Will he recognise me, do you think?"

She shrugged. "How must I know?"

Before he could respond, the hand on the clock above the nurse's station clicked over, triggering a chime. The waiting visitors stood and moved towards the ward doors, bracing themselves: for pain, for boredom, for the necessity of not showing these things in their faces. They put their hands against the closed doors, let the light from the little windows fall on them, and pushed.

Elyse, too, was on her feet. The door to 38B cracked open, and in its sliver of light she turned to look back at him. He held up a hand – now, just now, I'm coming – and she gave him a grave smile and went on in.

Mark, he thought. Look who I've brought.

Con was still seated. His legs lay stretched out before him, nerveless. Get up, go in, he thought, but his legs wouldn't listen.

They wouldn't walk him over there. The door sighed closed and he could not imagine the strength it would take to push it open again.

In the end he wrenched his legs to the side, balanced himself above them like a man getting out of a wheelchair, and toppled down the corridor to the lifts, the matron's contempt searing his shoulders.

As always, it was easy to keep on walking, walking, although he was very far from his home. It would take him two hours to get back to the flat, by which time Elyse would be there, and angry, and probably changed into a fresh outfit, like the whole evening hadn't yet happened, like they were in some impossible repeating loop.

Lorraine never met Elyse. When he first came home to help his mother in her illness, it had been one of the first things she'd said to him: "Do you have someone? A girl?"

"A girl."

She tapped the ash off her smoke. "Don't tell me," she said. "She's gorgeous. Stylish. You always went for those ones. Put-together people." Lorraine laughed. "What does she do then? This girl."

Con was smiling despite himself. Put together: it was perfect for Elyse. "She's a dancer. Actress. That sort of thing. Entertainment."

His mother nodded, lips knowingly pursed.

At that moment, in fact, Elyse was moving in the periphery of his awareness, circling closer and closer to Cape Town; she was on her way. The thought excited him, even if, on Skype, Elyse seemed depthless and distant. She pressed her fingers to the lens and he smiled and pressed back, unsatisfactory though this was.

"English?"

"No, South African actually. She's coming back to live here."

Elyse had got a job running a children's theatre group. They'd made no promises to each other, but when he'd told her about his mother and she'd said, yes, she would be going home too towards the end of the year, he'd wondered if it was because of him, if Elyse's bright generosity and certainty extended that far.

"That'll be nice," said Lorraine.

They were seated at the old kitchen table in Woodstock. He'd taken a taxi that morning straight from the airport and found his mother sitting there, reading. It was a quiet scene, and he was visited by equal desires to wake her from her reverie and to keep it intact. Perhaps just sit quietly beside her, pick a book for himself from the shelf. He was intrigued; she'd never been a big reader. When she looked up, she gave a start as if she hadn't heard him coming at all.

He pulled a chair out and took his seat, and smiled at her. She laughed aloud and clapped the book shut in a celebratory way, as if it had just been a prop set before her until he made his appearance, something to make her waiting seem more natural. He realised why the house was so quiet: no barking from the yard, no parakeet squawking in the corner. A black kitten came to touch its small dry nose to his palm, though, and that was almost like old times. The air of the house was cross-hatched with fur, from cats alive and cats long gone.

He was happy to see her. In his years away, the memory of her face had become vague, obscured by a corona of knick-knacks that circled her like an asteroid belt around a distant planet. But he'd found her not so much changed after all. Lorraine had the kind of face and body that doesn't get ruined, it just grows smaller and denser with age. Her skin seemed unlined, her hair dark. He wondered how much of its chestnut had always been dye.

The house seemed small, too, and dirty to his adult eyes. A brown house: brown glass in the windows, brown door, brown ceramic pots lining the path to the front door, a brown garden of half-dead plants in dry beds. He resisted the mundane observation: how small the place had grown. It wasn't true: this house had always been too small for everything in it. She was alone in it now.

Her final boyfriend was gone – fucked off as soon as the diagnosis came through, she explained.

When he told her of his plans to move back, she asked, "What will you do? For work?" She'd never asked him about his job before.

He shrugged. "Find something." Then to change the subject: "Where shall we go tomorrow? Kirstenbosch?"

She tilted her head uneasily. "People don't really go there, now."

"What? Don't tell me they've fenced that off too. Jesus."

"No, no, it's just … I don't really like it up there any more."

"Wow." He looked at her with sad surprise. "You used to love going to the Gardens. With whatsisname, Clive."

"That tosser." But she wasn't smiling. "It's not safe, so close to the fence. All kinds of wild animals up there now. And there's armed guards, they'll shoot you if you get too close."

"Jesus!"

She looked at him timidly, as if his swearing alarmed her. "Although they have tours … with a guide, and guards, you know. It's expensive. Mostly for tourists. You want to do that?"

"No. That sounds awful."

From old habit, he found himself lifting up objects in Lorraine's house, peering into cupboards, leafing through the detritus. Looking for clues. The house was full of the same old shit; in his bedroom he found two old posters crammed behind the bed, their painted sides sticking together. DON'T FENCE US OUT, they said. DON'T FENCE US IN. Never could decide.

But something had changed: the stacks of material seemed settled, compacted by time. She hadn't shifted anything for a while, had added nothing new. There was a film of dust over every pile of magazines, on the embroidered cushions and the rows of chipped mugs. In a strange way it was soothing: the house was at peace at last, its mudbanks settled, its secrets fossilised within.

"I don't have time for that sort of thing these days," said his mother when he asked her about going to the auctions. "No energy. I'm sleeping a lot."

Later, in the garden, they sat and drank sweet white wine and watched the sun go down. The sun seemed very bright on the horizon; he squinted against it and turned his eyes up to the mountain. Cloud was starting to pour off its edge, endlessly cascading but never reaching the streets below. Grey figures curdled and broke up there, rearing and subsiding.

"Lion's Head," said his mother, pointing – as if he didn't know, as if he'd never lived here. You couldn't even see the whole lion from here, this tired old suburb lacking the City Bowl's mountain views. "The sunset used to be lovely, from up there. Before the squatter camp, of course." Con heard the disdain in her voice; her politics had never been very deeply rooted. He shifted in his seat, looking around for a change of subject. His eye caught something bright in the grass. He reached down and picked up a small red-handled screwdriver. Whatever happened to the old toolbox? Its contents no doubt scattered by the entropic forces of the house.

He tossed the screwdriver end over end by its tip and held it up for her to see. "Remember this?"

She smiled vaguely. "Never seen it before."

"I thought it was my father's."

"Oh, it could've been! I just don't …" She shook her head slowly. "You were always asking, when you were a kid, is this thing my dad's, is that thing my dad's. You know, I just said yes, a lot of the time. I didn't want to disappoint you."

"How about the Ark?"

"Hey?"

"Noah's Ark. The wooden one?"

"No memory. Sorry."

"God. The table, at least? The kitchen table?"

She screwed her eyebrows together, but then her expression cleared. "Oh, the table. That was him, yes, definitely. He was good with his hands." She paused, and then said again, gently, "You know, he wasn't here for long. We weren't … together very long. I was young."

"Sure."

"And then he got sick."

Con hesitated. "So what was that? You never really said. Some kind of virus?"

"Did I say that? Oh. Oh no, Con, it was dumber than that." Her voice apologetic. "It was drugs, a stupid overdose. I guess I didn't want to tell you. He wasn't a happy man." She sighed, then rasped a laugh. "But despite all that, he was nice, you know? Charming. Total sweetie in fact."

That made Con smile. Of course. He focussed on flipping the screwdriver over, flip and catch, flip and catch, and nodding, nodding. Around him he could feel the house deflating: all the pockets of air between the junk, where his father had resided, collapsing with a sigh.

He thought he might take the screwdriver away with him. Always useful, screwdrivers. But he could feel his mother's eyes on the spinning tool. Quietly, he stilled it; lowered his hand and slipped it back into the grass where he'd found it, back into the matrix of the house, into its place in the complex strata of nameless history. He felt his mother's anxiety subside.

The next day, on the long green lawns of the botanical gardens, Con and Lorraine laid out their picnic in sight of the fence. She was wrong, it turned out: people did go there, of course they did. It was much more crowded and diverse than he remembered Kirstenbosch being in the past: families and young couples spread out on the grass, music playing, small kids running around. His mother sat very upright in the centre of her patchwork quilt, knees pulled up, as if drawing herself above floodwater.

He bent on impulse to kiss the top of her head. She didn't look up. She started tensely laying out the food – little Greek deli things in plastic tubs – and flinched when two children, dressed in gaudy costumes, came running past. One, a girl, had a princess outfit on; the smaller boy was wearing pyjamas in tiger stripes. It seemed an old-fashioned game: chasing, with weapons. When Con said he was going to the toilet, his mother glanced up at him, alarmed.

"I won't be long," he said.

Instead of the toilet block, though, he went round the back and on up towards the fence. It was much as he remembered: cylindrical steel bars, topped with a wicked serrated edge. Unbroken by a gate, it seemed completely impregnable – although those kids, he knew, could wriggle through if they tried. It was very high, a good two metres tall, winding off past the edge of the picnic site and folding through the trees. He wondered if the stories of big game up there were true.

Intrigued, he peered through the bars. On the other side, an old track led off into the trees in a broad zigzag, but he could see that the path had been eroded, with new bushes growing in the middle of the track and fallen boughs slanting across it. He could see a cluster of mushrooms at the base of a young bluegum. Golden, undisturbed. He was surprised to see the alien tree.

He tried to picture himself as a child in there, darting between trees, lobbing hard green pine cones. Something about the complete stillness and emptiness on the other side of the gate made him afraid for that phantom kid, lost under the ivied archways of the fallen trees. Just as he turned away, his eye caught a movement around the curve of the disused path – something small and black scuttling away.

He looked at the people on their blankets with their beer coolers. The mountain at his back felt like a gentle vacuum sucking him towards it. He imagined folding a curtain of leaves across himself, lying down and pulling a comforter of pine needles over his bones.

Someone was watching from the corner of the block. A uniformed guy sitting on a folding chair, holding a gun. He saw Con looking and raised the weapon from his knees.

"Just pellets," he said. "For the baboons."

Was that a baboon he'd seen, running off in the distance? No, it hadn't had the gait of an ape. It had seemed more doglike. Someone's runaway pet?

"So no one goes up there?"

The guy shrugged. "Oh no, sure," he said, "you can go. They got permits, guides, whole package. It'll cost you though." He handed Con a small pamphlet from his top pocket.

Con glanced at the prices and handed it back. "For tourists, then."

"Sure. They can pay. They like to go up, do the safari. They got eland, wildebeest. They say they're going to put some lions on the mountain, even."

"Seriously, lions?"

"Crazy, hey? They're breeding them down there, in that new complex." He pointed in the general direction of town. "There by Rhodes Mem. There's a whole new thing going on."

snake

Mossie was standing under the tree outside the Lion House, as he knew she would be. She drifted over to him like smoke settling on his clothes, his skin. He remembered his mother's musty odour: cigarettes and sweat and sweet eastern scent.

Con was a little out of breath, and the sweat was chill on his skin. He'd walked, fast, all across the city from the hospital, jogging at times. It had taken a while; the day had faded, the sky growing soft and purple as a lake and the cars switching on their pilot lights, approaching white and receding red, as he crossed their glittering wakes.

It was not intentional; not a route he'd plotted or planned. It was just where the walking had taken him: not back to Elyse's flat, but up, back up again to the blue-green mountain.

Con did not touch Mossie. Instead, he started down the path towards the gate. When he glanced back she was following slowly, a strand of hair caught between her slightly open lips.

"You know I can't take you all the way in."

She nodded.

"But I can show you. Come."

The evening had taken on a velvet density. Together they walked down the pale path, past the sign of the golden lion. No guard at night, with the staff cuts. He closed his hand around the keys in his pocket, heavy and cold. The first gate gave way.

He led her along the familiar path, to the grass corridor between the prefabs and the den. The early moon lit the ground only in patches and he felt his way across the space by memory, dodging the spade leant against the wall and the edge of the concrete trough. Then through the small door into the lion enclosure.

They stood for a moment in the circular space. He could sense Mossie trembling next to him. He pointed to the barred gate and she almost leapt towards it, putting out her hands as if to push them through the grille. Quickly he pulled her back, shaking his head. Mossie started to speak, and he put his fingers to her mouth. Her lips were slightly open, her breath warm. He guided her to sit next to him on the grass, an arm's length away from the cage. They waited there for a long time, long enough for their breathing to fall into synch.

And Sekhmet roared. Con had never been so close before. The sound reached in through his ears and grabbed him by the guts and shook him like a bird in a big cat's mouth. The bars of the cage trembled and resonated.

When the last tremor died, Mossie was panting, mouth open. Her eyes were very dark, as if her pupils had expanded massively, like someone on drugs, and he knew what it was: the spike, the rush, the beating heart. He was feeling it too. Without thought, responding to her flushed and open face, he leant forward and pressed his mouth against her cheek – to still her, to hold her back. His teeth pressed softly into her flesh. And she tilted her head towards him and turned the bite into a kiss.

The mobile warmth of her tongue in his mouth. And before he could gather himself, the scene had changed, and she was moving more forcefully, with some new scheme, some plan. She put her hand on his throat and pushed him down hard, her other hand at the buttons of her shirt. Every sensation was precise, intensified: the cold ground against his back, the pinpricks of the grass against his hands and neck. And it was as if her clothes had already been shaken loose by the rumble of the lion's voice, because they came off so easily. Her eyes still huge and black as she twisted out of stockings, shirt, panties, bra, the whole cumbersome apparatus of her clothes, dozens of items it seemed, left boot, right boot, the feathered pendant at her neck, the zips so laborious, a long-sleeved vest with buttons, peeling herself free until she was pale against the dark sky. The body revealed was barely human, formless, turning, never holding still long enough for him to get a lock on it, to see it all in all – full breast, pale buttock, dark patch between her legs. And then she was on him, at full stretch, hands pressed into the grass either side of his head, warm breath in his nostrils. He lay there, thinking: me, me too, how am I supposed to shed this skin all on my own?

But she had that under control too. Without releasing him, keeping him pinned, she freed the buttons of his shirt, breathing deeply through her nose, mouth closed in concentration. She drew the wings of his shirt to either side to bare his chest, and then worked at the belt and the fly, and pulled down his trousers to his ankles until he was lying half-dressed, half-unpeeled, and she was astride and already pushing herself down onto him – the liquid heat of her, skin still cool to the touch – with her forehead bent to touch his and her eyes blank as she moved against him. The movement of her body knocking the top of his head lightly against something hard, over and over until he realised that it was the bars of the cage, and pulling away from them just as he shuddered into her, thinking: don't turn your back …

When she was quiet again, she moved her weight off him and lay by his side. His mind was empty, his body dissolved in the dark. He lay for a long time staring up at the stars, which appeared and reappeared, as high, unseen black clouds covered and uncovered them like a child's hands in a game.

At length he turned away from her so they were lying back to back and he faced the darkness of the cage. He kept one hand draped behind his back, holding her fingers loosely in his so that the turned back didn't seem too cold. His eyes drank the darkness. He opened his mouth and let the fuzz and buzz of the evening roll out, breathed it out into the black space on the other side of the bars. Losing it all, losing the words; they tumbled out of his head. He let the black roll into him, the black and the silence.

It was quite a bit later, perhaps, that the quality of the blackness changed; and perhaps he'd slept, or was sleeping still. But he was aware that the dark beyond the bars was no longer empty; it had grown full, plumped with breath and blood. It moved, shifting against the bars, seeming to bow them towards his face. Slowly, he let his hand travel outwards from his body, finding the metal, which seemed warmer now, and through, passing between the bars to touch – very, very gently, with tips of his fingers – some warm, almost feathery surface.

Sekhmet had come to the bars and laid herself out, was pressing her length against them as if offering her warmth, or seeking his. Con shifted his own body closer, and slowly, millimetre by millimetre, brought his face near. He could feel her heat against his cheeks and forehead, smell her reek. At last his fingers came to rest, very lightly, on her spine.

He seemed to hold his breath forever, but at some sleepy, barely conscious point he must have exhaled; and then drawn in the lion's breath, a potion, a sleeping draught.

V. THE LION DREAM

I recalled queer stories I had heard of human beings that could turn themselves into animals, and although I am not a superstitious man I could not shake the feeling that it was a spook thing that had happened ... The way he had first sniffed at me and then lain down beside me that day under the withaak ...

– HERMAN CHARLES BOSMAN, from "In the Withaak's Shade", 1947

hound

They were only going to be gone for three days, two nights. After all, this game park wasn't hundreds of kilometres away in the bush; it was right there, in the middle of the city, on the top of the mountain. A new joint development by the Department and a private safari company. They'd converted the old reservoir pump-station into a high-end tourist lodge, and ringed the area with more fence. *Take a seat at our Table*, said the promotional slogan.

Con had been hesitant to tell Lorraine about their destination, expecting disapproval, but when he finally did she seemed, if anything, slightly jealous.

"Fancy," she said. "Nice for some of us."

Gerard drove them up there on the Saturday morning, pulling into the new parking lot that had been chopped out of the forest at Eagle's Nest. Inside the high-roofed office, built like a log cabin out of peeled pine trunks, a map covered one entire wall.

"You can walk here," a woman in a dark-green uniform explained, her wooden pointer tapping the map. It showed the reservoir, the lodge, and an uneven oval area around it. "You see this circular track; that's a nice day-walk." She traced the boundary. The fence was a dark broken line, sutures in the paper. Inside its bounds, the map was detailed, showing pale-blue water, dotted brown paths, streams and picnic areas; the contours were etched in fine green gradations. Over on the edge of the map was another small filled-in oval: the cable car and its surrounds. Everywhere else was blank white paper. "Out here, you can only go with a permit. And a guide." Pointer in hand, she turned to indicate a couple of men slouched at a table in the corner, presumably waiting to be hired. They looked up warily from their card game; one nodded.

"Why do we need guides?" asked Mark, cheeky.

"Because of the tigers," his sister answered him with a frown. "Silly."

Con had been avoiding looking at Elizabeth, but now he risked a guilty peek at her top lip. Was it still red? Scarred? Nothing obvious. He brought his finger to his own lip.

The guide smiled. "No tigers, no. But there are still things up there that can hurt you. Don't worry, though, the fence is very strong. Very high."

They had to load all their bags into a dark-green Department four-wheel-drive; their own wasn't allowed into the reserve, which seemed, as Gerard remarked, ridiculously officious. A warden drove them through the gates and up the broad forestry road. As they ascended, long zig, long zag, Con saw the city recede, reduced to a pale matrix of orange roof tiles and grey concrete, like a mud wasp nest daubing the roots of the berg.

Up at the top, next to the old reservoir, a wooden chalet had been built, dramatically cantilevered over Orange Kloof. Big picture windows looked out over the dam in one direction and down the kloof in another. Inside, the fittings were like a smart hotel's, with rustic touches: rough-hewn beams in the ceiling, a smooth clay floor. Exclusive, too – there was just this one solitary chalet, no other buildings in sight. Con understood, again, how wealthy his friend's family actually was: this was not a place his mother could ever afford.

Over on the other side of the dam, the fence wasn't visible, lost behind the rocky inclines, but down in the notch of the kloof, Con caught its new-metal gleam. He imagined his mother on the other side, shaking the bars – small, bedraggled, trailing a misspelt banner in the mud.

Before the sun went down, Con and Mark took a walk down to the reservoir along the well-marked path. Then a narrow stream-bed led them away from the water up a small rise, stopping short when they hit the fence. Beyond, they could see a broken landscape of grey rock and grey-green bush, the sea visible in the fall-off to the right, and ahead the mountain rising in a series of long flanks towards the high plateau.

"This is boring," Mark said. "It looks so wild in there, and we can't even go through."

"Actually, you know, we can."

"How?"

"Look," Con said, grasping the bars, turning his head to the side and pushing it through, then back again. Sore on the ears, but he didn't flinch. "Come, it's easy, I've done it before. Just get your head through."

"So no electric shock, then," Mark said sourly.

Con ignored this, embarrassed by the memory of his lie. "Look." It wasn't actually easy, but Con knew it was possible. He pushed his head back into the gap, rotated his shoulders and dragged his torso through, his chest and thighs. He stood up and laughed and held out a hand to Mark.

But Mark couldn't. He shifted this way and that, trying to fit his suddenly oversized head and rigid shoulders through the gap, black fringe flapping. It wouldn't go. Then he tried to do it the other way around: feet first, then knees and hips. He got as far as his waist and then stuck fast, twisting and angling. His feet flapped, his knee rapped the ground. "Ah, my nuts!" he yelled.

Con felt the laughter expanding inside him, like yeast rising. Mark gave a panicked whine and scrabbled at the ground, eventually righting himself. The bars stood quietly between them.

"What the fuck, man, you crazy," he said. "You'll get chowed by a hyena. And the sun's going down now. I'm going back."

Con gave up and the laughter shook him like a spasm. "You could climb over."

Mark kicked the fence. "No, I fucking couldn't. Come on, get back this side; we'll get in trouble."

"I just want to go for a little walk. Just to see. I won't be long."

"Con, you can't – there's wild animals there."

"I'm just going to go over that little hill, then I'll come back. See what I can see."

"Fine, suit yourself."

Mark turned and walked away, down towards the reservoir, his easy lope replaced by something stiff and self-conscious. It was one of the few times Con had seen his friend lose physical grace.

Alone, Con had the distinct impression of eyes between his shoulder blades. He turned, back to the bars. The sun was going down, staining the sky to one side with rust but casting the dips and folds of the mountain in shades of grey and slate. It was very quiet up here, with the promise of cold. When Mark was with him, filling the space with talk and breath and brightness, he hadn't noticed the silence or the chill, or the subtle palette. Against the blue air, the skin of his own hands in front of him looked too bright, attracting attention.

To walk out there, into those blue valleys and slopes, away from the fence and the dam and the path, would be to have tone and warmth and words drain gradually away, until you were the colour of stone – a quiet, cool thing; until you could lie down with the stones and blend right in.

Con pressed and struggled his way between the bars again. It felt a little harder now, as if he'd grown a tiny amount, or the gaps contracted minusculely. A small panic of entrapment forced him through, and he leapt away from the bars, skittish.

Laughter behind him. A lithe white shape, glowing in the dusk.

"Elizabeth?"

She was showing off, weaving through the fence, in and out, in and out. She was such a skinny little thing, she barely touched sides. "Look, I can do it easy!"

She seemed to have forgiven him; to like him, even.

"Brilliant. But, Lizzy, you shouldn't have come out here – you know you're not supposed to follow Mark around." He held out his hand. "Come, we better get you back, they'll be worried."

They walked together for a few minutes, hand in hand. Her fingers were cold and slightly sticky. Con had never looked after a child before. It felt surprisingly natural. He cast around for something to show her – an interesting stone, an insect. Her white nightie was smeared with dust.

"Did you see any tigers, Con?" she asked. "On the other side of the fence?"

"Sure," he said. "And stegosauruses too. There's loads of them on that side."

Con was worried about the board games that had been brought along: Scrabble, Monopoly, decks of cards, checkers, all just for three days. The Scrabble especially made him tense. He'd been surprised when he saw the boxes, back at the house when they'd packed the car; they didn't seem like things to take camping. Now that he was here, of course, he saw that it wasn't really camping they were doing. Margaret and Gerard had seemed entirely uninterested in the mountain; as soon as they'd arrived they'd poured themselves gin and tonics and gone to sit on the deck, commenting on the sea and the city below. When Con and Elizabeth got back from their walk, the older Carolissens were still there, staring out at the blood-red sunset, Gerard's pipe glowing. They seemed not to have noticed the children's absence.

Mark was in a bit of a sulk. He hardly said a word as they ate dinner, picking through the braaied meat and salads that had been prepared and left for them in foil-covered dishes by invisible Department employees.

"Can we make a fire?" asked Mark suddenly halfway through pudding. "Con's good at making fires. His father taught him."

Mark's confidence in his abilities warmed Con's cheeks, then drained them as he realised a demonstration would be required. But to his relief, another invisible Department functionary had already done most of the work, arranging wood in a neat pyramid over a bundle of kindling and firelighters. Still, there was pleasure in being the one to light it, watching the flames almost immediately lick the wood, and seeing Mark's face light up orange as the last streaks of the sunset faded behind him.

"Cool," Mark said, leaning in.

Elizabeth appeared quietly between the two boys and pushed her head close to the flames too. The siblings had such similar hair: two black fringes catching the light, in danger of frizzling in the flame. Soon Gerard and Margaret joined them with their drinks. When Gerard poured each boy a half-glass of red, the taste was overwhelmingly rich in Con's mouth, something lush and rotten: he wasn't used to wine. He felt his tongue grow soft in his mouth, and the release of a tension he hadn't been aware of, located somewhere at the back of his jaw and also around his lips. His mouth opened, letting the night and the flamelight in. He could smell his own fruity breath. He sat cross-legged, feeling the dark flowing in and out as the others' voices moved smooth and slow around his ears. Unlike Mark's illicit whisky, the wine left him content to be silent and to listen. Lizzy's laugh was a high note in the stream of deeper voices, like a frog calling from a river, or maybe it really was a frog. His eyes must've fallen closed at some point because then he was dreaming, dreaming of running through grasses, everything lit orange as though he were seeing through a lens of flame …

"*Shht*," someone hissed sharply, and he came awake, although he wasn't startled. He felt gently and involuntarily recalled to a shallower plane, as one's body surfaces in a rush of bubbles after a deep dive.

Everyone was strangely still, rigid in their circle around the fire, staring straight ahead of them. They looked like kings and queens, thought Con sleepily, or statues of kings and queens, on stone thrones … he could make out no expression on their faces. His legs had gone to sleep and were starting to prickle with pins and needles, and he wondered how long he'd slept like that. They've almost let the fire go out, he thought, and leant forward to fix it.

"What—"

Mark reached forward to grab his elbow. "*Shut up*," he hissed.

"I think we should go in," said Gerard softly.

And then they stood, and stiffly turned their backs on the dark and went inside, leaving their empty plates and glasses. Margaret had grabbed Elizabeth's hand, was almost dragging her through the door. Con was mystified – the night was young, the stars like white fire, the fire still alive – but he followed them indoors.

They were acting like frightened people. Like a family hushing each other while a robber picks the locks. Gerard was bolting the door; Margaret was switching on lights and pulling at the orange-and-brown curtains, enclosing them in a muffled box. Then everyone was talking all at once; Elizabeth, with spots of pink on her cheeks, was giggling in a high mechanical way. Mark was at the bright white fridge, smashing up ice cubes. Their busyness was sore on Con's ears. He felt fragile and tenderised by the dark, as one is burnt by the sun; the light inside the house hurt his eyes and made his skin sting.

"What's wrong?" he asked Mark softly. "Why did we come in?"

"Didn't you hear it?"

He shook his head.

Mark gave a short laugh. "God, I can't believe you! It was like this … *roaring*. Like, there is something *seriously* big and scary out there. You really didn't hear?"

He shook his head again. Although a memory surfaced: some kind of deep resonance in his dream, some echoing vibration in his own chest …

"That guy fucking lies," said Mark. "There are fucking *lions* out there."

Gerard clapped his hands together. "Perhaps a game of Scrabble?"

Later, when everyone was asleep, Con lay on the floor in his sleeping bag. In his pocket he fiddled with the high-value Q tile which he'd stolen from the Scrabble set earlier, unable to find a place for it in a word. It would be mortifying if he were discovered with it in his pocket. If this were his own home, he'd be able to lose the tile easily – slipped into a crack in the floorboards or behind a pile of mismatched Tupperware. But the cabin, though luxurious, was sparely furnished. He'd have to drop it in the bushes. The mountain, in its own way, shared elements with Lorraine's house: the jumble of things, the chinks and crannies.

The Scrabble game had gone as badly as anticipated. The tiles were hostile, a row of flat teeth bared on the little wooden stick in front of him. Everyone else at the table – even Elizabeth – made them hop and clatter and utter extraordinary words, but for Con they remained clenched and silent. It had been a humiliation, especially at one point when Lizzy, who'd edged close enough to him to see his letters, had sneaked her hand across and rearranged his tiles to say BUTTER. He blushed in the dark to remember it. Butter!

The air inside the cabin was close. Mark was snoring softly next to him, a tenor echo to Gerard's grunts in the room next door. Con was filled with a smarting, babyish homesickness: for his mother's house, for its hiding places and silences.

He slipped from his sleeping bag and padded barefoot in his pyjamas into the lounge, then fiddled with the lock on the sliding doors and went out into the black.

The night was clear and cold. The handrail on the observation deck was gleaming under the moon, the metal still new. The silver was echoed in the shine on the reservoir, and further up by a glimmer from a distant segment of the fence. He grasped the railing and swung himself down into the dark.

He could feel the damp earth and the small stones under his bare feet. He spat on the ground, thick night-time spittle, and felt the satisfaction of putting something of his body into the landscape. After a while his eyes adjusted to the deeper black. He needed a pee but didn't want to do it in sight of the house, so he started to walk towards a low rise. Up there, he thought, perhaps he could see the city.

As if his body wanted to lose the weight of the Carolissens' heavy meals, his bowels stirred too. He pulled down his pyjamas and crouched down, taking a shit right there, the warm, sweet stink of it rising up between his thighs. A kind of honesty; a bodily truth you shouldn't tell. Nothing to wipe with. He used a tuft of grass, roots unwilling to give, too scratchy. Dirty. When he pulled up his pants he found in the pocket the Q tile: ten whole points. He hurled it into the dark. Pushed on.

As he reached the top of the rise, the fence came again into view, a little below him. It seemed to glow with its own power, as if some magic burnt in it, colder and stronger than an electric shock. He opened his mouth to the crystalline sky and sang into the wind: nothing with words.

Far off he could hear something coming, a joyful urgent yipping, and it reached into his head and tweaked his dreams awake. Beyond the fence a moonlit plain, in motion: although the air was still, shadows streamed across a silver field like dapples on a spread wing, like leaves before a storm. A scatter of barks, a yelp. A hunt, although he couldn't see the prey.

There were people following the dogs. On foot. Every sound was very sharp: running feet, even the gasp of a human breath, although they were several hundred metres away. Then a singular breath detached itself from the other noises and started to climb the hill towards him: someone panting, sniffing. Unmistakeably human. Coming close. Con didn't move. He didn't creep or hide or shift. He stayed very still. His body dissolved in the darkness.

When the human came up the path, Con saw it was a young man, lean, dark-faced, bare-chested, panting slightly, but with a quiet fortitude; he wasn't unfit or tired, just exerting himself with purpose and direction. He passed within an arm's length. Con might have put out a hand and touched him on his shoulder. A long-legged dog followed behind the man. Pale, with strokes of shadow for ribs. It looked up at Con, and sniffed him busily when he put out a hand. Its fur was wet and warm. Then it gave his hand a lick and bounded on. Down below, the hunt had moved through the valley and was gone, leaving no trace, no clue as to what its quarry had been. Impossibly passing through the line of the fence, as though it wasn't there at all. The dog's saliva grew cold on his hand, and the sky was light along one edge.

Returning down the slope, he saw a yellow light kindle in the cabin. The Carolissens were up. He felt light's banner falling on his face: back to the world of being seen, of talk and Scrabble. He slitted his eyes against the glare.

The curtains were still drawn against the dark, light filtering through the coarse weave. The fabric glowed orange, making the whole building look like a paper lantern about to float off into the night. Con came up close, and saw the hundreds of thousands of tiny winged creatures thronging the panes.

He was surprised by a tall figure standing at a tilt on the deck. He came up next to Margaret quietly, with half a bold thought to startle her. But she turned towards him quite calmly, as if she'd heard him coming, and put one long finger across her lips. He waited.

"Listen to them. They're making breakfast. Talking, talking."

And they *were* talking in there, Mark and his father, their voices musical, interjecting high and low. Although he could tell they were arguing, their voices sounded relaxed, almost happy. As if things were easier between them, as if some blockage to the flow had been removed.

"How they go on," she murmured, "when we're not there." She turned her face to him with a smile. "You've hurt yourself."

He looked down, and saw for the first time the blood on his hand, brilliant in the dawn light. He remembered the warm, wet fur of the dog. Margaret was wearing a long old-fashioned nightgown – another strange thing to bring camping – and the desire to press his bloodied hand against her whiteness was momentarily unbearable. She was watching him with a cocked head.

"No, it's not," he said. "It's not my blood." Ineffectually, he scraped the blood off the ball of his thumb onto the banister.

She reached out a pale hand and gripped his wrist. It was perhaps meant to be a comforting gesture, but Con was startled and he stared a little rudely at the hand, gripping with surprising strength. She shook his wrist back and forth a couple of times.

"Mark has told us the story about your father," she said. "We are so sorry."

Con nodded. What story? Which one?

"It must've been a terrible time for you, for your mother."

Con, masked in darkness, cloaked in darkness, thought that perhaps if he just opened his mouth the truth might flow from it.

She peered down at him as if peering into his mouth, observing the birth of words. Then she laughed, a little gasp. "Oh, I'm terrible. Don't mind me, Constantine. I'm just nosey. You don't have to talk about it if you don't want to." She rested her hand on his shoulder, a further warm shock.

"Grub's up!" called Gerard from inside. "You two, stop plotting and conniving out there. We have bacon!"

lobster

After breakfast, Gerard decided that they should do the eight-kilometre circular walk. Only Margaret demurred, arranging herself on the shaded deck with a hat and sunglasses and a novel. "I'm not much of a hiker," she said.

"I'm also going," said Elizabeth.

"No, love, it's a bit long for you. And hot."

"But I want to see the tigers and the steggo-sores."

"No," said Margaret firmly. "You're staying here with me."

"Boys only, then!" said Gerard, thumping the ground with an ancient walking stick he'd brought from the house.

But it didn't work, this heartiness. Somehow they didn't have it in them. The group that set out on the hike didn't balance. Gerard and Mark were asymmetrical, wonky without Margaret and Elizabeth. And Con had no weight in this arrangement. Soon the hiking party became strung out, dislocated, Gerard striking ahead with his walking stick wagging, Mark dawdling behind him in a sulk. And Con stuck right at the end, forgotten.

Mark and Gerard's mutual irritation had built up again over breakfast, and now vibrated in the air between father and son. It was pleasant not to hear their footsteps crunching in the gravel. There was no sound at all, just Con's own breathing. He felt released, his shoulders lifting in the intense relief of being alone, unseen. Solitude enlarged him, his body forgetting its boundaries. He paused, leaning against a smooth boulder at the side of the path. Pressing its cool, granular surface with his palms and cheek.

Lizzy came around the curve. Trotting, determined. She stopped when she saw him. He smiled and she came closer.

"I thought you weren't coming," he said. Her face was pinker than he'd seen it, more flushed even than when she'd been crying.

"I sneaked off," she said, delighted. "Don't tell!"

Not again, he thought.

But there was this thing, with Elizabeth: she made him feel calm, happy in a delicate way, like watching a tiny new fern uncoil. He could never tell Mark that. And it was much more restful to be sitting here with her than to be strung on the buzzing wire between Gerard and Mark.

"Listen, you should go back. It's a long walk. Really. Your mom will be pissed."

She snickered at the word, then grew still. "But I want to come. Please?"

"No, serious. Go back." If she were a stray dog, he thought, he'd chuck a rock at her. To miss, of course. Just to give a fright and send her in the right direction. "Tomorrow I'll take you for a walk," he said. "I promise."

"To see the steggo-sores? Promise?"

"Ja, I promise. Just go back now, okay?"

She looked over her shoulder, back up the path. A little hesitation.

"It's easy," he said. "Just go back along the fence. It's not far." I should go with her, he thought. Make sure. But he didn't move. He gave her a wave. "Go on now."

And so she went. Turning and trotting back the way she'd come, pink-faced. Around the bend and out of sight. Con sighed and stood and started off in the opposite direction, but without enthusiasm.

The path around the reservoir was clearly marked, paved and edged; but intersecting with it were smaller, non-human routes traced in the bush, leading away to the water, and in the other direction to the fence and the higher ground beyond. He might as well explore while he was here. No rush. Let the others go on ahead. They wouldn't care if he stayed behind.

He took one narrow track and then the next, which petered out until another, made by hooves or paws, emerged again and led him on. They seemed designed to help him. He walked with a sense of great peace: this was easy. Soon he had lost sight of the main path, the dam concealed behind the gentle rise of the rocky ground.

Coming down into a cleft in the rocks, he saw a twist of pale-brown water. He followed it uphill for a while, until he saw the fence again, dipping to cross the stream. He squatted and cupped his hands in the flow. He didn't drink much, just enough to clear the film from the inside of his mouth. He took off his shirt and tied it around his waist, looking down and flexing his arms and noting the swell of his biceps. That was new. He was growing into the world. Still shorter than Mark, but broader than before.

He was standing on a tiny perfect beach, a lick of clean white sand laid down on the curve of the stream. A breeze down here, cooling his forehead. He closed his eyes. The light, sun-warmed air played across his chest and his belly, goosebumping his arms. Quite alone, but exquisitely seen by sky and hills. He loosened his trousers and stepped out of them on the sand, penis hard up against his belly. Dick, cock, he thought, the words they used at school. Penis was his mother's baby-bathtime word. He jerked off quickly, came on himself. Then stepped into the water, which here – unexpected munificence of a thin mountain stream – cupped a knee-deep pool, richly amber, still cold from the night.

He crouched in the stream, washing himself, splashing and grinning like a kid at the seaside. Then sat quietly on his haunches, closing his eyes and feeling the rush of the water around his thighs. He may have sat there for a long time.

A shadow fell over his eyelids.

Con pricked his ears and listened as the cold crept over his skin and tightened his nipples. Something big. A brushing sound. And then a sniff: deep, resonant. He swayed, squeezing his eyes shut, leg muscles cramping. His thighs began to burn. There was the sensation that a large creature was moving alongside him, like a ship passing. A raking noise in the sand. The air barely touched his sun-hot cheeks, as light as the breeze off a hummingbird's wing. The creature moved, but the shadow lay frictionless on his face. And cold, colder than a terrestrial shadow should be. He could so easily open his eyes. But to do that would require a decision to see.

It took a good four or five seconds for the shade to move off his lids. Sunlight again. He clenched his eyes tighter. Eventually, he could hold the pose no longer and tumbled backwards into the water, eyes breaking open, gasping and cowering. But there was nothing there. The small valley was empty, exactly as it had been before. He stepped stiffly through the water to the shore. The sand was cold under his feet, and slightly damp, as if the passing shade had altered the local climate. Shivering, he pulled on his T-shirt. The whole day had cooled, skeins of cloud coming over the sun.

The pants were not as he had left them. They'd been dragged to the side and scattered with sand. Something had shown great interest in his jeans. Something big. Dig marks all around them, great, deep gouges. He kicked sand over the traces, his and whatever else's, not looking too close. When he shook the pants out and pulled them on, they felt different. A patch on the thigh was cool and damp, as if something had drooled there. He felt a tightness in the back of his throat, the hairs standing up all over his body.

Things were getting in his way now, he'd lost the landscape's confidence. The thorns grabbed at him, the little stones bit his feet, the branches wanted to mark him in blood. Hopping on one foot and then the next, he put his shoes back on and scrambled to higher ground.

When he heard the sounds of something moving through the bushes in the riverbed, he juddered like a plucked wire and sank to his knees. But almost immediately he knew it was nothing to fear. It was a human gait, an uncertain footfall. A boy.

Mark was picking his way through the bush, stumbling and tripping. Con could see that the animal pathways weren't clear to him, that he didn't know how to place his feet. He came to a halt on the slope directly beneath Con and leant against a rock, panting. Con could see the tracks circling where his jeans had been, exactly where Mark now stood. A jolt went through his groin at the memory of the cold shadow passing, the smell of it, still reeking up from the jeans he wore.

Mark was foreshortened, head bowed; the top vertebrae protruding and vulnerable under a pink sheen. Anything might jump down there and snap that brittle column. But then he raised his head and shouted, "Con! Con, stop fucking around." There seemed to be something wrong with his voice: it was shaky and weak, absorbed at once by the rock and bush. Still, Con's impulse was to shut Mark up, so as not to draw the shadow back.

Con had to take a moment to bring moisture and words back into his own throat. "I'm up here," he said scratchily. "I'll come down."

When Con got close, he saw that Mark was flushed, his mouth set tight. "Been looking for you!" he gasped. He turned and hurried up the far bank, a steep scramble.

"Sorry." Had he been gone that long? As Con followed, the wind came up in an accusatory gust, strumming the fence. He glanced over his shoulder; the landscape was washed with shadows and uncertainty. The grass ruffled and twitched like an animal's pelt. As it stilled, he noticed the heat.

When he caught up, Mark was squinting down the gravel path. Con felt a kind of shivering disappointment, a spell broken. The world was back, with its paths and fences. The sun was high; it was later than he'd realised.

"Why are you freaking? It's not like anyone could get lost here …"

Mark shook his head impatiently. "It's my dad. Look."

The stooped figure up ahead, rippled and refracted in the heat off the gravel, was a desolate one: a dust-caked tramp, an injured wanderer. There was something wrong. As they came closer he could see that Gerard was panting and flushed, dabbing at his brow with the back of his wrist, shirt-sleeves pushed up.

Gerard reached out and grasped Mark's shoulder.

"We need to get him back," said Mark. "It's so hot. We've been walking all over."

Con, following behind, watched the two of them, Gerard leaning on his son. Their shoulders were the same shape. Mark's bowed neck, usually tanned and silky-skinned, was red with sunburn.

The heat wasn't abating. At first, Gerard held on to the back of Mark's shirt as if he were dragging a naughty puppy along the road. But the road was long, and as they walked Con started to see a shift in the balance of strength between the two in front of him. They slowed to accommodate this delicate transformation. Mark seemed to be walking taller, squarer, while his father slumped, leaning ever more heavily. Con saw the older man's controlling grip tighten and become a clutch. Mark held firm, putting his arm around his father's shoulders. They were walking so slowly! Con could run rings around them, could sneak up behind them without a sound.

Gerard had a handkerchief out, was wiping his face with it; then he draped it over his head. The handkerchief was wet through, but soon it dried and started to waft behind him as he walked. It looked ridiculous. Con could smell the older man's sweat on the breeze.

Gerard stopped and looked up at the sky. "Water," he said. "You boys got any water?" His voice rasped in his throat.

"Con, you got any water?" Mark repeated.

Gerard's throat clicked as he swallowed. "Been walking for hours," he said. Gerard seemed to totter, then force himself on, then stop short. Mark, strangely, turned to face his father and put both arms around him. Con was embarrassed. What were they doing, hugging?

Mark bent his head to look up into his father's eyes. Con caught a glimpse of Gerard's drooping face – brick red, unnatural, shocking. A devil mask. As Con watched, Gerard seemed to slip through Mark's circling arms, melting like wax and falling to his knees at his son's feet. Mark stared at Con, white through the sunburn.

Con was alert, focussed. Something shuddered in the light, and it was as if he could all at once see further. Perhaps a small cloud pulling itself across the sun, damping the glare. As he came up to the two, he grasped all the facets of the situation: the lengthening shadows and the cooling sky, the glint off the distant fence, the light breeze coming up, and off around the curve a pewter gleam which he recognised as the roof of the lodge. They were almost home.

Gerard was down on all fours on the orange gravel, gasping. Mark stood to one side, hands at his sides. Little boy, thought Con. Little kid. "Mark," he said sharply. "Mark. Let's get him down there to the water." Together they helped the old man, staggering, down to the shore of the reservoir. There was no shade or shelter here, but at least there was water.

"Go get someone. There by the house. Go."

Mark headed off, walking at first and then jogging. Con knelt in the sand beside Gerard. For the second time that day he took off his T-shirt, laying it over the older man's head. The cloth was thin; the sun came through tiny holes, sprinkling Gerard's baked-red face with spots of light. Gerard was breathing in short, dirty pants now, his cheek laid on the gravel, eyes closed and mouth open. The shade wasn't enough. Con crouched over the man's face, sheltering him with his own body. He could feel the heat on his back, the greater heat coming up from below. Mark was still in sight, too far from the house. Too slow to do any good.

Con took the water with his cupped hands and poured it onto Gerard's face, his wrists, thinking: hot blood, cool it. He made him drink and drink again. He took off Gerard's shoes – thin-soled town shoes, ridiculous. Rich-smelling socks. He washed the long bony feet. The smell and the touch of the older man's damp skin combined with the dread in Con's gut to form an awful, sensual tension. Gerard's breathing had stilled; his face seemed paler. His eyes were thin wet slits under the lids, but Con didn't look at them too closely. He lay down next to Gerard on the sand, took his hand. What else was there to do? He closed his eyes and waited for disaster to fall on them, or for its shadow to pass them by.

It seemed a long time later that the sound of an approaching engine made him open his eyes. There was a dark-green vehicle coming up the road, and a guard stepping down. Gerard was opening his eyes and sitting up, and Con felt a wave of elation. Whatever beast had stooped over them had withdrawn, was receding, was tiny in the distance. He had seen it off.

Mark stood a little outside the circle, white at the lips. Con stared at him, wanting to catch his eyes and share the triumph, but the other boy didn't look his way. Gerard was helped to his feet, eased into the vehicle. Mark and Con climbed in the back and soon they were back at the chalet.

It was only after Gerard had been taken inside that Con noticed something else was wrong. That fatal imbalance. Margaret of course had seen it already; she'd come back out and was standing on the path, her long figure sloped to the side with anxiety, as if the world had tilted. "But where is Lizzy?" she said.

"What do you mean?" said Mark. "She's here ..."

"No – didn't she come with you?"

"No ..."

Mark and Con exchanged looks.

"She went with you this morning; I let her go because she was making such a fuss," said Margaret, voice rising. "I put sunscreen on her, I watched her go after you. She always follows you, you know that."

She was moving up the path as she spoke, faster, starting to run. It was the park guard who went after her, taking her arm, talking her still.

Con and Mark just stood there, two dumb kids, not looking at each other. Con felt light and sick, like all the blood had left his body and run into the ground.

He'd been wrong, so wrong. The questing shadow hadn't been looking for him, or for Gerard. It had come for the youngest of them, the weakest, as wild things often do.

—

The rangers took them all down to the lower forestry station. Heatstroke, said the paramedic who came to look at Gerard. What a strange word for it, Con thought: like stroking a cat's fur, a heavy hand pressing down. As Gerard's high colour faded, Con felt himself think these cold thoughts, and recognised that he too was changing hue.

The Department guides looked for her for all of that day, and the next, and the next, and for the whole of the following two weeks. But Elizabeth wasn't anywhere in the five square kilometres of mapped terrain. She wasn't in the reservoir. Con knew what had happened. The little girl had slipped straight through the fence and into one of the cracks in the world, into a different place. And he, Con, had shown her how to do it. He'd given her the route and the technique, and had told her what to go looking for, on the other side: wonders. Lions and tigers and stegosauruses.

And just like that, the Carolissens were broken. There was a moment in that first long and feverish day – when the Department officers were out searching and the helicopter was scouting back and forth, and Gerard and Margaret and Mark were inside the chalet, waiting for the transport to come – when Con looked at the family and saw that it was mortally wounded. Some crucial piece had been torn from its body. They all sat silently, quieter than he'd ever known them, but around them the air writhed.

And Con knew that it was he who'd done it, who had called something savage into their lives. They should never have let him in, brought him along. While they sat at the table inside, he stayed out on the deck, punishing himself with the sun.

When the guide called out to him, Con went to the door of the chalet and cleared his throat. "Lift's here," he said, but it seemed his voice was too soft, or his language wrong, because the three of them just sat there dumbly; they didn't even look up. "We can go down now," he said, louder. This time Mark did meet his eye; and in his sky-blue gaze Con saw a kind of horror, as if when he looked at Con he saw something utterly alien.

—

Later, none of them seemed to notice him leave. He walked all the way home from the Carolissen house, hurting with every step. When his mother opened the door, she gasped and said, "My god, what happened? You look like a lobster!" It was the first time he realised what the sun had done to him.

She made him bathe in cold water, which was excruciating, and then brought him a tube of aloe vera ointment and smeared it on his back and shoulders and neck as if he were a little boy again. It didn't embarrass him; the outer layer of his body was dead to her touch. It was the worst sunburn he'd had for years, that he could ever remember having. He was feverish with it. There were giant blisters on his shoulders, and for days afterwards he was peeling off transparent skeins of skin, a clear liquid weeping from his flesh.

That first night home was the first time he had the lion dream. In it, the lion stood over him and breathed on him, pushed its burning, matted mane into his face, and he turned away but couldn't escape it. Cool, I need to cool down, he thought, waking at last prickly and inflamed and trapped in the coil of his sheets.

He didn't go to class the next day or the next, and when he finally returned his skin was healed and Mark was no longer at the school. In his absence, Con returned to being a quiet boy at the back of the classroom. After a while, though, girls came up to talk to him, asking after his friend; and he found he could speak to them now, saying words that Mark might have said.

The next time he saw Mark was at a memorial service for Elizabeth that took place at the Carolissen house a few months later. He wore a suit, his first. Lorraine had found it for him at the Salvation Army shop and it felt like the proper thing: slightly cold, meanly cut, old and very black. The only person who paid any attention to him at the wake was Margaret, who took his arm in her strong grip, a painful acknowledgement.

He opened his mouth, and it seemed the suit put words into it, because he said: "I'm so sorry. I wish there was something I could have done."

And astonishingly, these stiff and leaden words were the right ones. Margaret squeezed his arm and leant down to kiss his cheek. Dully, he registered the lesson: that weightless phrases sometimes work better than none at all.

As for Gerard and Mark, neither one of them would look at him, or speak a word.

VI. THE HUNT

O Sekhmet, Lady of Flame, Lady of Slaughter
Eater of Blood
The one who captures the wanderers' spirits
Who opens the mountains,
For whom the desert animals have been killed
The one who shines
Who hates the thief
For whom heads are severed
Who fills the ways with blood
O Sekhmet, Lady of Vegetation, Generous One
The Curled One, Lady of Obscurity
The one who moves in light, who terrifies the gods with massacre
O Sekhmet, Luminous One, preeminent in the mansion of fire
Who causes the acacia to bloom

– From "The Litany of Sekhmet", inscription from the Temple
of Horns at Edfu, *c.* 237–57 BCE

meerkat

Waking in the lion den, Con was immediately, keenly alert to his surroundings. The scents of the early-morning world were crisp and deep. Mossie had flown; he was alone. He buttoned his clothes against the chill, and slept again.

The real dawn was colder, and he was snatched into it by a shrill alarm, startling him half to his feet before he realised it was the cellphone in his jacket pocket. He barely recognised the ring. He didn't reach it in time, and for a moment sat staring at the strange number. He was blank, unable to think of the name of a single person who might be calling. The lion cage was dim and cold, dew standing on the grass, the sky leaden. There was no sign of Sekhmet in the cage; her black home was as cold and silent as a ruin. His clothes were wet with dew and stuck unpleasantly to his body. He hauled himself to his feet, stiff and decrepit. Scrolling, he could see there were many texts from Elyse, the last one at four a.m. He couldn't bring himself to read them, but they radiated fury.

There was a movement in the observation window. A group of schoolchildren were gathered, laughing. He must've looked dead lying there, or drunk. He lunged towards the glass growling. He could see the kids tumbling back from the window, overjoyed – squealing, by the looks of it, but soundless behind the pane. Still little enough to be half-afraid of their own make-believe.

Then he spotted their teacher, a glowering young woman, coming up behind them. He stood up straight, adjusted his collar, grinned and gave her a jaunty wave. Just then the cellphone rang again: same number. He didn't want to answer it, to break the silence and spoil the mime show. But the caller wasn't giving up.

Like a demonstration of twenty-first-century human behaviour in some alien museum, he clicked the phone and brought it smartly to his ear, still smiling at the teacher. Succumbing, even through lion-proof glass, she quirked her mouth back at him.

"Constantine!" cried the voice on the phone. He knew it at once, although she sounded out of breath.

"Margaret?"

There was a loud crashing, and a surprised little "Oh!"

"Margaret, are you okay? What's going on?"

"Oh, Con, Con, Constantine! Oh, *thank* you!"

And then the line went dead.

He was greeted by a large removals van in the road outside the Carolissen house, the garden gate chocked open by a stone. For a moment his heart stopped, as if it were an ambulance sitting there, lights flashing.

A man came out, carrying a meerkat family on a plinth. The arrangement obscured his chest and head, so Con could make out only a pair of long blue legs, two workboots. Con went over and took one end of the bulky display. The workman nodded his thanks. Together, they manoeuvred it out of the front gate and into the road, where the van was waiting. Inside, the van was packed with Gerard's animals, stacked tightly together.

Together they wiggled the meerkats into place between the legs of a blesbok. The man nodded again and went back inside for another load. Con followed him vaguely, half-heartedly smoothing out the wrinkles in his shirt.

Around the side of the house, he spotted Margaret in the wicker chair under the plane tree. Before he could speak, she was gripping his arm.

"Constantine. I must thank you. I would never have managed this without you."

"I don't understand … where's all this going? Are you selling it?"

"Selling? Good lord, no. That lovely girl is taking it all away – for free!"

"Girl?"

"Oh, I'm so old these days, I can't remember names – you know. Your friend. That lovely, lovely girl …"

Ah fuckit, he thought. "Elyse."

"Oh, I like her *so* much. It was so good of you to give her my number."

It took a few beats for him to grasp this. "She's taking the animals? What – what's she going to do with them?"

"Oh, I didn't really ask. She has some idea … for a show. She does that, doesn't she? Shows?"

"Yes, yes she does."

"Sounds marvellous."

"But, Margaret – you didn't want to keep anything – the hummingbirds? Something small like that, for yourself, a keepsake?"

"No! I want all of it out, out!"

"But—"

"Out! Everything. Tell her!"

Con sighed. "Is she inside?"

Elyse was in Mark's old room. She'd pulled down the curtains and opened the doors wide, and when he came in she turned to him in a sparkling cloud of dust. She looked fevered, high colour on her cheeks. Con felt he hadn't really looked at her for a long time. She was very beautiful. There were two more overalled men behind her, rooting about in Mark's belongings, but Con couldn't look too closely; the sense of defilement was too strong.

"Quick work," he said.

Today she was dressed in dungarees and a denim shirt with rolled-up sleeves, bandanna tied around her hair. Rosie the Riveter. She wasn't actually working, though; her clothes looked new and pressed, another costume. He felt conscious of his own slept-in clothes, the strands of dry grass still clinging to the knees, the breath of the lion cage. Her flush, he saw, was not exertion at all; it was a kind of excitement. And anger. He was angry himself.

"Mrs Carolissen has kindly donated her collection. I offered to help her move it out. We're going to use it in the production."

"You called her?"

"I said I was going to. I gave you a chance to help." She turned away from him sharply. "Careful!"

The two men blundered past, carrying the lion on its plinth between them. As they came past, Con caught the animal's cracked eye, its teeth stained by the clumsily applied green paint, the tennis ball jammed into its mouth like a gag.

When he looked back at Elyse, she had done a quick change, slick as any backstage transformation. Now she was smiling, composed.

"I'm going away," she said. "There's this weekend workshop. I wasn't going to go, but now I don't see why not. When I get back I would like you to be gone from the flat."

Her voice was so warm he could hardly find rejection in it. It sounded like an invitation, like a special offer. Con was grateful for her professionalism. He should've known that it would be like this in the end, with Elyse: clean, no delaying or procrastination. Just a dance step, one two three.

And then she was gone, so quickly she left two vortices of dust particles sparkling in the room in her wake. They made him think of the delicate whorls of golden hair on Sekhmet's chest, and just above her eyes.

Everything was emptied out. Mark's old room stood stripped even of curtains, its glass sides showing nothing but reflections of leaves.

"It doesn't look like anyone lives here any more," he said to Margaret, and then wondered if that was an unkind thing to say.

"I love it," she answered with a squeeze of his forearm, and then sneezed, delicately. "Those things made a lot of dust, didn't they?"

So Con stayed to sweep the house out with an old-fashioned straw-headed broom. Because that didn't leave things as clean as he wanted, he searched for and found a Hoover and vacuumed every rickety floorboard and kink and angle, dragging the machine all the way up the circular staircase, poking the plastic nib into corners and along the skirting boards in Margaret's bower. Like sanitising a crime scene: every mote of hair and fleck of skin sucked away.

Clean, clean, down to the bones. He switched off the machine and stood still as the roar faded from his ears. The house was hollow and relieved, lying quietly like an animal purged of parasites.

Everything was perfect now, squared away. Ready. A precious minute, two minutes of silence, until the soft palm of the wind patted the window frames and set time in motion, and the trickle of dust began again.

He put his head out of the window to call Margaret, who was sitting in the shade. She took a long time to come back into the house; it was a good while before he heard her walking stick tapping the bare boards.

The old woman stood for a moment in silence, looking around. "My god," she said. "My god."

He held her arm as they walked through the house. She made him take her all around the circuitous ground floor, into every corridor and pantry. Her eyes were wide, starring at the bare walls as if seeing wonderful shapes or pictures in them. There was something touching about the way she stroked the plaster. It made him think of a young girl, given her own room for the first time. I could stay for a bit, he thought, light-headed. Take one of the smaller rooms. Keep an eye on things, help out.

"How lovely this is," she said. "The space. I should've been living like this all along. It feels like we've made room for something new. For a great arrival!" She beamed at him, and held out her bony fingers in celebration. "You've given me a grand present, Constantine."

And, yes, that was right: Con felt like he'd done something capacious, generous. He couldn't remember when last he'd felt that way. "The house does seem very big, now," he said. "Will you carry on staying here, alone?"

She looked at him as if he were joking. "But my dear, I won't be alone! Mark will be with me here. When he's strong again."

The photos were gone from the table, and the paintings from the wall. All that was left was the postcard of Saint Jerome and the lion, the tiny ghost in the wings, never closer, ever approaching.

"Of course," he said softly. "Of course he will."

"Leave me now, dear," said Margaret, laying a hand on his wrist. "Thank you for everything. I'll be fine."

She seemed so frail, although illuminated from within by a kind of exhilaration. He kissed her on the cheek and left her sitting there, looking at her little postcard as if out of a window.

Coming home to the empty flat was an enormous relief. He felt like he did when he was alone at the zoo: childlike, playful, released into the space.

Con spent the rest of the day sleeping, making himself sweat under the too-heavy duvet, not changing his clothes. He kept the curtains closed, avoiding the sky-blue accusation. He watched TV in the evening, ate cold pizza, drank whisky, slept again. He didn't worry about the days to come. On Monday he'd go to work, maybe ask Amina about getting paid. Tonight he could sleep in the office, no one would know.

On the Sunday morning he shaved and trimmed his hair, cut his fingernails and cleaned them, flossed. He felt better and better. *More human.* He laughed. In the bathroom mirror he checked his smile, bared his teeth. It was very quiet in the flat then, and cold.

Before he left that afternoon, he cleaned the house, as he'd done at Margaret's. He did it slowly, methodically as always, moving in a trance from room to room, wiping down all the surfaces, washing the plates, washing the windows. More thorough than usual, even. Erasing every fingerprint.

He hadn't brought many possessions to this home, had had nothing when he moved in here, and so extracting himself was easy. For old time's sake, he opened Elyse's closet and stroked her dresses, her lacy goods; he opened the drawers of her dresser and straightened out the lipsticks. There was nothing here he wanted to take away. He found the wooden lion at the back of her underwear drawer and weighed it in his hand for a moment. In the end he put it in his pocket along with his zoo badge and his keys.

He left the cellphone and almost all the clothes she'd bought him. Just one suit, one shirt, one pair of shoes. He knew what he looked like: an out-of-work violinist, an undertaker, a shabby minor politician. It was okay. As far as he was able, he was leaving clean.

Already he found it hard to conjure up her face, although he could summon each of its features, perfect and isolate: big eyes, bowed mouth, the curl of hair on her brow. Perhaps one day he might be able to see it whole again.

What he did remember was how she had looked from behind, face turned away, as she approached the door of Mark's hospital room and placed her hand against it, and the fluorescence from within had fallen around her like light from another realm. In that moment, in her white clothes, she hadn't looked like a joke nurse. She'd looked like a bride.

Walking out the door, he felt light and spare. He'd been here before. Usually when leaving a house, a situation, he'd slip the keys into the postbox or the mail slot in the door. A ritual of no returns. Women's keys, usually, with their fobs decorated with humorous doo-dads and other indicators of personality: lucky charms, pictures of loved ones encased in Perspex, novelty bottle-openers. Each time he felt that he'd shed a burden, something that slithered down through the metal slot with the keys and left him lighter.

Reaching now into his pocket, he became conscious of a wrongness. He'd not consciously noticed it when he came home on Saturday, but, he realised, he'd been subtly aware of it all the time: a lack. He lifted the keyring to his eyes. Something was missing. His eyes flickered when he saw that it was the work keys. They must've come off the ring that night in the paddock. Annoyed with himself, he pushed Elyse's keys through the mail slot too hastily, turning away without savouring the moment.

The wooden toy in his pocket knocked against his hip as he walked down the stairs, three flights, and out into the road. It was a beautiful late afternoon, clear but warm, the sky purple, the sea a few shades lighter, salt in the air. He glanced up at the balcony and saw the closed shutters, and the flat seemed like a musical box that had closed its lid on the ballerina within. Although perhaps the music continued, inside. He remembered his excitement when he first came here, thinking he might stay. The childish pleasure he'd taken in Elyse's house, her things. Now he turned away with only a slight frosting of the heart. Elyse would have a lover within the month. Musa, if he had to guess.

antelope

Immediately it was clear that something bad, the worst, had happened. Above, two helicopters puttered back and forth like they did in fire season; but there was no smoke, and these were police choppers. The Lion House parking lot was empty except for three squad cars, and there was no one on the pale brick path leading down to the shining lion sign. He walked it alone, step by step, feeling his legs grow light and his face lose blood. Something bad.

The ticket window was closed, a blind drawn down behind the glass. The front gate was open and strung with police tape. He ducked under it. Something very bad.

As he entered the courtyard, Amina came out of the bathroom block. Con couldn't make out her expression. After a moment's hesitation she walked deliberately across the brick towards him.

"What is it, what's happened? Was there a break-in?" he asked.

Amina looked at him and gave an off-kilter laugh. "Break-in? Break-out more like it."

He walked fast, overtaking her, straight towards the lion cage.

The outer door was swung wide. He'd never seen it pushed back so far on its hinges. The great bolt hung loose, the padlock dropped to the ground. And the inner cage open too, full sun for the first time on the grubby straw where it had never shone before. He walked inside, in a dream. He saw the hollow her body had made in the bedding.

The door into the enclosure, too, was open. He ducked under the low arch and out into the sun, expecting what, blood on the grass? Mossie's broken body. But there was nothing: no sign, no clue, no trace. No keys, but he knew that already. The keys hadn't slid off his ring, they'd been worked off by fluttery fingers, sometime in the night. He walked over to the viewing window and placed his hand flat on the pane. The lights were off inside and the late-afternoon sun was striking it just so. All he could see was himself, as in a mirror.

Perhaps this is what she saw, he thought, all those times he watched her through the window as she ate, or paced, or lay in the sun. Perhaps when she gazed back, it was not him she was seeing, never the meeting of gazes he had imagined. It had always only ever been her, the last Cape lion in existence, staring at her own reflection in the glass.

Amina was crying in her office, with her hands in her lap. Elmien was with her, her round face tightened at the lips.

"The keys." Amina shook her head. "I always knew there were too many keys – all the volunteers. Any one of them might have made a copy. Sold it to someone, for something. Canned hunting. Muti. Who knows."

"But how could they take her away?" said Elmien. "She was—"

"In a truck, a bakkie," Amina snapped. "Drugged her, dragged her …"

Elmien met Con's eyes. It was impossible to imagine. A lion was not moveable property. Con dropped his gaze.

"Go home, both of you. It's over now." Amina blew her nose, tossed her plait over her shoulder.

Elmien and Con left together, side by side but not touching or speaking. At the foot of the golden lion they said their goodbyes. Elmien held out a large, warm hand and he clasped it, imagining that his own palm was chill with guilt.

At the top of the path, blue lights sizzled on a police car, and several uniformed policemen stood smoking beneath the trees. They ignored Elmien as she walked past but turned to Con as he approached.

"You work here?"

"Yes. I was … actually with the lioness."

A balding cop took out a notebook and looked Con up and down. "Name?"

"Con Marais."

The cop jotted it down. "You got anything in particular to tell us, Mister Marais?"

He shook his head.

"Then in that case I'd ask you to clear the area, sir. If we need anything further we'll be in touch."

In the parking lot there was another police car, as well as a big green double-cab bakkie. On its side was the silhouette of an antelope head, in black. The men leaning against it weren't cops; they were dressed in khaki and camo, like soldiers. Arms folded, they watched Con come towards them, and he felt puny under their gaze. One of them tossed a cigarette butt to the ground – a criminal offence so close to the fence, Con happened to know. They were both tall men, one lean and dark-skinned and one a heavier white guy. Two long rifles leant up against the vehicle between them, like equal members of the hunting party. Con knew little about firearms, but he could see these were serious: spare, coolly functional implements with telescopic sights, stocks darkened by long use. A third man in sunglasses was sitting in the driver's seat, talking on a phone.

Con nodded a greeting. "I'm from the Lion House," he said, holding out his hand. Giving it time, the white man unwound a heavy arm and took Con's hand in a searching grip. At his throat hung a pendant – some kind of tooth on a leather thong. Con thought of showing his lapel badge, but it seemed girlish, gilt. "You guys with the Department?"

"Subcontracted. We're a private operation."

"Hunters?"

"I'm a tracker." The leaner man's voice had a rustling timbre.

"You're going to catch her?"

"Could be."

The driver got out and walked purposefully to the gate in the fence behind them. What came into Con's head was the photo he'd seen in Margaret's house of Mark: a hard, tanned man, dark hair clipped almost to the scalp. "Let's go, it's getting on," he said. The other two turned away, Con immediately forgotten. Buzz-cut pushed a code into the locked gate, and then the three of them slid through, closing the gate behind them.

Con watched as the men bent their heads together to glance at the ground. The tracker went down on one knee in a smooth, almost balletic movement, pointing at something in the grass. Then he was up on his feet and the three of them started to move up the slope, along the track to the old fire lookout, guns on backs. Tight, springy strides, making time, heads lowered. Buzz-cut turned his head briefly, but with the dark shades, Con couldn't tell if the look was aimed at him.

He trailed the fence towards the monument, keeping the hunters in the corner of his eye. Soon he lost sight of them among the trees. The helicopters still up in the sky, blades turning, too high to hear.

He found himself searching the ground too, looking for – what? Blood, maybe. Paw-prints. It was silly; he was no tracker. Still, he couldn't shake the sense that hidden in this picture was a clue.

The fence was leading him higher, up onto the shoulder above the memorial. It was cool, the mountainside in shadow. The sun was touching the flanks of the bronze lions below. And there it was in front of him: a mark in the sand. Could those be pads of a paw, even the indentations of claws? It wasn't clear. He touched the spoor, then glanced back to where the hunters had disappeared. Quickly, he kicked soil over the tracks, then swept leaves across the area. He stood quietly for a moment longer, ears reaching into the still air, finding nothing: no insects, no gunshots, no purrs or rumbles. Not even the birds spoke in the trees, as if they'd been struck silent, as if something had passed beneath them not too long before. He closed his eyes and saw them: a messy-haired girl, leading a lion on a leash of flowers.

The fence ran down again into a little dip where the bush had grown close against it. It looked dead, that bush. He moved closer, and saw that it wasn't rooted, was in fact a stack of dry twigs and leaves laid in the hollow. He tugged at the branches and they came loose in his hand. By the time he'd cleared them, his hands were scratched and he was sweating. Revealed was a gap below the fence where a small stream passed. A weakness in the fortifications: where the water cut a path, the bars didn't meet the ground. The soil had been dug away further to allow a large body or bodies to pass.

He crouched in the trench and gripped the bottom edge of the fence. A trickle of water was already coming through the seams in his city shoes. He tried to wrap himself into a neat ball and ease under, but it wasn't so easy. Con felt the bulk of his adult form keenly as he twisted first one way and then the other, then straightened out and tried to post himself feet first. The stream ran straight through his clothes and he felt a gash on his thigh as the trouser-leg ripped. But then he was on the other side, looking back at the city through the bars.

He turned his back on the view and took a slanting route up towards the tree line. He thought he recognised a tree here, a rock there, landmarks from childhood walks before the fence. Up, up. Past the grey boles of ancient pines, tangles of emerald grass poking through the stonework of an earlier time, centuries-old terraces and waterworks all tumbled and overgrown. Across abandoned paths, up into the mountain, emptied of people now, differently occupied.

But everything was extremely quiet. No living creature visible. Were they hiding? Was the silence the sound of a mountainful of prey, hunkering down to watch a great predator pass, a queen returned from exile? Or just the silencing effect of three men with guns?

But there must be some wild things about, because here was something like a path, not human-built, but circuitous, subtle, pressed into the grass with animal logic. He followed it. The grass was still wet with dew, the earth damp and fresh-smelling. Spiders had been busy here, their spangled trip lines laid. Every now and then he found something that might be part of a track: the suggestion of a heel-strike, a scuff-mark, a broken branch. Once, a golden hair caught on a twig; it floated away as he reached for it. He scuffed all traces out, although he knew he was leaving a trail of his own, as clear as writing.

He thought only of Sekhmet now. If he were an animal, he could leave a signal for her, a marking, a scent. If she were human, he might know her thoughts, deduce where she would go. Just once he called, softly, into the trees: "Here, girl, sweet girl." But it was like calling the cats in from his mother's garden: if they heard, they never came.

The slope grew steeper, the day darker. Con's wet leather shoes were pinching and slipping; his torn trouser-leg flapped at the ankle. The path dwindled and died, and soon he was pressing his way through an impossible thicket of thorns and tangles. He felt a surge of indignation: this tangled path she was leading him down, into spaces not meant for human bodies, into mouse holes, into rats' nests. Why was she making it so difficult?

Con thrashed through the bushes into clear space, coming up over a rise to find himself looking straight into a pair of dark glasses on the other side of the clearing. He dropped to his knees until all he could see was the cracked bark of the fallen tree in front of his face. After a moment, he peered over the log. The man, twenty metres away, still seemed to stare at him, but showed no signs of seeing. Although the hunter was the one in camouflage, it was Con who was hidden.

All three men were gathered in the clearing, looking at a patch of grass at their feet. One man spat onto the ground. The burly hunter was circling, pushing back tussocks of grass with the side of his boot. The tracker went down on one knee, and then held up two fingers, marked with red. Whose blood? There was no kind of body in the grass.

Quietly now, Con thought to himself, quietly does it, as he eased himself back into the trees, step by backwards step, a tape rewound, a photo undeveloping.

He circled round the clearing, traversing a few hundred metres and then up again. The encounter had shocked him into movement and he hiked strongly, urgently. The taste of blood in his mouth. The world blue-grey, sharp-edged.

The evening was cooling and the darkness pooled at the base of the trees, in the hollows. And on, and on. He walked and walked. He knew it was foolish, dangerous; on either side he sensed the dark gorges of the mountain dropping away, skeletons in their pits. Down wasn't a possible direction, so he headed up, up; up to where the night was gathering. As he climbed, the lights of the city fell away behind him, and for a while he walked through utter dark.

eland

Con lay on his back, feet on fire and face of ice, and gazed at the night sky. The wind sliced through his ruined clothes – his violinist's trousers and shirt – and into the flesh. He seemed to be at the edge of a crevasse.

This high up, the night mountain emits its own darkness; as if it casts a shadow upwards into the sky, hiding itself from the view of the city, hiding the sky too. What was visible to Con was a secret sky, perhaps even containing different stars and planets to the ones the city folk could see, if they looked at all. Or perhaps the same ones, arranged in subtly different constellations, as they were aeons ago, or aeons in the future.

He slept for a while, or perhaps not. At some point, a pale light began to burn softly in front of him, or was it behind his eyelids; and for a moment he was dizzy, turned around, because there should be no light like that up here. It wasn't an electric light, not a city light; not a light of this time. Greenish, lunar, almost phosphorescent. It flickered like fire, but coldly. It made the dark shiver.

He was on his feet again, no pain or weariness, and before him a gleaming slope. He walked up to its crest, and looked down into a basin of silver sand.

A bonfire burnt there, with dark figures moving before it. Some seemed to be dancing in a row, raising their hands to clap. And beyond the fire, a great corpse lay. A pale mound like a beached whale, glowing greenish-grey in the light of the huge moon, which had broken free of the cloud. There'd been no moon at the start of this long night.

The creature's flank was breached with a dark slash, and a puddle stained the sand around it. Human figures crawling over the body, hacking at the meat. When the bonfire flamed higher, Con could see the soaked earth around the leviathan was ruddy, the hands and the faces of the hunters too. The smell of burning wood, of roasting meat, came drifting up to him and he savoured it; but there was no substance and no warmth in it. And he felt a great cold sweeping up out of the sand basin, which belied the fire, the meat, the people below; it was an empty cold, of things long gone.

He tucked into a ball and pushed himself in under the stiff, unwilling arms of a low-lying bush, which scratched and bit him all night long.

When Con woke he didn't recognise where he was, huddled beneath a shrub that maliciously held a thorn to his neck. Nothing looked familiar; he couldn't be sure what direction he'd come from the night before, what way he'd faced, down which slope he'd blundered. He seemed to have tumbled into a damp hole. When he scrabbled his way out of it, he still could see nothing. The world was cloaked in a white mist, the sun only a pale intensification to what he must suppose was the east, if this was morning. That was no help. He appeared to be on a flat, rocky plain, which meant that he was on the top of the mountain, which meant that any direction he took could take him off the edge of a cliff. He plunged ahead anyway, walking through a solid wall of mist with every step.

It was their sounds he heard first, transported to him by the dense air: laughter, a nose blown, English words. And then the shock of colour: red jacket, blue cap. A group of humans around a fire, with a small stone cottage behind them. Not dancing. No butchered beast.

The men whipped round when they heard him coming, startled, and he realised that he'd approached in complete silence, his feet soft on the ground in their ridiculous leather-soled shoes. How strange he must look to them. He tried to smile, but he wasn't sure that's what his face was doing. So he held out his open hands – I come in peace! He found he was giggling.

"You lost?" a man asked him, although surely this must be plain.

Con walked towards the group. It wasn't easy; his legs seemed to be dissolving beneath him. And seeing their heavy boots and thick flannel shirts and trousers with many pockets and padded jackets also with pockets and woollen hats and dark glasses and gloves, he realised how bone cold he actually was. A long, hard shudder took him, gripping the back of his neck and shaking him all the way to his toes, and he nearly stumbled.

"Can I ask you what you're doing here? You know you need a permit. To be up here." The small hawk-faced man had his hair caught back in a ponytail. He seemed to be in charge.

With frozen fingertips Con reached into the damp slit of his trouser pocket. He realised he'd lost his wooden lion, somewhere up on the mountaintop. It seemed like the right place for the last survivor of the Ark. At last he fished out his badge, the gilt eye dull and childish in the white light. He showed it on his palm like police ID.

"What the hell's that?"

"He's from the lion place," said a square man with a black beard and gappy, immature-looking teeth. "The zoo."

"You with those other guys?"

"No," said Con. "Well, kind of."

The men looked at each other uneasily, and then back at Con. "They said they were tracking something, but they wouldn't tell us what," said the bearded guy.

"I tell you something, my friend," said ponytail man, stepping forward and taking a corner of Con's sodden shirt between two fingers, "you're not set up for it. You been up here all night? And those shoes."

Con looked down, embarrassed. "I know, I … got off course."

The men laughed, but not in an unfriendly way. They seemed puzzled: "You must be fucking freezing."

By force of suggestion, he felt his body rippled by another heavy shudder.

"Guys, get him a jacket, blanket, something."

"No, look, it's fine …" The trouble he was having speaking was because there was no sensation in his face.

"Come on over by the fire."

The heat of the fire was good, was so deeply, sensually good that for a moment he was speechless with gratitude. He crouched down facing the flames and cupped his body to gather the warmth on his chest, on his crotch. He turned his hands in it, bathing his skin in the glow. This was real flame, not the ethereal green bonfire of the night before. "This is beautiful," he said, grinning. "Just beautiful."

"Take those things off."

Con peeled off his shirt, his sodden and ruined shoes, his long damp trousers that clung to him so slickly they looked like wetsuit leggings, his underwear. It didn't occur to him to be shy. He was already such an alien body here.

He let the fire lick the last of the night's dew from him. Then he allowed these hospitable men to dress him again in their own clothes: a down jacket with multiple pockets, smelling of men's sweat; a flannel shirt and somebody's old army trousers; fleece-lined gloves. One of the men even gave him a pair of hiking boots, and when he protested the man just gestured with his pocket knife at his own feet in socks and said, "Blisters. I'm staying right here today." He nodded at the hut behind him, and carved off a slice of jewel-pink biltong, which he passed to Con.

"Thank you," Con said, again and again.

The meat was salty and delicious, more delicious than biltong had ever been, and softer and redder.

The men were different from the trackers he'd seen below. There was something sheepish about them, something soft. He noticed plump bellies and cheeks, smooth hands, neatly trimmed nails, shiny high-end camping equipment that looked barely used. The hawk-man, who was off to one side, fussing with gear, was something else. He had the alert, controlled bearing and taut skin of an outdoor sportsman. A fit little guy, small and wiry. Con assumed he was the guide.

"Who are you guys then?" he asked.

"We're just a bunch of friends," said the bearded man.

"Like a club, you could say," added another, tall and sandy.

"We like to hunt."

"So they let you *hunt* up here?" he asked.

"Well … you've got to get your hands on one of these special permits. Not cheap though."

Con chewed on his biltong, pondering this. After all the Department publicity about preserving species, it seemed bizarre.

"It's mostly just for the thrill of it," said the sandy man confidentially. "For the experience. You know? And Kruger's so pricey these days …"

"What kind of animals do you get?"

This seemed to be an uncomfortable question. The hunters swapped glances. Beard shrugged. "Well – we were hoping for wildebeest. They're supposed to stock springbok too."

"But we haven't seen a thing," interrupted a short man with aggressive eyebrows. "Not one single fucking meerkat. And it's our last day, we need to bag something."

"It's like some shooting party's come through here before us, cleared the place out."

"So it wasn't you I saw, last night?" asked Con.

"We didn't do fuck-all last night; it was too windy even for a braai. We stayed inside." Eyebrow guy jerked his head at the stone house. "Waste of fucking time."

There had been no wind up on that silver sandplain. And a giant moon. The memory made him shiver.

"Right, we need to get going," called the hawk-man, adjusting the straps on his rucksack. "Before the sun gets much higher."

All Con wanted to do was wrap himself more deeply in the scratchy blanket and fall asleep again by the fire, next to the comfortable man with the biltong and the stinking socks. But the thought of this lot blundering into Sekhmet out there … the lioness wounded maybe, or hungry … He forced himself to his feet. Amazingly, he didn't seem to have blisters.

"You okay, man?" asked the biltong eater. "You need to go down, get a doctor, something like that?"

"No," he said, "I'd like to come with you. If that's okay? I'm fine."

They looked at him warily.

"If I don't make it, I'll stop and come back, I promise. I won't be any trouble."

"You don't look too hot, mate."

"I'm fit, I'm good to go." He did a little star-jump, clumsy in the borrowed boots, which were a size too big. But actually he did feel good, energetic. He could see at a glance that he was in better shape than most of these guys. The sun was coming up, kindling a white glow in the depths of the mist. "So what are we after?" he asked. "What's the target?"

"Whatever we can find, man, whatever we can find."

Hawk-man was up at the front, leading fast – so fast he was in danger of leaving the others behind in the mist. Con caught up with him and matched his stride. The man gave him a quick sideways glance. He was balding at the temples, with a dramatic black widow's peak and eyes and skin of a similar coppery shade. Fierce and small and hook-beaked. He would have been an obviously handsome man if everything had been scaled up by ten per cent, but as it was he seemed miniaturised. His nose had a sharp bend in it, polished by the early light as he turned to face Con. He was dressed functionally, but with an edge of eccentricity: bits of ancient, olive-drab army gear mixed in with vintage khakis, all worn and patched and none too clean. No modern high-tech fabrics, nothing like the clothes on the pro hunters Con had met the day before. The outfit seemed to have grown on him like a pelt.

"Con," said Con, awkwardly holding out his hand as they walked. Without breaking stride, the other man turned and grasped it in a brisk, businesslike shake, then skipped ahead again. Graceful, thought Con. He can move.

"Richard."

"So you're the leader here," smiled Con.

Richard acknowledged this with a crisp nod. His voice was resonant, belonging to the ghost of the much bigger man he was meant to be. He was quiet, though, sparing in his words. The rest of the party chattered and joked behind them, surely scaring off even the dimmest wildebeest.

"So," Con persisted, "how much is this hunting permit?"

The man spat into the bushes. "You're South African?"

"Yes, of course." Sometimes it happened: people mistook him for a foreigner. His travels had left a trace in his accent, had straightened up his vowels from their slouched southern-hemisphere positions.

"This is my permit." Richard tapped the stock of the gun on his shoulder.

Con walked stiffly on, unsure how to respond. The man was fatiguing to talk to. Fuckit, he thought. I can be silent too.

Five minutes later, the man seemed provoked into elaborating: "Don't really need it. Just give the Department guys a little extra; they're cool with it. Look the other way." A few minutes later: "You like to hunt?"

Con considered. "Not really. I've never really done it."

He felt surprisingly strong. Richard increased his pace as they walked, perhaps testing him, but Con kept up easily. He could walk forever. Meanwhile he was scanning the surroundings, watching for a glimpse of yellow fur, a flash of eye, of tooth. But he already knew that it was hopeless; the bunch of jokers behind them were making so much noise, any animal would hear them coming a million miles away.

Richard knew it too. "Can't wait to get this lot back to base camp. Feed them lunch, say cheers. Amateurs."

Was Con exempt from this judgement? Maybe his appearance in the night, skinned and torn-shirted, had been more impressive than he'd realised.

"So you really didn't catch anything last night?" he ventured. "Because I thought I saw … something. A kill."

Richard looked at him sharply. "Maybe it was those other guys. What did they get?"

Con shook his head, troubled. "Something big." He held his arms wide. "Like a really big animal, like a …" He was going to say elephant, but that seemed so unlikely that a kind of shyness prevented him. "Pale. Maybe an eland …?"

Richard laughed. "Yeah right. Eland."

"No? I thought they'd stocked the mountain with antelope. Bigger things."

Richard shook his head, laughed again. "Maybe they did. They didn't last long though, if they were ever here. People bring their dogs up here, you know? Hunting dogs. Illegals."

"They can get in?"

"There's a million holes in the fence." He gave Con a shifty, amused glance. "You got in, didn't you?"

"But then what do you catch?"

"You'll see."

"No lions."

Richard laughed, suddenly boyish. "I wish!"

Con could look down on the crown of the smaller man's head; he was that much taller. Richard didn't seem weighed down by his gear, although he was carrying more of it than anyone else. But the size of his gun, which he also carried on his back, seemed disproportionate.

"You want me to carry anything?" But as soon as he'd said it, the little man stiffened and drew away from him, offended; Con realised he'd made a mistake.

"Stay on the path," Richard sniffed. "Don't want to add to erosion." And then he was striding off again, eyes on the ground.

Up here in the mist, the mountain floated like a dream inside a blind brain. It was clear that fencing it off had been effective: the vegetation was shoulder-tall, and the smaller paths had almost disappeared under grey-green bush. If the rest of the country was out, some strange countercurrent was in effect up here on ountaintop island: things looked lush, almost tropical. At intervals, Richard hauled out a panga to lop off low-hanging branches. The wooden steps that some long-ago Parks functionary had laid into the path were coming adrift; a winding section of boardwalk had rotted. As the mist cleared and the sun came through weakly, the birds started up, and Con thought that there were more of them, and louder, than he'd ever heard. But they saw no animals, except the smallest. Bird tracks, the odd beetle. At one point, Richard darted off the path, pointing at something in a crack between two rocks. Con went over to see. It was a noose made of nylon cord. The hunter cut it loose with the tip of his blade and held it up for inspection. "Poachers." But the snare was empty, the threads frayed and brittle. It looked like it might've been there for decades, waiting in vain for an unwary paw.

Con wished he knew more about lions – their tracks, their traces, their faeces, their kills, their calls. Why hadn't he taken more care to learn about Sekhmet, all those long days in the office in front of the computer, or wandering around the empty cages? Why hadn't he thought how she might live, if she were free? He wished he had a hunter's knowledge.

Richard stopped short again, bending to poke at something on the path with his panga. A kill. A bent back, twisted, spilling ants from its black feathers. The crow was surprisingly big. Perhaps more so at the feet of Richard, the scaled-down man. Richard bent to pluck a feather from the wing. He held it out to Con, but Con shook his head, repulsed. There were ants crawling on the shaft.

Richard shrugged, blew hard onto the feather to knock the insects off, and pushed it into his hair, just where it was gathered into the ponytail. That'd impress the punters, thought Con.

Con touched the bird with the tip of his boot. "What did this?" he asked.

"Cat. Cat's work."

—

They walked for two hours and then stopped for a coffee break. A couple of members of the party had gone astray. Richard made a fire and brewed coffee while they waited for the others to join them. The hunters seemed tired; they were sipping docilely from their tin cups when they heard a shot fired. Richard swore under his breath. Then the bearded hunter appeared up on the ridgeline, gave a hoarse croak and came hop-sliding down towards them, gun flailing in a way that made Con want to duck. He had a black substance smeared on his cheeks, and was wearing a fluoro vest over a voluminous camo jacket. As he came up to them, Con could hear the whispery sound of his thighs brushing together in their high-tech fabric.

"It's a cat?" he panted, more asking than telling. "A big one? I think I got him?"

Con felt his throat clench.

Richard scowled. "You shouldn't have been up ahead," he said. "Where's this cat?"

The man gestured wildly over the hill.

Con was on his feet and running. It was only when he was over the rise and halfway up the next one that he realised the others weren't following. He turned; they were behind him, gathered around something on the ground. Whatever they were looking at was so small, he'd gone straight past it. He made himself wait until his breath had slowed. The shot of adrenaline had winded him; he was as out of breath as anyone in the overweight hunting party. He walked slowly back.

A small shape twitched at the feet of a ring of silent hunters. The cat's belly was a mess of innards and blood-caked fur. Its pink mouth gaped convulsively.

"Wild cat," Richard said. "African wild cat. Pretty rare."

Although everyone could see it was just a ginger tabby.

Richard knelt down and put a knife to its throat.

Sickened, Con turned back into the mist and walked in the opposite direction. Away.

—

He marched straight until a sheer drop stopped him, then stood panting with the air dead in his ears. It was all dead, dead, dead. There were no lions here. Not for three hundred years. This mountain was finished, cleaned out, dried up, used up, shot out. Nothing. The misted-out sky was blank as a painted wall, the things around him – these rocks, these crumbs of damp, quartz-salted earth – each as crisply defined in the diffuse light as a relic in a museum case, and as drained of life.

Again, time slowed and dissolved. It might have been half an hour, or two hours, that Con walked. No texture in the gauze of mist, no variation in the small boulders hunched like creatures long fossilised. There was life here, but slow: secret, green beings holding their leaves completely still; and the immeasurably ancient lichens, which did not care to note his passing. It might have gone on like this for days, unchanging, if it were not for his grim determination to get to the edge: of the plateau, of the map, of this endless day.

And at last, against pale mist, he noted a stain rising. The smell of wood burning. He traced the smoke down to where it was rooted behind a boulder. Something moving there: a small person, swathed in a bright orange anorak, stirring a pot on a campfire. At first he thought: Mossie. She hadn't crossed his mind since the night before; he'd almost forgotten her existence, so much did Sekhmet fill his mind.

But then he saw her face and the way her sleeves, too big, draped over the back of her nimble fingers. Con laughed. "Thandiswa."

She looked up at once, bright-eyed, eager, already smiling to see him. "Con! What the fuck! What are you doing here?"

"Me? What about *you*?"

"I told you, silly. This is my other job." She wagged a spoon at him. "But you! You look like something ate you up and puked you back out again."

Con leant down to kiss her cheek.

"Eina, jees, freezing!"

"Sorry." Con smiled and rubbed the tip of his cold nose. "So this is the job on the side? You're what – a wilderness hostess?"

She laughed. "Cook. Nanny. Sherpa. Pay is good though."

"Why didn't I see you yesterday?"

"Oh, I saw you. But I stay out of the way. I do the logistics, set up camp ahead of the group. It spoils it for the punters, to see me. They like to think it's just them, just people like them, you know? They also like their food to appear by itself." She lifted a ladle of stew. "Want some?"

He was actually starving. He nodded.

"They won't be back for an hour. Here."

She dished a dollop of stew onto a tin plate and handed it to him. The plate was hot in his hands, the food fragrant.

"No reason why we couldn't have nice china plates, proper food. Camping food these days is really excellent, you know? And we bring it all up the back way in a truck; there's a good road. But these guys, they like to get a little hardship in the deal. Otherwise they feel cheated."

"Don't they feel a little cheated anyway? There's no game here."

"You'd be surprised what people feel content with. We pick up a few dassies, most times. Sometimes a klipspringer or two. Birds, even. I'm sure by the time they get down and back to the office, it's turned into the Big Five." She shrugged. "But, ja, I don't think this permit thing is going to last much longer. People like Richard are losing money. If someone wants a big trophy they can just go to one of the game farms, they'll sort something out for you. It's not hard. You can get anything."

"Lions, too?"

Thandiswa just laughed. "Not ones with black manes, no."

The electronic beeping was strange to hear, up here. Thandiswa pulled a phone out of her pocket, checked a text. "They're on their way. The great white hunters. Better get moving."

She started to clear away the cooking utensils. He helped her move the potjie off the coals, stoke up the fire again, arrange the camp chairs in a neat circle around the fire, and erase all traces of her presence. Then, quietly, before the hunters arrived for their lunch, Con and Thandiswa slunk away like ghosts.

They came over the rise to see the bowl of the reservoir below them, silvered, and next to it the old wood and glass chalet.

"What is it?" Thandiswa said, seeing him stop short.

"I've been here before."

Up close, it was looking rather the worse for wear. The orange curtains he remembered were gone, and dusty sunlight flooded the space where he'd sat with the Carolissens and played Scrabble. The glass door had to be shoved open against a swell in the floorboards, where it had scraped an arc in the wood.

A table with a couple of chairs, empty coffee mugs. The bunk beds that he and Mark had shared were still there, bare of mattresses. Dead flies were heaped on the sills. In the main room, an emergency radio murmured softly to itself about mundane departmental matters: a broken pump, a truck with a flat tyre, a suspicious person spotted near the fence. Someone had been using twists of newspaper to kindle a fire.

"You okay?" asked Thandiswa.

"It's just … strange to be here again. This place used to be fancy."

"This dump?" Thandiswa laughed. "Fancy people want fancier than this, now. It's just a place to store shit. The guides use it." She looked at him. "You came here? When?"

"Before your time."

"I heard a bad thing happened, years ago. A kid got murdered, something like that. Nobody wanted to stay here after that. Do you remember that?"

He shook his head. "Urban legend."

While Thandiswa packed away the cooking gear, Con walked around the old pavilion, out onto the balcony. Below in the gorge, the undergrowth was lush and tangled, much more overgrown than he recalled. He realised just how tired he was. The variegated textures of the bush and trees broke into a shifting grid of greens and greys, dots of blue and yellow. Any kind of shape or shadow possible in there.

He felt a light hand on the small of his back. Thandiswa. "You weren't really looking for her, up here?"

"Who?"

She was silent.

"Of course I was looking for her. I'm her keeper."

She regarded him for a moment, shoulders sagging. "Here, let me show you something." She went inside and brought out a folded newspaper.

Con reached for it eagerly; it was as if he'd been up on the mountain for months, everything seemed so delectable: food, water, warmth, company – and now printed matter too. He couldn't remember the last time he'd felt such a hunger for reading. He swiped his fingers across it, flattening out the page. This morning's newspaper. The paper was cloud-grey, friable in his hands, softened by the ambient moisture; into it, the black words were incised. They seemed uncannily crisp and dark; the photo of the child was vivid. So much meaning packed into such a thin tissue. He let it sink in; the headline and the small print. He felt Thandiswa's eyes on him and carefully, without looking up, folded the newsprint into squares and squares again and slid it into the pocket of his borrowed jacket. His heart beat once, twice, secretly against his fingers, before he withdrew his hand into the cold. She was watching him curiously and he gave her his charming smile. He felt it break as he did it, break like the sunburnt skin on his lips.

"Oh," he said. "Oh, I see."

The wind whispered coldly in the corners of the world, and he felt very high up, very far away. The mist was starting to clear now, eaten away along one edge by a rim of pale gold, lifting like ragged curtains to reveal the city, which had been there below them all along.

Manenberg — A nine-year-old girl was fatally mauled by an unknown animal on Saturday evening. Nadja Baard went missing after taking a shortcut through a field near her home after school. Her body was found by concerned relatives in the early hours of Sunday morning, in nearby bushes. Neighbours report seeing a "huge lion" leaving the scene of the attack. A police spokesman said the animal is more likely to have been a large dog, and requested members of the public to come forward with any information.

The news was filed from a rough suburb, beyond the shadow of the mountain.

"Down," said Con. "She went down. Not up. Down there. I've been a fool."

Thandiswa just shook her head. "That poor little girl," she said.

Thandiswa drove him in silence to the entry gate. Her fingers flickered on the combination lock, punching in the code. "Perks of the job," she said with a glance at him as the lock popped open. "It's not six six six."

As he passed through the gate, Con wondered if this would be his last crossing. He raised a hand to Thandiswa in thanks, and started down the winding road.

VII. FABLE

And after [St George] said to the maid: Deliver to me your girdle, and bind it about the neck of the dragon and be not afeard. When she had done so the dragon followed her as it had been a meek beast and debonair. Then she led him into the city.

– From *The Golden Legend*, compiled by JACOBUS DE VORAGINE, Archbishop of Genoa, 1275

pigeon

Con felt like he hadn't slept for days. He came down into the city light-headed, swinging his arms. The sun glanced off the sea and directly into his eyes, bringing tears.

He walked and he walked, and the city rose up to meet him like a bowl lifted to his mouth. The sun was waiting for him on the lip of the sea, and everything shone golden into his eyes. He walked in a dream, whole neighbourhoods passing him by in stop-motion: now a glowing bank of shops, now a field of broken tar. He no longer knew where he was. As he travelled, he seemed to pass through every street he'd ever known, every neighbourhood of significance, different but the same: here surely was the house where the Green Lion club had met, and here an apartment moulded in much the same way as Elyse's flat, although that was surely impossible, because the sea seemed to have drawn back, and for a while he was walking through some long-ago blue dusk with grasses brushing against him and not a house in sight, and here was his old school, and here perhaps his mother's house.

He found himself at length on the edge of the city in the failing light, in a zone of warehouses and mechanics and spares shops, everything chill and shining, with the taste of metal in the air. The workshops and places of small business seemed wonderfully ingenious, so busy and well meaning and resourceful, but also with their mysteries – what even were these things? Cogs and gears and levers.

A man came up to him and asked brusquely, "Can I help you?" and Con realised he was running his hands through a tub of bright nuts and bolts, letting them spill through his fingers like grain. He pulled his hands regretfully away and smiled and shook his head and drifted back out of the shop.

He lurched on down the road, stinking and limping from the night. And this is how you lose humanity, he thought; it doesn't take very long. He was confused by his clothes, by how small he seemed to have grown inside them; then he remembered the hunters. Of course the clothes weren't actually his. The camo jacket and army pants were big and shapeless, not at all like the narrow-cut clothes he usually favoured; his feet slopped in the hiking boots. The discomfort reassured him that his feet at least were still his own.

He felt gingerly in the borrowed jacket. God, there were a lot of pockets in this thing. Why hadn't he noticed before how heavy they were, freighted with clunky items? Like a bum, he sat on the pavement and turfed out his finds. The first thing he found was a shiny silver compass. It looked brand new, and expensive. Next: a box of waterproof matches. A snack bar, which he immediately ate, his hunger surprising him. A silver whistle. A Swiss Army knife. He looked at the little pile of items and felt overwhelmed with gratitude, almost to the point of tears, like a shivering polar explorer stumbling on a stash of rations buried beneath the snow. Right here, courtesy of some other human being whom he had already forgotten, was everything a person might want. Warmth, direction, sustenance, protection.

But none of these things was much good to him now. He needed assistance of a higher order. He sighed and slid his fingers into a zip-pocket in the trousers. His fingertips found something smooth and weighty, and recoiled from its supple, skinlike texture; but then he realised what it was and pulled it out. A wallet. Cards and cash. Quite a lot of cash. For a while he looked at the very fine engraving on the fifty-rand note – a lion! The animal scowled to the right on one side, while Mandela stared to the left on the other, amused. Carefully, Con packed everything back, placing each item into an appropriate pocket, stood up and continued on his way. The money had cheered him.

He stopped at a bar with a couple of outside tables, although no one sat there: the evening was growing cold. Inside, drinkers thronged, but he was content to watch through the window, entranced by the people, moving their tongues and their lips and their fingers, making words in the warm light. When a waitress came with enquiring eyebrows, Con managed wordlessly to imply the need for a beer. It was delivered, and he passed over a crisp pink note and drank deeply and the taste was cold gold. He was filled with admiration for the bevelled edge of the wooden table, and for the regular glossy curves of the bottles he could see behind the bar. He wanted the place to stay open forever, the same people to stay talking and smiling at each other across their drinks, all human, all alive.

He laid his head on the table. Perhaps he slept a little. When he opened his eyes again, the place was empty.

"Can I get you something? Coffee?" A small figure was standing with the lights of the bar behind her. Again he thought: Mossie; but then she moved and her hair flared blonde. He couldn't make out the expression on her face.

"No, no, that's okay," he said, on his feet. "But is there a phone I can use? I'll pay."

There was still enough cash to call a taxi and to pay the driver. So wonderfully simple, having money. You handed it over and people understood. He told the taxi driver quite clearly what he wanted and the man grasped his need immediately. Con seemed to be able to talk to people in a new way, an extraordinary way: clearly, frankly, with no charm or deceit, but deeply, into their souls.

Steering with one hand, the driver passed Con something in a greasy plastic bag. Koeksisters, sweet and filling. Con's mouth watered at the smell.

"My wife makes it," said the taxi driver.

For a moment he felt incorporated into some simple benevolent economy. Into a family, even: like a cousin, almost a brother. He had tasted the wife's baking.

"Where exactly do you want to go?"

When he leant between the seats and pulled out the carefully folded piece of newspaper to show the driver the small article, the driver nodded and said, "You want to go see where that happened? That little girl? Shame, hey."

The paper almost came apart in Con's hands, splitting along

the fragile folded seams, and the colours seemed translucent. It was very dark outside now, dark and cold.

"Are you sure?" asked the taxi driver. "It's late. It's not a safe area."

Con nodded.

When they got to the place, the taxi driver stopped alongside a field between houses. Letting the engine run, he said again, "This isn't a safe place. I can wait for you to do what you need to do."

But Con looked out at the black field and couldn't say for sure that he would ever emerge from it again. The kind taximan might wait forever.

"No, you go on," he said. "I'll be okay."

"You know people here?"

"I know people."

He huddled the sloppy coat around him and was glad of its warmth and its fuggy smell, which had grown familiar. He raised his hand to the taxi driver and waited for him to pull away. It was lonely, to see the red tail-lights sliding into the dark. The nearest streetlamps were a block away.

It took him a moment to grow aware of sounds. Even at this late hour, life was all around, whistles and talking and a car revving. There was a group of people standing in front of the houses down the block and they looked at him curiously. He didn't feel afraid, just shy. There was nowhere to hide but the dark, so he walked onto the field, as if he knew the right direction. It was a flat lot of frayed grass that glinted in the streetlights with broken glass, which crunched under his feet like frost. Since when did it get so goddamn cold in Cape Town?

He walked quite far, until the lights around the edges seemed equidistant stars. Right here, in the centre of this field, he felt as far from humanity as he had ever felt.

Then he saw a small patch of deeper black angling towards him. He shivered. The figure stopped short, a stroke of dark paint against a dark ground.

"Who's there?" called Con softly.

"Who's there?" came the reply, teasing. And Con realised that the figure was small, the voice a child's.

They walked towards each other blindly, groping, as if pained by the shards of glass underfoot.

"Who is it?" said the child again. A little girl, hands in pockets.

"Nobody," said Con, unsticking his tongue. "Nobody. I'm just here to see the place – the place where it happened. The other little girl, was she … your friend?"

"Are you from the TV?" She came closer and he could see her face now, smiling. She didn't come up to his chest, even. Why was she up so late?

"No … I'm just interested. I'm from …" He felt in his pocket for his zookeeper's badge but it seemed to have gone, or got confused with the objects in the hunter's jacket: he felt a slippery mix of metal, the compass, the pen, but none had the right weight or edge. He touched the knife, but it slithered into a seam like a silverfish.

The girl clicked her tongue chidingly – a comforting sound, intimate, tucked between tongue and cheek. "Here," she said, "I'll show you."

She walked off in a new direction. As she passed through the beams of the far streetlamps, a white fire briefly traced her silhouette. He followed her to some mysteriously significant co-ordinate of the dark field.

She gestured at the ground with a closed hand. "It was just here. I saw it."

"You saw it happen?"

The child nodded.

"Were you scared?"

She just laughed and held up her fist. "Look." Something in her hand caught the stray light and glinted. Strands of stiff hairs or grass.

Con stepped forward to look more closely, reaching out – but she snatched her treasure away and danced back a step, giggling and waving her whisk at him.

"I got that lion! By the tail!" She darted forward, touching the tickling ends of the hairs to his lips, giggling. Then, relenting, she took his hand with icy fingers and pressed her gift into his palm. "Goodbye, Mister Man," she said, and then she was gone, slipping away towards the far lights, extinguished.

He clutched the handful of stiff hair. He was sick of this obscurity, this darkness in his eyes like mountain mist. He felt he hadn't seen clearly for days. Why couldn't there just be lights? Not even a torch in the fat hunter's stash. It seemed a black crevasse had opened in the ground before him, but he forced himself to take a step, and then another, falling over and over into the pit of darkness, heart beating with the panic of the fall, stumbling, faster and faster towards the distant lights.

When he got back to the road, the taxi was waiting for him, after all. The driver was fiddling with his radio, shuffling blue and red lights with his fingertips. He looked up and smiled, and a gold tooth glinted.

As they drove, the driver continued to magic the radio, catching wisps of music and snatches of voice.

"How late is it?" Con asked.

"Late, late," said the taxi driver. "Listen."

A newsreader was speaking to them. A million things were happening out there in the world: scandals and calamities, old lovers reunited, murders foul, great works of art and business. A lioness was moving through the city; she had been spotted in Strand, in Rondebosch, in Gugulethu. In the light from the dashboard, Con looked down at his palm. He held a few coarse strands of synthetic fibre, unravelled perhaps from a nylon cord like the one used to make the snare on the mountain. Not even grass.

He closed his eyes, and saw them, the girl on a lion's back. They were riding away, up into the high lands, into golden grasslands, grass to the horizon.

The taxi's fake leather cradled him, and he slept.

jackal

He must have told the taxi driver the address. Because here he was, inevitably. In front of the familiar door. Mark's house. He'd lost his jacket somewhere along the way, and everything that was in the pockets. He stood with his fingertips resting lightly on the plastic buzzer, not pressing. Then he turned and went around the back of the property, back to where the old bluegum still leant, the bricks of the walls built carefully around it like a wound healed around a thorn. He looked for the old footholds in the broken wall, smaller now, made for narrower feet. He put the tips of his toes into the holes, found places to hold. The wall was disappointingly low, although the drop on the other side was heavier for his old bones. He sat with his back against the garden wall, and for a while the ghost of a child, which one he wasn't sure, came and sat with him too, companionable.

When he was ready, Con came through the garden to the house. He found her face in an upstairs window, the only one lit. Margaret seemed to be sitting quite still, staring at a wall; waiting for something to arrive.

And then another face, in a different window. A clean, familiar profile. Con could see them in their separate windows like icons in gilded frames, then together in the same frame – a magical moving portrait; and for a moment he was back in an art gallery somewhere far away, watching bright images shift and communicate mysteriously behind glass. The two faced each other, heads gently bowed.

Like a dog he crept close to the walls of the house. No, not a dog – a jackal, something wild and shut out from human warmth and exchange. The door was locked, of course, but the coir mat was a welcome of sorts. Con curled himself up small, there on the threshold, and fell asleep like a creature that doesn't know a floor from a bed, as long as it's a place to lie. Grateful, so grateful for a place to lie.

In the morning he woke in the dew, shivering, and stood up with a painful flare of feeling through his limbs. He wiped his hands carefully, sparingly, on a small patch of clean shirt that remained. Everything was ripped, soiled, barely clothing. The house was very quiet. He put up his hand to knock and then lowered it, not wanting to break the peace.

Con walked around the side of the house. He could see Mark's empty room, a glass box varnished with reflection. There was a narrow figure standing inside it, obscured in shadow. But Con knew him at once: the stance slanted like his mother's; the profile pronounced like his father's. As Con watched, the figure opened the door of the room, stepped out into the sun. A shadow spilt out onto the grass, elongated, barely human.

Mark's hair had grown long, and a beard fell onto his chest like a prophet's, flecked with grey. He was very pale. Heavy-rimmed spectacles. The same, different, changed. Con wanted to run up to his old friend and put his arms around him and exclaim, my friend, what has happened to *you*? Ageing had never been on the cards for Mark, yet here he was, unaccountably damaged by time.

The hurt ran deep. Mark came walking across the grass, not with the striding lope that he'd perfected at age fourteen, but with a stiff pendulum leg-swing. Some deep rewiring or short circuit producing this jarring step, step.

He had not yet seen Con. He was making for Gerard's old chair beneath the tree. Getting there took ages. Eventually, Mark had found the chair-back, walked himself around it, turned and lowered himself achingly into the seat. The orange cat came leaping up onto his lap as soon as he settled.

As Con came towards him, Mark looked up, and his eyes behind the thick lenses were the colour of veins. Con went down on his haunches next to his old friend, who observed him with gentle pleasure. A strange thing, to look at the face of someone you loved in childhood. You search for, and briefly find, the boy beneath the skin; he meets your eyes brightly, but then the aged face slips sideways into place again, over the ageless bones.

Mark was still a beautiful man. His eyes were wide and blue as ever, but guileless now. The sly knowingness had been burnt out of him, leaving, still, his grace. One hand moved rhythmically over the cat's back. Every movement seemed a careful adjustment of ligaments. It was only then that Con saw: one of Mark's sleeves was neatly pinned back, just above the elbow. Nothing below that. The other hand stroked, stroked the fur.

There was a joke in here somewhere, Con thought, an awful joke, truly bad taste, but he couldn't quite bring it to mind.

"Mark," he said softly. "How are you feeling?"

The cat was very old, the hair thinning on its back. It sat tight on Mark's lap, hoping not to move at all, ever again. The sun and a stroking hand were its sole desires now. "Old boy," said Mark. "This old boy has been in the wars."

Mark sat delicately in his chair as if unable to put much weight on any part of his body for fear of splitting a seam, cracking a fragile mend. He wore a soft, knitted cap, and Con wondered if the skull beneath it was shattered and held together like a soft-boiled egg in its shell. A long-sleeved blue shirt was buttoned to the neck; loose grey tracksuit pants. Between the pale face and the pale bare feet was a hidden country of potential pain. Skin removed and stitched back on. The stuffing coming out. Bits left off, bits gone missing. Was that the pale worm of a scar, creeping up his larynx? When he turned his head, it crept back under the collar. The face was unscarred. Dmitri must have been gentle with him, Con thought, to spare this much.

"Help me with this … bro?" Mark pointed at a box of cigarettes and a lighter lying on the ground at his feet. "Tricky." And his voice was the same, just a shade deeper, a shade slower, as though some of the words required a moment of particular consideration before he released them.

Con fitted the cigarette to his own lips, clicked the lighter, held the flame to the tip. He was careful, conscious of the smartness and economy of his own movements. He managed with one hand, and reflected that Mark could well have lit his own smoke. But he'd wanted Con to do it for him.

Mark took the cigarette and dragged on it, then grinned at Con through the smoke. "You look like … shit."

Con laughed. "Fine one to talk. So, are you going to get a …" He flexed his hand in the air, making pincers. The word-lag was catchy.

"A hook?" Mark laughed. "Captain Hook, for sure. Maybe …" He clapped a hand over one eye.

The door of the house opened and Con saw Margaret standing there, leaning on her cane. She started forward, then stopped when she saw the men together. Con straightened up and waved. She didn't come forward, though; just raised her hand in greeting.

"Old lady. Better … go in," said Mark, and started to rise from the chair, leaning heavily on one hand to lever himself up.

Con put out an arm to help him, but then hesitated, his fingers a few centimetres from Mark's back. He was uncertain whether to touch; what hurt it might cause.

"S'okay … Lemme do it," said Mark. Righting himself at last, he set off determinedly down the lawn to the house, limp swing, limp swing. He paused just before the door to call back: "Come again, bro. Another time, yeah? Good … to see you. Get a …" – long pause, some trouble with the tongue – "… get a *suit*."

Mark raised his arm, as if signalling across a great distance with the sparking end of his cigarette, and then Margaret gathered him in – light arms around him, also not quite touching – and the door to the house closed behind them.

Pain, and the easing of pain. A long thorn, drawn from the flesh.

VIII. JEROME

Each day brings its toad, each night its dragon.
Der heilige Hieronymus – his lion is at the zoo –
Listens, listens.

– RANDALL JARRELL, from "Jerome", 1960

lioness

In the sunny courtyard, the animals are arranged in tableaux, in naturalistic postures. They are sheltered from the sky by awnings, but are open to the air; you can go up close. One mother rests her toddler on the back of a springbok, and Con asks her not to do that, for fear of damaging the antique model. But generally, the mood is relaxed. The children are encouraged to touch and experience: stroke the fur, put their fingers in glass eyes, pass their hands between the rows of teeth. Things have changed around here, since the Lion House became the Green Lion Centre, devoted to the interdisciplinary conjunction of Arts and Natural Sciences, under the joint auspices of the Departments of Environment, Recreation and Culture. As part of the rebranding, the golden lion at the entrance has been given a tasteful green tarnish. Dmitri, beautifully mounted in a reclining pose, has pride of place at the entrance, next to Elmien's ticket booth.

Generally, the development has been a success with the public. The cafeteria is open again, and families are sitting in the sun under parasols, sipping milkshakes. The crowd is cheerful, diverse. Some have T-shirts featuring the faces of kittens or wolves. They are young and old, from all walks of life, but all clearly animal people.

The new focus has been good for staff morale, too. The money crisis is over now. The work is light; these animals don't need swilling out or bloody feeds. Most of the old cleaning staff got their jobs back, the cafeteria waiters are busy, and there are even some new volunteers. Thandiswa has moved on, of course – she's working at the Transfrontier Park now. Amina's had her hair cut, and taken out the greys.

Everybody seems rejuvenated. Even Gerard's poor animals have been given a lick of paint: they are brighter, friendlier, less macabre, their spots and stripes definitely more vivid. This was the work of Elyse and her friends. With that theatrical energy he still finds alarming, they'd taken up needles and thread, paint and latex, and knocked Gerard's stuffy old trophies into some more appealing, kid-friendly shape. And why not? It is, after all, a Centre for Arts and Science now, and taxidermied animals are its perfect emblems. Never particularly rigorous scientific documents, these ones are now almost wholly imaginary creations.

The only specimen not to have found a place here is the young lion with its tragic green fur. Con keeps that in his office, to remember. He is growing accustomed to it, and often spends time staring into its one button eye. Speechless, it offers him the tennis ball, a game of catch that can never begin or end.

A figure appears up on the battlements of the den, looking down on the crowd. Hybrid: a muscular human fitted with a tail and a swept-back pair of spiralling horns. His skin is spotted with eyes of black paint. He lifts some kind of trumpet – no, it's a kudu horn – and winds it. It is only when he speaks, summoning them inside to the performance, that he is recognisable as Musa, of the resonant voice and wandering hands. The crowd gets to their feet and makes their way out of the sun and into the den.

Inside, the space is as dark as ever, but filled now with neat ranks of chairs. They've taken down the glass viewing pane; the grass enclosure, opened up, functions as a stage. Ramps allow access to seating around its edge, so the faces of the audience ring the space. Small children race down the aisle to sit at the very front. Con stays back, though, taking his place at the rear of the dim auditorium.

Another sounding of the horn, and in the subsequent silence Elyse's friends come stalking out, each in creaturely form, in striped leotards and fake-fur manes and hooflike shoes that dangle from their limbs like weights and clop to the ground. But the costume cannot conceal the humanity of the bodies, naked beneath the paint: lithe, hairless, clever.

They dance instructively; they dance the fables. He watches the figures stretch and swivel on the stage and Con is filled once more with a kind of uncomprehending wonder. They dance in a row, the stork dance, the frog dance, the dog dance; it's hard to make out which one is Elyse, but he identifies her by her long stork-legs, the stork bill that sways before her face. They do this every Friday and Saturday evening, with a Sunday matinee. It is a good gig, regular work. In the dark he's never sure if Elyse can see him; he keeps very still.

All around him the children breathe and smile. They are decked in their mascots, their familiars. They all have little metallic toys, robots or cars, dangling off their bags now; the fashion for furry animals is gone. Their faces are lit by the glamour on the stage.

Elyse has now shed her animal form and is dressed as a little girl, with pigtails. Despite her tallness, she seems plausibly childlike, her movements unformed, her face limpid. He is enthralled as ever by her transformations. He likes to watch her like this, with no way to speak or be spoken to.

Musa is sonorously narrating a story about a lion who came to a little girl and held out his paw to be healed. Elyse walks through a field of waving grasses, artfully created by banners of silk held by actors on either side of the stage. At the sound of a recorded roar she throws up her arms in surprise, dropping her bunch of wild flowers. The children scream with delight.

When the lion enters stage left, the effect is gorgeously achieved: the animal is amazingly realistic, its limbs manipulated by four silent black-clad players with sticks. The lion pauses, bows, roars, attacks – and limps. First it does a rolling circuit of the front of the stage. The puppeteers are excellent. They have observed the movements of a lion's walk so well – not too fluid; there is the suggestion of heft and muscle there, and the pain of a wounded paw. The unwillingness of a heavy creature, trapped. Con sees a zoo animal, wearing a track along the front of a cage. At the limit of the stage, the lion lurches, its giant head swinging out, almost far enough for the kids in the front row to touch or imagine being touched by a string of lion spittle. Again, they squeal on cue.

It is close enough for Con to see how the lion has been made – a cunning articulated frame of canvas and wood. Its jaw has been hinged, its eyes substituted with brown glass orbs that are too big, cartoon style. As the great head sways past, its big blank eyes meet his for a second, but there's nothing there except his own reflection, caught in a too-small chair among the rows of human young. The glass eyes reflect the light from a camera-phone flash and the image is dissolved. The lion turns way.

On stage, the play takes a turn for the charming; the lion goes to the girl and lays his head in her lap. The children are enthralled. One of the littlest rises involuntarily from his seat and goes forward to be close to the stage. "It's so nice for them to see real animals," murmurs one of the parents next to him.

Con rises and goes out the back of the auditorium, into the courtyard grown cool and dim. Behind him, the den fills with a deep recorded purr.

He sits at the edge of the courtyard, where there is a view of the city below, and lights a cigarette. It is on evenings like these that he feels the need. When he turns away from the view, he sees a small woman on her own, standing before the great eland, staring up at it with hands folded before her. "Oh, but he is beautiful," she says softly to no one in particular. She moves on to the zebra, the oryx. She does not let a single one pass by without her notice. At last she circles back to the eland, and lays a hand briefly on its enormous muzzle. Then she leaves to go back to wherever her home may be. Turning, before she vanishes into the dark, to give Con a little wave, which he returns. It is not Mossie, but one of these days it might be. Con can easily see her here with the members of the Green Lion Club, greeting the animals, performing their stations of the cross. He'll be glad to see her.

Although Sekhmet is gone, she still features regularly in newspaper reports. She is sighted now and then in ever more fantastical circumstances: scaring off muggers in an alley off Long Street, or leaving her footprints at the tomb of the Muslim saint in Faure. She is held captive in a backyard shack in Lavender Hill and used in dogfights. Further afield, a group of boys at initiation school in the Transkei reported that she came strolling past their huts in the middle of the night. She is kept by a famous playboy in his Sandton penthouse, brought out at parties wearing a jewelled collar. There was one sighting of Sekhmet in Durban, walking down the beachfront at sunrise. She has never been photographed.

There have been no further confirmed attacks. A small bronze plaque in the courtyard, close to where Con sits now looking out at the city, commemorates the short life of Nadja Baard, the child who died. Con makes sure to keep it polished. Often there are wild flowers laid on the stone, although he has never seen who puts them there.

For Con, the lioness is everywhere. He sees her form slipping around every corner, her eye peering from every window, her growl behind the traffic rumble. Right now, she's watching him from the mountainside, hidden by the leaves; he feels the weight of her gaze upon his back. At other times, it's as if he himself is looking through her eyes, viewing the world through a lens of golden fluid. He can see for leagues. Sometimes, on the other side of the fence, he glimpses things from the corner of his eye – a swaying branch, a child in the leaves, a tawny flank. An eye, a wing. But he doesn't look up, much, at the mountain any more. There is no need.

He likes it here best late at night, after the actors have left, when the crowds have gone as well, when Amina has taken the funders round the corner to the restaurant and it is just him alone. There are paths to patrol, exhibits to clean. He is responsible for these old animals. He moves from one to the other, dusting, touching, stroking the wounded pelts, noting which pieces need repair. It is important to preserve things. Many of the species in the collection have vanished from the world, lost completely now.

A few hundred years, Con thinks, looking at the eland, who is staring out onto the Flats with a melancholy to rival Rhodes'. That's how long it takes. In another hundred years, how many more creatures will have attained this desiccated calm? Imaginary beasts, existing only in museums of lost and impossible things.

He sits in his office and works into the night, the lamp throwing its small circle of heat around him. He may be here for a long time. He may grow old at this desk, may grow a long beard like the saint. But one day, there will be a lioness in the corridor, her footfalls soft but growing louder. He will not hear her coming. Already perhaps she is outside, approaching, still small in the background of the picture; but soon she will be here. Much larger, much closer than she appears.

ACKNOWLEDGEMENTS

To my agent, Isobel Dixon; to Umuzi, in particular Fourie Botha and Beth Lindop; and to Martha Evans, my editor: my eternal thanks for their championing of this book, their great care with the text and their patience with me. Thank you also to publicide for the fiercely lovely cover, Genevieve Adams for immaculate proofreading and Fahiema Hallam for the lucid page design.

Many people have been very generous over the last four years with help and advice, and some gave their time to read the manuscript at various stages. Thank you particularly to Diane Awerbuck, Darrel Bristow-Bovey, Greg Fried, Karen Briner, Jeanne-Marie Jackson, Lisa Lazarus, Eustacia Riley and Rachel Zadok.

Especial thanks to John Coetzee, Patrick Flanery, Damon Galgut and Ivan Vladislavić for their invaluable time, critiques and support.

Opportunities to work on *Green Lion* were given to me by the Hawthornden Castle, Bellagio Center and Caldera artists' residencies; and by the Gordon Institute for Performing and Creative Arts at the University of Cape Town, where I held a year-long fellowship. My gratitude to everyone who helped my entry into, and passage through, these wonderful programmes, including Ken Barris, Imraan Coovadia, Michael Cope, Ingrid de Kok, Leon de Kock, Jonty Driver, Michiel Heyns, Ashraf Jamal, Alan Morris, Pilar Palacio, Jay Pather, Hamish Robinson and Katie Weinstein.

My thanks also to the Natural History Museum, London (especially Richard Sabin) and the Scottish National Gallery (especially Graeme Gollan) for allowing me private access to their precious holdings.

Thank you to the late John Spence of the now defunct Tygerberg Zoo, for kindly showing my sister and me around and explaining his work with the lions; thanks too to Lorraine Spence for allowing us access.

Finally, uncountable thanks and love as always to my mother, who started this all; to Andrew and Olivia Rose-Innes, who keep me going; and to Peter Colenso, for being so steadfastly at my side.

Sincere apologies to anyone I have inadvertently left off this list.

I gratefully acknowledge the permission granted to reproduce the copyright material in this book.

Thanks to Margaret Atwood for allowing me to use a portion of her poem "Sekhmet, the Lion-headed Goddess of War, Violent Storms, Pestilence, and Recovery from Illness, Contemplates the Desert in the Metropolitan Museum of Art", from *Morning in the Burned House*, first published by McClelland & Stewart, 1995, as an epigraph. Reproduced with permission of Curtis Brown Group Ltd, London, on behalf of Margaret Atwood. Copyright © Margaret Atwood 1995.

The extract from Van Riebeeck's journal on pg 11 is taken from *Precis of the Archives of the Cape of Good Hope, January 1656–Dec 1658, Riebeeck's Journal, &c.* by H.C.V. Leibbrandt, Keeper of the Archives, Part 1, Cape Town, W.A. Richards & Sons, Government Printers, 1897.

On pg 67, the summary of ||kabbo's account is taken from the *Second Report concerning Bushman Researches, with a short account of the Bushman Native Literature Collected*, W.H.I. Bleek, Report presented to Parliament of Cape of Good Hope, 1875, pg 11. The original account was told to Lucy Lloyd by ||kabbo (Jantje) (11), 1871. I accessed this via the wonderful Digital Bleek and Lloyd, lloydbleekcollection.cs.uct.ac.za.

"||Kabbo Tells Me His Dream" on pg 133 is from the collection *Return of the Moon: Versions from the /Xam*, Carrefour, 1991, reprinted with the kind permission of Tanya Wilson, Hugh Corder and the literary estate of Stephen Watson. My deepest appreciation.

The verse on pg 101 is an extract from "The Hunting of the Greene Lyon, Written by the Viccar of Malden" in Elias Ashmole, *Theatrum Chemicum Britannicum*, London, 1652, pgs 278–79.

The line from "Jubilate Agno" on pg 157 is from Fragment B, Part 2 of Christopher Smart's manuscript.

The Herman Charles Bosman quote on pg 187 is from the story "In the Withaak's Shade", published in *Mafeking Road*, Dassie, Johannesburg, 1947.

On pg 211 I have given my own paraphrasing of "The Litany of Sekhmet", translated and adapted into English by Richard Reidy from the French text *Sekhmet Et La Protection Du Monde* by Phillippe Germond, Ägyptologisches Seminar der Universität Basel, 1982.

The lines on pg 243 are from William Caxton's 1487 translated edition of *The Golden Legend*.

The Randall Jarrell poem "Jerome", quoted on pg 255, is from the collection *The Woman at the Washington Zoo*, Atheneum Publishers, 1960.

Every effort has been made to trace copyright holders and to obtain their permission for the use of copyright material. The publisher apologises for any errors or omissions in the above list and would be grateful if notified of any corrections that should be incorporated in future reprints or editions of this book.

HENRIETTA ROSE-INNES is the author of the novels *Shark's Egg*, *The Rock Alphabet* and *Nineveh*, and the short-story collection *Homing*. She was awarded the South African PEN Literary Award in 2007 and won the Caine Prize for African Writing the following year. Her novel *Nineveh* was shortlisted for the 2012 *Sunday Times* Fiction Prize and an M-Net Literary Award.

Her short stories have appeared in various international publications, including *Granta*, *AGNI* and *The Best American Nonrequired Reading 2011*, and her work has been translated into several languages. In 2015, the French translation of *Nineveh* won the François Sommer Literary Prize.

She divides her time between Cape Town and Norwich, where she is completing a PhD in Creative Writing at the University of East Anglia.